Broken

Samantha Baca

Cover Design: Jack'd Up Book Covers

Content Warnings:

Violence
Stalking
Murder: including of a parent, spouse, and infant on page
Suicidal thoughts/ideation on page
Foul language
Explicit sex scenes on the page
Removal of human body parts
Consumption of said body parts (by an animal, not by a human)

Contents

Contents

Contents

<u>Darkness</u>
Sloane

There's a darkness that lurks inside all of us.

Some more so than others.

But it's there. Always trying to claw its way out.

Eating away at any happiness it can find and consuming your soul until there's nothing left.

Soon, you'll find that you prefer the darkness.

That you'll yearn for the peace it brings you when you get to spend time with it.

Because in this darkness lives your greatest fears.

Your worst nightmares.

The very thing you would never wish upon another human.

Yet you'll allow it to consume you.

To turn you into something you don't even recognize.

It will take away everything you've ever loved and remind you why you stopped living.

Everyone has this darkness inside of them.

Everyone has that climactic event in their life that unleashes it.

But some of us have *someone* who is responsible for all of it.

He was my darkness.

My reason for not wanting to live.

He took everything from me.

And now it was time I showed him what the darkness of hell looked like…

<u>Massacre</u>
Sloane

"Do we have to go?" I whined as Gabe wrapped his arms around my waist and planted a kiss on my nose.

"Yes. We haven't been to see your parents since Nicky was born. It would be good to get out of the house for a bit. Get some fresh air."

"I get out of the house," I objected with a scowl as I looked down at the baby asleep in his car seat that Gabe had just put him in.

"I know you do. I'm just saying that it would be nice to visit your parents. Your dad calls all the time. He's worried about you."

"There's nothing to worry about. I'm fine. The baby is fine. Everything is fine." I threw my hands up in frustration. I didn't want to get into the many reasons why I hated going back to my hometown.

"It's been three months, my love. I know that you've never been close to your mom, but I can't help but want Nicky to grow up knowing his grandparents. Plus, I know how much it hurts your dad not to be as involved in his only grandson's life as he could be. I'm not trying to guilt you into any of this. I just thought maybe we could try *together*."

He gently squeezed my chin between his thumb and pointer finger as he lightly kissed my lips. I knew he was right about it hurting my dad not being involved with my son, and I hated that.

"But it's so cloudy outside. What if there's a bad storm? I don't think we should chance taking Nicky out in this."

"It will be fine. I promise you. I won't let anything bad ever happen to you or Nicky. You know that. You two are my whole world."

I sighed heavily, knowing I wasn't going to win.

"Fine. But do they know we're coming?" I asked, already making a mental list of everything we needed to take with us. My parents lived a few hours away, but I already knew that the moment we arrived, they would want us to stay the weekend with them. More so, my dad, but my mom would go along with it to make him happy.

"I'll call once we get on the road. I've already packed the essentials, but if you want to pack your stuff, I'll go load the car."

I nodded and rolled my head on my neck, trying to relieve some of the mounting tension. No matter how hard I tried, I couldn't ignore the feeling that something bad was going to happen.

Half an hour later, we were on the road as I sat in the passenger seat and gripped the seat tightly. Gabe reached over and placed his hand on my thigh to calm me, but it was pointless. My leg bounced nervously as I stared out the window, just waiting for something to happen.

As if the universe could sense my unease, a dark cloud above us burst, releasing a torrent of rain that made it impossible to see the road ahead. Gabe pulled his hand away and gripped the steering wheel as I felt him try to slow down on the two-lane highway.

The ringing in my ears got louder as I closed my eyes and waited for the impact. Thankfully, it never came. I opened my eyes and found Gabe completely focused on the road in front of him, though it was hard to see through the rain that was coming down in sheets in front of us. Soon enough, the storm passed, the clouds parted, and a comforting stream of sunshine floated in.

By the time we got to my parents' house, Nicky was waking up from his nap. He wasn't usually a fussy baby, but that didn't stop me from getting out of the car and making him my sole focus to avoid my mother, who was waiting for us on the front porch.

"Oh, Jack, darling. They're here!" she called from the steps before making her way toward the car.

My father opened the screen door and smiled, adjusting the ball cap on his head as his eyes met mine. My dad and I had always been close, ever since I was a little girl and found an interest in sports instead of baking. That always irritated my mother, which was part of the reason our relationship had always been strained. She wanted her only child to be exactly like her, while I did everything in my power to be the complete opposite, which was also why we hadn't spoken since Nicky was born. She had given so much unsolicited advice in the hospital right after I had him that I had wanted to protect my peace for a while and avoided her calls to check in after they went home.

"Hey, sweet pea," my father said, pulling me into his side as he hugged me and looked down at the baby. "How was the drive out here?"

"Scary," I admitted with a nervous laugh as my mom watched me. "We got caught in a bad storm and couldn't see anything for a few miles. I'm just thankful that we made it here in one piece."

"Always so dramatic," my mother said, waving her hand as she reached for the baby.

My glare was icy as I clutched him tighter to my chest. Her eyes fell as she nervously tucked a strand of hair behind her ear and looked away. Not that there was actually a hair out of place. That would never happen because my mother always had to be perfect, and that included not stepping foot outside her house unless her appearance was immaculate.

"The storm was pretty bad," Gabe said, coming to my side after unloading our stuff from the trunk. "But the good news is that we're here now."

"Yes, well…" my mother started and then stopped abruptly from the look my father gave her.

"Go ahead and head inside," my dad said, guiding me as he put himself between me and my mom. "It's supposed to be nice tonight, so I thought we would head over to watch the football game if you guys are up for it."

"Sure," I replied as a genuine smile kissed my lips. "I would love that."

Growing up in the small town of Oak Creek, Colorado, meant that most of our entertainment came from the local high school sports. My dad and I always went to the football games on the weekends, while my mother would come up with an excuse why she couldn't attend. But it never bothered me any. We had more fun without having to worry about her.

We went inside and put our stuff in my old room, which my mother had turned into a guest room the same day I moved out. She insisted it had nothing to do with our falling out back then, but that she needed space in case anyone came to town and needed a place to stay. In all my life, I had never seen my parents have company that stayed longer than a few hours. More importantly, neither of them had family they stayed in contact with, so it was just me and Gabe who came to visit.

"Do you think I should put Nicky in his pajamas now?" I asked Gabe as I rummaged through the suitcase to find the ones I wanted. "It can get cold quickly, and I don't want him to be uncomfortable. Maybe I should take his thick blanket." I knew how brutal the cold could get here in the fall.

I looked up to find the man I loved standing in front of me with a gentle smile on his lips.

"I think he's fine in what he's wearing," he replied as he pulled me next to him, bringing my focus to his mouth as he licked his lips. "I'll pack a bag full of stuff for him before we go. If you want to change so *you're* warm, I would do that now. You know how impatient your mom gets when she *has* to go to these things."

I chuckled, knowing he was right. I glanced down at Nicky, who was lying in his portable crib, looking up at us. He was one of the happiest babies I knew, almost never fussing about anything.

I grabbed a pair of fleece-lined leggings and a thick hoodie before heading into the bathroom to change. It felt weird being back in my old house, but at the same time, there was something calming about being away from the big city. We had called Denver home for years now, but sometimes, I really missed how slow-paced things were here.

By the time we got to the game, my mother's mood was as sour as the lemonade my dad bought us from the concession stand. It was never the best, but it was our tradition to eat as much junk food as we could at the game before going home to get scolded by Mom. She had rolled her eyes when he came back earlier, arms filled with hot dogs, cotton candy, and bags filled with peanuts. He passed them around, putting a hot dog right under her nose as she snubbed it and looked away. He laughed it off and adjusted his ball cap before pulling the hot dog out of the foil sleeve it was in.

The game was as good as you could expect for a high school football game, but it was the energy of everyone around us that made it fun. I'd seen and said hello to those whom I remembered from when I used to live here, grinning when they all took an interest in my baby. It felt nice to be surrounded by people who were genuinely happy for me. That was the nice thing about small towns: you practically knew everybody.

We had just finished eating when Nicky woke up in the carrier that Gabe had strapped to his chest. He took him out and kissed his face before turning him around to see the game. Gabe bounced him on his knees while holding Nicky against his chest and making him wave at the high school cheerleaders.

I grinned, my cheeks almost burning, as I watched my husband and son enjoying a football game together, just like I used to with my dad. The crowd roared as one of the guys on our team intercepted the ball and ran it down the field for a touchdown. We stood up and cheered, the joy around us contagious.

Right after we sat down, three men wearing black leather jackets and low-hung beanies on their heads walked by, blocking the view of the game as they stopped in front of us. A chill snaked down my spine as I felt Gabe tense beside me as he turned Nicky around and held him tighter against his chest.

"Are you Hugo Sanchez?" the one in the middle asked as the other two kept their hands in their pockets and scanned the bleachers. Everyone's attention was still on the game, except for those right next to us who had gone dead silent.

"No," Gabe rushed out quickly as I stared at the guy's face, taking in the small black widow tattoo under his eye and the scar above his right eyebrow. The one in front of me turned his attention to me, the clearest blue eyes locking onto mine as the guy in the middle let out a heavy sigh and cocked his head to the side. The guy on the far right lifted his hand, a snake tattoo wrapping around most of it, as he pointed a gun at Gabe.

"I don't even know a Hu—" Gabe started before his breath slipped out of him as a bullet pierced him right between the eyes.

"NOOOO!" I screamed as I watched his body fall back from the impact.

Everything happened in slow motion as I lunged in front of Gabe, taking Nicky as another bullet whizzed past my head. I grabbed Gabe's shirt and tried to hold him upright as Nicky screamed in my arms, blood soaking through his clothes.

Gunshots continued around us as I stared down at my son, horror filling my eyes as I realized that he'd been shot.

"NOO!!" I screamed again, praying as hard as I could as I pressed my hand against Nicky's back to try to stop the bleeding.

"God, please don't take them," I begged, closing my eyes as I struggled to hold onto my family. I squeezed Nicky tighter against my chest and kissed his face as his cries started to slow. "I love you, baby. I love you so much. I'm so sorry. I'm so sorry, my love."

I saw my dad trying to make his way over to help me, but before he could get there, a bullet hit him. He stumbled back, clutching his chest as blood immediately stained his cream-colored shirt red as it poured out. My mother wailed as she reached for him.

There was a sharp pain in my shoulder, but I ignored it as I screamed at the top of my lungs and leaned over my family, trying to shield them as their blood soaked my clothes.

I cried out for someone to help us.

Anyone.

But my cries went unanswered as people rushed around us while pure chaos ensued, and the gunfire continued. I closed my eyes and prayed harder than I had ever prayed before. Hoping for a miracle.

Broken

Numbness
Sloane

"I'm so sorry for your loss," the doctor repeated as he stood beside my bed and clasped his hands in front of him. "We did everything we could, but we weren't able to save your husband. Unfortunately, the damage was too extensive."

He continued talking, but I couldn't hear the words. Nothing could stop the overwhelming numbness I had when I looked at the bag beside me that had Gabe and my dad's stuff inside it. The white Colorado Rockies ball cap I had given my dad for Father's Day sat on top of the bag, red splattered across it from the blood. Whose blood? I had no idea. In a matter of seconds, my entire life had ended.

The number of people who were injured far exceeded those who died, but it had turned into a complete blood bath as the three men shot their way out of the crowd and escaped. I wasn't sure that they had a final death toll just yet, as the small town hospital overflowed with those who had been shot.

"What about Nicky?" I asked, my voice barely above a whisper.

The doctor shook his head and then gathered the strength to speak the words that would shatter my heart.

"I'm so sorry, but we've done everything we can, and while he's on life support currently, there are no signs that he will recover." His voice cracked, breaking my heart along with it. "I can take you to see him whenever you're ready."

What he really meant was that he could take me to say goodbye to my baby because not even the best doctors in the world could have saved him. I balled my fists at my sides and held in the hateful words I wanted to hurl at the doctor. It wasn't his fault, but I had been hopeful that there would be a miracle that would save my baby's life.

I had done nothing but curse God from the moment I woke up in the stupid hospital bed. It wasn't fair that I was there and they were all dead. I wanted to be dead, too. What kind of life was I supposed to live without them? Not one that I wanted to live.

"How's your pain?" the doctor asked, trying to pull me back into the conversation after I refused to acknowledge what he said.

"Fine."

"If it starts to become uncomfortable, just push the call button, and a nurse will come to administer pain meds. It's important to stay on top of the pain so it doesn't get out of control."

"Maybe I deserve to feel it," I muttered, looking away from him and catching a glimpse of my mother sitting in the corner of the room with her knees pulled to her chest.

For once, she didn't look perfect. Her hair was a mess, and her clothes were covered in blood, much like mine were before they took me to the operating room. I had been shot in my shoulder when I leaned over to shield my family. But I wished it were my heart instead. Perhaps then it wouldn't hurt as badly as it did now.

I watched her, looking completely disheveled, as she rocked back and forth on the floor, trying to console herself.

"I'll come by later to check on you." The doctor offered a small smile and stepped out of the room.

I closed my eyes and willed my brain to be as numb as my body was as I drifted back to sleep and prayed that I wouldn't wake up.

****

Seeing Nicky had been absolutely gut-wrenching. His lifeless body hooked up to all of the machines to keep him alive broke me in a way I had never felt before. My mother went with me, both of us sobbing uncontrollably as we stared at him, knowing there was nothing that could be done for him. While the machines kept his body going, he was already gone.

We sat quietly in the room, waiting for the nurse to come back and let me know when I would be discharged. I didn't want to stay in the hospital any longer than I needed, yet I had nowhere else to go. My life ended the moment my family was taken from me, so I was stuck in this futile state of existence for the time being.

There was a gentle knock on the door before it was pushed open, and an older man stepped inside, closing it behind him. I'd met him a few times at the church my parents attended.

"Sloane, Karen," he greeted as he held his hands in front of him and bowed his head. "I'm so very sorry for your loss. Please know that I'm holding both of you very tight in prayer during this difficult time."

"Thank you, Reverend Blue," my mother said, the first words I'd heard her speak since I woke up to this nightmare.

"The congregation has been discussing setting up a meal train for you ladies once you're ready. I told them I would pass along any special requests if you have them."

"No, thank you. That's not necessary, but we appreciate the gesture," my mother assured him while I sat numbly in the bed.

What neither of us was bothering to say was that there was no amount of kindness anyone could give us that would make this situation even slightly better. Our family had suffered an unfathomable loss, and nothing could heal that.

Uncontrollable sobs washed over me in waves as my mother climbed into the bed beside me, careful not to touch my shoulder as she held me. It was the first and only time that I could remember having this sort of connection with my mother, but I didn't focus on that as we fell apart together. The door closed a few minutes later, and I knew we were by ourselves. I didn't have the strength to comfort her back because I barely had the strength to want to keep living.

****

I sat in a chair with sunglasses hiding my red, swollen eyes as Reverend Blue said a prayer as he stood behind the three caskets. Tears silently slid down my face as my mother squeezed my hand. There was a large turnout for the funeral, but I couldn't tell you who was there. My mind was numb, and living was a chore in itself. Not only that, but this wasn't the only funeral the people of Oak Creek would be attending this week. The amount of grief that weighed on this town was more than any of us could bear.

One final prayer was said before people quietly got up and paid their last respects before leaving. I remained seated, refusing to leave. Birds chirped in the tree above me, singing a beautiful song as a gentle breeze floated past me.

There was no one left other than my mom, who stood off to the side, thanking a few of her friends for coming. I knew that the next step was that their coffins would be lowered into the ground, but when the two men approached Nicky's, I lost it.

I got up and rushed over, throwing myself on top of it as if I could stop this from happening. They stepped back and gave me space as I held onto his coffin and wept for my son. A guttural scream ripped through my chest, shredding any remaining life I had in me.

Strong hands wrapped around me, comforting me as I continued to cry.

I didn't have to look up to know who it was. I leaned into his embrace and allowed myself to be consoled by the first man who ever held my heart.

"I've got you," Everett said, allowing himself to sink to the ground with me as he continued to hold me. "I've got you."

I didn't bother to tell him that he'd said those words to me before. The truth was that I used to think he broke my heart. But back then, I didn't know what a broken heart really felt like because a broken heart was nothing compared to the shattered one I had now.

Old Flames

Everett

I couldn't focus on anything other than holding Sloane in my arms as she fell apart. My heart ached for her as she gripped the side of the casket that held her baby, my throat raw as I wanted to scream with her. I wanted to get my hands on the assholes who did this and rip their throats out for causing her so much pain. For causing all of us so much pain.

"I've got you," I whispered as her body relaxed against me, and she clutched my shirt as sobs wracked through her. "It's okay. I've got you, Sloane."

I knew my words did nothing to make things better for her, but I hated the thought that she felt so completely alone right now. I had gotten the call about my brother when it happened, and came back immediately, but my world crashed around me when I heard the news about Sloane's family.

"Thank you," Sloane's mother said softly, standing beside us as she gave me a slight smile. She didn't bother to try to get Sloane to stop crying, which surprised me. I hadn't seen

Karen be this soft or caring to Sloane in my entire life, but grief changes people.

"I'm so sorry about Frankie. Your mother was just telling me that his services are tomorrow. Sloane and I will be there," Karen said as Sloane slowly pulled away and looked up at me.

Her eyes were hidden behind her dark sunglasses, but I could see the tears still running down her face.

"Frankie?" Sloane asked as she started crying again.

I nodded, my jaw tight as I struggled to keep from falling apart in front of her.

But Sloane knew me better than anyone. We grew up together and had been best friends since kindergarten. We dated in high school but broke up right after graduation when I got accepted to New York University, where I studied criminal law before joining the FBI. I asked her to go with me to New York, but she declined. She wanted to be close to her dad and moved to Denver instead. Trying to act unaffected by my baby brother's death wasn't going to convince Sloane that I was alright. She knew how close we were, even with a ten-year age gap between me and Frankie.

"Oh my God," Sloane sobbed, her body trembling as a new wave of grief washed over her. "He was just a baby."

"He was getting ready to celebrate his eighteenth birthday in a few months," I replied sadly. "I was planning to come home for it before he went off to Harvard in the fall."

"I'm so sorry," she cried, removing her sunglasses to wipe at her eyes with the palms of her hands. "Like my mom said, we will be there for his service."

"Thank you."

Sloane looked around, the crowd of people already gone as the workers stayed a distance away to give her space.

"I don't think I can just leave them here," she said, her face falling as new tears started. "I need to see that they're laid to rest properly. That it's done with respect."

I nodded as her mother agreed. I stood up and extended my hand, helping Sloane as I nodded to let the workers know they could get started. I guided Sloane and Karen over to the seats that were still out when Sloane suddenly stopped and turned around.

We gave her space as she went to the casket her husband was in and laid over it, giving him one final hug.

"I love you so much. Take care of our baby in heaven for me."

I turned my head to give her privacy as I wiped a tear from the corner of my eye.

Sloane came and sat down, her sobs echoing around us as Karen lowered her head and started crying. I stood behind them and placed a hand on each of their shoulders, trying to give them whatever strength I had.

Jack's coffin was lowered into the ground first, then Sloane's husband's. Her baby was last, and I knew it had to be destroying her to see it because it wasn't even my baby, and I felt like the life was being ripped out of me as his coffin was lowered.

I gently squeezed their shoulders as I made a silent vow that I would find the monsters responsible for this and make them pay.

Nightmares
Sloane

Dark eyes locked onto me as he lifted the gun and pointed it at my face. I stared back, challenging him to pull the trigger. But he just tossed his head back and laughed, the black widow tattoo crinkling on his face as he pushed me out of the way and grabbed Nicky instead.

Nicky wasn't a baby anymore. He was a little boy. Beautiful brown eyes and rosy cheeks that lit up his smile. He looked from the man to me, sadness washing over his face as he stared at me.

"Save me, Momma," he whispered right as the gun went off.

I startled, springing up in bed, throwing the covers off me as sweat ran down my back. I gasped for air, struggling to catch my breath. My heart drummed loudly in my ears, making it impossible to hear anything else. I quickly looked around, trying to gather my bearings as I reminded myself it was just a dream.

Well, technically, a nightmare. But why bother calling them that when my entire life was a nightmare? I had the same dream almost every night after Gabe, my father, and Nicky were murdered. Every single night, I would stare at the man with the black widow tattoo beneath his eye and beg him not to kill my family.

Sometimes, he turned his attention from them to me, shooting me once before going back and murdering them before my eyes. Other times, he took his time slowly killing each of them as I screamed until it woke my mother.

I couldn't bring myself to go back to Denver after Gabe died, aside from the one trip I made with my mother to gather whatever belongings I wanted. But there was nothing there anymore. Aside from a few pictures I had kept on the mantle, nothing else seemed to matter to me. We packed up everything else and donated it before listing the house for sale.

Things were better overall with my mother, but we didn't dare talk about our past, just like we avoided talking about our present. It was like we were two lifeless souls left to wander the Earth and keep each other company in doing so. Neither of us had a purpose anymore, and thanks to my father's life insurance, my mother didn't have to worry about anything financially. I had gotten enough from the sale of the house and Gabe's life insurance that I didn't have to worry either, yet there wasn't enough money in the world to drown out the depression that lingered over both of us.

I got out of bed and quietly used the restroom, careful not to wake my mother. Who knew if she was even sleeping? Two months had passed since our family was murdered, and yet we both continued as if it were just yesterday. Sometimes, it felt like it was. There was no moving on from the soul-shattering grief that overwhelmed me. No relief from the ache that burrowed so deep in my chest it felt like I was constantly dying.

When I got back to my room, I was too awake to try to go back to sleep. I glanced at the clock, groaning when I saw it was barely two in the morning. It would be hours before I would be able to fall asleep again, only to have to wake up and get the day started. Not that there was anything exciting waiting for me, but still, my mother insisted that we at least make an effort to move forward.

I grabbed my pencil and the sketchbook from my dresser and plopped down on the bed. I opened it and flipped through the pages, each one filled with the image of the man who killed my family.

When I first started sketching him, it was always the same image that was permanently engrained in my brain: him pointing the gun at Gabe and taking his life. That image haunted me more than anything else, and even drawing it didn't do anything to push it from my subconscious. Then, I started to have recurring nightmares and began to sketch out those instead. It was almost like I was giving myself a glimpse into what my future could have been as I watched my baby progress and grow up a little bit every night, proof of his changes on the pages.

I hated what had been robbed of me, but even though the nightmares were terrible, I couldn't help but notice the features that changed as Nicky got older. His baby face thinned out, and he went from looking like I did as a baby to looking just like his dad. When my nightmares turned to him being a toddler, I noticed the dimples in his cheeks that mirrored Gabe's. And when he became a little boy last week, I cried when I realized that he was a spitting image of my husband. My heart ached to see what could have been, but I knew that this was all I would ever have of him. Images that my subconscious created as it tortured my soul with what had been ripped away from me.

I flipped to a new page and began sketching, capturing the haunting image of Nicky as a little boy, with fear in his eyes as he begged me to save his life. I moved quickly, turning my head to the side to avoid getting the page wet as the tears ran down my face.

Justice

Sloane

"I'm sorry. I wish there were more I could say, but unfortunately, we don't have much information. We're doing everything we can."

The sheriff of Oak Creek shoved his hands into his pockets as he delivered the unnerving news to my mother and me as we sat at the kitchen table. The same table that neither of us could bring ourselves to eat at anymore. I lost track of how many family dinners we had at this table, and every time I looked at it, I was reminded of losing him. The joy and warmth I used to feel from family dinners were forever gone, and that hurt deeply.

But in all fairness, it wasn't like we ate that much these days. It had barely been two months since their tragic deaths, and aside from my mother's friends and the people from church popping in with premade meals for us, neither of us took the time to cook, let alone eat. Grief was actively consuming both of us, and I was ready to let it have me.

"So, what happens now?" my mother asked, fresh tears pooling in her eyes. "We just let the monster that killed Jack run free?"

"Until we know who it is, there's not much we can do about it." Sheriff Dowdy responded.

"It wasn't just Dad," I said quietly, hating the ice-cold hatred in my voice.

"Yes. I know," my mother said, her voice tight.

"Say. Their. Names," I growled, my eyes narrowing on her.

"The sheriff is well aware of whose murders he is investigating," she snapped, returning the look I gave her.

"I don't give a flying fuck. I want *you* to say their names and stop acting like Dad was the only one who lost his life that day."

"I'm well aware of how many people we lost that day."

"But yet you can't bring yourself to say, Gabe and Nicky. Why, Mom?" Tears filled my eyes as I looked into hers, wondering if there was anything left of her soul.

"Because, Sloane, I can't say their names without picturing my only grandson in that tiny coffin. I can't say his name without seeing you cradle his lifeless body as you screamed in agony. I can't stand the thought that you lost the love of your life. That we both did. I don't say their names because it breaks what little bit of a heart I have left. They all suffered a painful, tragic death. And it kills me knowing that they all died while the monsters who did this are still out there, roaming free."

She gave a pointed look to the sheriff as she reached over and squeezed my hand gently.

"Trust me, Karen. We are doing everything in our power to find the assholes who did this," Sheriff Dowdy assured her before looking at me. "I want justice just as much as you do.

I attempted to press my lips into a smile, but it fell flat into a thin line instead.

"Well, that's not good enough," my mother huffed, pulling her shoulders back. "Can't you get the FBI or National Guard or someone to help? It's already been two months, and nothing has been done."

"I've reached out to the FBI for assistance, but I can't promise you that they'll be able to do much. I'm not at liberty to discuss anything, but this whole thing goes deeper than one tragic event. We have a bigger issue on our hands, and I'm sure their attention will be focused on that first."

"What is the issue?" I asked, completely ignoring his statement about not being able to discuss it.

He arched an eyebrow at me in warning, his old, scruffy face turning cold.

"Like I said, I can't discuss it."

"Can't? Or won't?"

He leveled me with a look, and I felt my mother stiffen beside me.

"I ask because some man killed my husband right in front of me. That same man asked him if he was Hugo Sanchez—someone no one in this town seems to know. So yeah, I think at this point, we're entitled to know what's going on—all of it. Because I'll be damned if my family died at the hands of a madman and justice is never served. If there's something bigger than just their murders happening—which I can tell there is by how your ears just turned red—we deserve to know."

"*I* decide *who* needs to know *what*. At this time, there is nothing more that I can tell you," he pressed.

I leaned back against the wooden chair and folded my arms over my chest.

"Do you honestly believe that whatever happened that day is just over now?" I asked, cocking my head to stare at him. "That this small town could have a massacre like that, and no one bats an eye? Who is to say that we've seen the end of this? Obviously, there were several witnesses there that night who saw what had happened. They could easily identify the men who did this if any effort were made to find them and bring them in. It's not just my mom and me who want justice. This whole town demands it. We've all suffered an immeasurable loss."

"I know that it might seem that easy from all of the cop shows on TV, but it's not. So why don't you worry about being there for your mom and let me do my job the way I see fit?"

I shook my head as I stared at him, wondering how someone who took an oath to protect and serve was doing the exact opposite. The nonchalant way he talked about this, as if it were a random petty crime and not a mass murder, blew my mind.

Deceit

Everett

"What do you mean you have no leads? It's been two months!" I demanded, throwing my hands in the air as I sat across from Sheriff Dowdy.

I had come into his office to check on how things were going with the case, only to find that nothing had been done. I ground my teeth as my jaw clenched to keep from reaching across the table and smacking that smug look off his face.

"These things take time," he grumbled, fussing with the papers on his desk instead of giving me his full attention.

"Then let me help."

"You have no jurisdiction here. Not only that, your brother was one of the victims. Even if you had jurisdiction here, it would be a conflict of interest to allow you to work the case."

"Are you kidding me?"

He finally set the papers down, folded his hands in front of him on the desk, and gave me an ice-cold stare.

"Look, I know it sucks. But like I've told everyone else, we are doing the best we can. We have limited resources and are trying to get help where we can."

"But—"

He held his hand up and stopped me.

"You know as well as I do that you cannot work this case without letting your feelings get involved. Not only was your brother murdered, but your ex-girlfriend lost several members of her family. I have reason to believe that your judgment would be clouded and that you would retaliate instead of bringing them to justice the right way."

I arched an eyebrow as I leaned back in the chair and rested my ankle on my knee.

"You act like we're talking about someone who was wrongfully accused of a crime they didn't commit instead of discussing the three men who came in and brutally murdered several people in what you all are calling a case of *mistaken identity*."

"Innocent until proven guilty is the part you seem to be overlooking," he countered.

I threw my hands in the air and stared at him in disbelief.

"What about the video footage Stan got? I don't know how much more proof you need than a video of them committing the crime they're being accused of. Not only that, but why aren't you taking the video and getting it analyzed? Facial recogniti—"

"You mean the footage that stops right before the shooting started?" he said, interrupting me.

He held my gaze as he arched an eyebrow.

My face fell as I processed his words.

"What are you talking about? You and I both know that there was more. Stan showed me himself before he handed it over to your—"

I stopped before the words could fall out of my mouth.

"Sorry," I said, shaking my head as I pushed a hand through my hair. "You're right. I thought Stan said it had captured the shooting, but it didn't. It stopped right before. I must have been so hopeful that he got it that I made myself believe that he did."

Sheriff Dowdy's face changed as he nodded in agreement. My jaw clenched even tighter as I processed the tangled web of lies he was trying to feed me.

"Well, I should get out of your hair so you can get back to it. If you need anything, feel free to reach out," I said, standing up and extending my hand in a gesture of goodwill, even though I felt anything but hatred for the man. He was hiding something—that was obvious by the lies he just spewed. What wasn't obvious was why.

He gave it a quick shake and studied me.

"I thought you were returning to New York soon?"

I pushed the chair in and shoved my hands into my pockets to keep from fidgeting.

"I was, but I decided to extend my leave. My mother isn't doing the best right now, and I want to be there for her."

"Well, I'm sure she appreciates it," he muttered, lowering his eyes to avoid mine.

I didn't say anything else as I turned and left, but knowing that my prolonged presence bothered him was all the justification I needed to stick around. Something was going on, and I was determined to figure out what.

<u>Breaking Point</u>
Sloane

I leaned my head against the bath pillow and closed my eyes, allowing the hot water to soothe me. The light scent of vanilla, mixed with lavender, floated in the air, calming my senses, which had been on high alert lately.

The meeting with the sheriff hadn't gone well, and while my mother was nicer to him about it, I had been fuming since the moment he left the house. In an effort to lift my spirits, my mother suggested that we go out to dinner and get out of the house for a bit. I declined, much to her disappointment.

It had barely been two months, and I hadn't had the desire to do anything, especially go out just to be bombarded with people wanting to extend their condolences over and over. That was almost as bad as the constant stares I received anytime I left the house. My mother didn't push, which I was thankful for. Instead, she went out with her friends and promised to bring dinner back for me when she returned, since I still refused to eat if I didn't have to.

I sank lower into the water, not caring about it spilling over the side of the tub. An immediate relief washed over me as the water covered my head, and everything went silent. I kept my eyes closed and held my breath, flirting with the edge of darkness as I contemplated how long I could hold my breath before death had mercy on me.

My mind was clear as I pictured Gabe and me on our wedding day, the smile spread across his face as I smeared frosting down his nose. The way he tilted his head back and laughed before capturing me in his arms and rubbing it onto my cheek as he nuzzled my face. A soft smile played on my lips as my heart raced. I ignored the tightness in my chest as I continued to hold my breath, a rush of warmth flooding through me as I remembered the day Nicky was born. The nurse smiled as she handed him to me, and I cradled him against my chest.

I knew I needed to come up for air, but I refused to leave these memories. This was all that I had left of them, and I wanted more.

But then the happiness that I had felt suddenly vanished as I heard a gunshot and saw Nicky on Gabe's chest as blood covered both of them. I startled, springing upright as I gripped the sides of the tub and gasped for air as the water cascaded to the floor.

I looked around, trying to orient myself as everything felt darker. The candle I had lit flickered in the corner of the tub, but everything else was bathed in darkness aside from the dim light the candle provided.

I rubbed my eyes, trying to clear the visions that haunted me as my heart continued to race. It happened every single time I replayed that moment. My therapist had encouraged me to push through them when they happened and to allow myself to feel whatever I needed to at the moment. But this time, it felt different. It felt real, as if it had happened again.

As I lowered my hands and looked around, I realized that it actually was dark in the bathroom and not just my imagination. I grabbed my phone and checked the time, finding a text message from my mom that she was heading home. That was over ten minutes ago, so she should be home by now.

I pulled the plug to drain the tub as I stood up and wrapped the towel around my body, trying not to trip and fall over anything. The sound of rain pelted the window as the wind howled in the distance. I knew we were supposed to get another winter storm, but I hadn't expected the power to go out with it.

I quickly got dressed and left the candle lit so we'd have light in the bathroom if we needed it until the power came back on. I opened the bathroom door and started to head downstairs when I heard my mom. I stopped, gripping the banister tightly as I recognized the fear in her voice. She wasn't alone.

"Please, don't," she begged. "Please…"

A chill snaked up my spine as I froze the second I recognized the voice.

"Tell us where she is," he demanded.

I crouched down, careful not to make a sound, as I lowered myself to see better. Standing in front of my mom was the man with the black widow tattoo under his eye. The other two guys from that night stood off to the side of him, scanning the room.

"She's not here. She's out. With friends," my mother lied.

Why were they looking for me?

"Go search the house," he instructed the other two guys as he reached behind him and pulled a gun out. He pressed it against my mother's forehead as his cold, soulless eyes stared at her. "Last chance. Tell me where she is."

The two guys had already started going through the different rooms downstairs as I covered my mouth and slowly took a step back. The wood beneath me creaked, drawing attention to the stairs.

My eyes widened in fear as the guy with the blue eyes rounded the corner and locked eyes with me. A devious smile crossed his face as he quickly began climbing the stairs.

I turned and ran, not having a plan other than getting to safety. I dashed into my bedroom, closing the door behind me as I heard his heavy footsteps down the hall. As quickly as I could, I shoved the small dresser in front of the door and threw on a pair of shoes before opening the window and looking down.

Sneaking out of this room countless times as a teenager worked in my favor as I moved quickly, trying to get down before he got past the dresser. I held onto the lattice and was almost to the bottom when I heard a gunshot. My heart dropped as I imagined my mother dying alone at the hands of the same man who killed my father, the same man who killed my husband and baby.

I dropped to the ground and took off running to the back of the house, where the detached garage was. I knew it would only be a matter of minutes before they came outside looking for me, so I didn't have time to stop and think about my mother or feel the pain that was radiating through me, knowing she was dead. If I were going to survive this, I had to move quickly and hide.

Rain poured down, making it hard to see past it as I stood at the side of the garage and tried to get in. The door always stuck, which was something my dad hated, but it was better than trying to go in through the front, where they might see me. Everything was cloaked in darkness with the dark storm clouds hanging above, which gave me an advantage to remain unseen for a little while longer.

I shivered as I willed my hands to stop shaking long enough to get the door open. Finally, it moved, opening barely enough to let me slide in. I pushed it closed the best I could, knowing that I didn't have the time to mess with it right now.

My parents lived in a small community with houses spaced out quite a bit. However, I couldn't stand the thought of these guys hurting any of their neighbors while looking for me. I had debated running over to the next house and begging for help, but I knew it wouldn't matter. They would find me and kill all of us before help could come.

I quickly scanned the garage, noting how much stuff had accumulated in it the last time I was there. The garage itself was large enough to fit three vehicles, but it seemed small, considering everything my parents stored inside it. An old car sat in the corner, a passion project my dad had once started but never finished, and in the middle of the garage was the boat he vowed to restore.

A puddle of water quickly formed at my feet, which would give them a trail to follow the second they got in there. I grabbed an old cleaning towel from my father's workbench and put it beneath me, wiping up the water as I quickly shuffled over to the boat. I grabbed the towel as I climbed in, wiping down everything I could along the way.

The boat had been filled with bags and bags of clothes that my mother planned to donate, but never got around to. I moved them as quickly as I could before lying down in the center of the boat and pulling them on top of me, making sure to leave a tiny hole where I could breathe under the weight of them.

I held my breath when I heard banging on the bay door before it was forced open.

"She's in here. Find her," a deep voice growled, sending a chill through me.

I stayed as still as possible, too afraid to even breathe right now. These men had murdered my entire family, and I wasn't going to give them the satisfaction of killing me, too.

Heavy footsteps surrounded me as I continued to hold my breath with my eyes pinched shut. I knew it wouldn't be long until they checked inside the boat. Loud clanging noises filled the air as they flipped things over and threw whatever was in their way as they searched for me.

The car door slammed, and the sound of old, rusted metal made my heart ache from memories of time spent here with my dad.

I slowly started counting in my head to keep myself both calm and distracted from the destruction happening around me. Glass broke and crunched beneath their boots as they encircled the boat.

Suddenly, I felt the boat sway as someone climbed in the back and started tossing the bags onto the garage floor. They were still a few feet away from me, but it would only take seconds for them to uncover me.

I pressed my lips together to keep from screaming as I heard sirens in the distance. Someone must have heard the gunshot at my mother's house and called the police. Either that or she was still alive and called for help herself. My heart fluttered at the thought.

"Fuck," a deep voice growled. "We gotta go. We'll come back for her later."

"But we know she's in here somewhere. Why not just find her and deal with her now?" the guy in the boat with me said as he tossed another bag over the side. There was only one small bag that covered the bottom of my legs, and if he moved it, he would find me.

"Because we have strict orders. Now let's go."

The guy in the boat grunted before jumping over the side. Heavy footsteps sounded in the garage as they ran out and left the bay door open as thunder rumbled in the distance.

Broken

<u>Support</u>

Everett

"I need help," Sloane said as she stood soaking wet and shivering on my mother's doorstep.

My heart accelerated as I noted the fear in her eyes. I stepped to the side, gently pulling her in as I scanned the front yard for any sign of danger.

"What's wrong?" I asked, closing the door and locking it behind her as she dripped on the floor.

"Evere—" my mother started as she turned the corner into the entryway and noticed Sloane. "I'll get some towels and dry clothes."

I nodded, my jaw already tight from the tension I could feel radiating from Sloane.

"Are you okay?" I questioned, leading her away from the door as my mom reappeared with a towel for Sloane before rushing off to her bedroom to find something dry for her to wear. I helped wrap it around her shoulders as she continued to shiver.

"They killed my mom," she rushed out, pressing her lips together as tears filled her eyes.

"Who did?"

"The same men who killed my family. Who killed Frankie. They came to my house and shot my mother when she wouldn't tell them where I was." She lowered her head and let the tears fall as her body shook.

I grabbed her and pulled her into my arms. I had so many questions, but right now, my only concern was that Sloane was okay.

"I found these sweats," my mom said, returning a few minutes later.

Sloane pulled away and wiped her eyes with the back of her hand.

"Thank you. I appreciate it," Sloane said.

I stepped to the side so she could get past me to change in the bathroom.

"What's going on?" my mother asked quietly once Sloane was out of the room.

I shoved a hand through my hair and exhaled heavily.

"She said that her mom was murdered in their house. The guys who killed Frankie showed up asking for Sloane. Karen wouldn't tell them where she was, so they killed her."

"Oh my God." She gasped, covering her mouth with trembling hands. "That poor girl has lost every single person in her family in a matter of months."

"I know."

The thought that Sloane literally had no one left ate away at me like nothing I had ever felt before. What was even more disturbing was how calm she was about her mother being murdered. It was like she was already so numb she couldn't feel the pain of losing the last person in her family.

"Where is she going to go now? She can't possibly stay in that house by herself," my mom continued. "And you said they killed Karen inside the house?"

I nodded. I didn't have many details, but I knew Sloane would be devastated to lose her mom, regardless of their rocky history. In the past two months, the two of them had gotten closer, and I was happy that Sloane had someone to lean on. Now, all of that was gone.

"I can't imagine wanting to go back to the scene of the crime—that poor girl. I'm going to make some phone calls, but you tell Sloane she's welcome to stay with us as long as she needs. I can make up—"

My heart ached at the way my mother's face fell when she realized what she was going to say—Frankie's room. Our house wasn't big enough to have a guest room, which left the only extra room as Frankie's. My mother hadn't changed a single thing from how he left it before he was murdered.

"It's okay, Mom," I assured her, gently touching her shoulder.

"Yes. Well, um. I'm going to make a phone call."

She walked off and headed into the kitchen right as Sloane appeared. The sweats were a little too big for her, but she looked warm and comfortable, which was all that mattered.

"So, what now?" Sloane asked, her eyes bloodshot from crying.

She had been gone longer than needed to change clothes, so I knew she had taken a few minutes to let herself fall apart in the bathroom. I didn't blame her. I had no idea what I would do if I were her and suffered so much loss in such a short time.

"Honestly, I don't know," I admitted. "I'm sure the police will take over handling things at your house, so it will be a while before you can go back. You're welcome to stay he—"

"I can't." She shook her head as she looked around the room.

"I know that we have a past, but—"

"No, Everett," she said, interrupting me. "I can't stay here because they're going to keep coming for me until they kill me. I won't put you or your mother in danger. I'll find somewhere else to go."

I opened my mouth to tell her she was wrong, but I couldn't. She was right.

They weren't going to stop until she was dead. They had already made that clear tonight.

<u>Safety</u>
Sloane

"I'm sorry, this is all they had," Everett said as he slid the key card over the lock and opened the hotel room door.

I yawned as I stepped inside and put the duffle bag on the bed. Everett helped sneak me over to my house, and I climbed into my bedroom to grab a few things, knowing I would never set foot in that house again. Thankfully, all of the police were downstairs in the kitchen where my mother had been murdered. Whether or not they had been in my room yet remained unknown as nothing seemed out of place or missing.

I grabbed the essentials like clothes and shoes, and then made sure to take the pictures I wanted and my dad's baseball cap. I was thankful that I had been stashing a large amount of cash in case something happened and I needed to make a quick getaway. I grabbed Nicky's baby book, desperate to hold onto what little memories of him I could, even though I knew it would never be completed. But the thought of leaving it behind felt like I was leaving *him* behind. At least this way, I would always have pictures of him as a newborn, along with his tiny hand and footprints taken in the hospital.

The hotel room was decent in size and overall nice. A king-sized bed filled the majority of the space, with a large window that overlooked the city. Which city? I had no idea. Everett drove for hours throughout the night, stopping only once to drop off the rental car and pick up another one that was waiting for him at an abandoned warehouse. I didn't bother asking who the guy was or what kind of deal was made. For now, we had a vehicle that wasn't traceable to either of us.

"The couch is supposed to pull out into a bed," he said as he set his backpack down on the bistro table by the window. "I can sleep on that."

I frowned and shook my head.

"The bed is big enough for both of us," I countered, too tired to fight him.

The clock on the nightstand showed it was already after four in the morning, but I felt like I could sleep for a few days and still not feel rested.

"I don't want to make you uncomfortable." He pressed his lips into a thin line as he looked at me.

"It will be fine. We should get some sleep."

He nodded but didn't press the matter as I kicked off my shoes and set the duffle bag on the couch. I pulled the blankets back as I slid in and shut my eyes. Within minutes, I was asleep.

****

"What time is it?" I asked as I rolled over and found Everett sitting at the table, looking at his phone.

"A little after eight. I was looking at food options for breakfast. Is there anything you're in the mood for?"

"No," I mumbled as I pulled the blankets back and lowered my feet to the floor. My head was pounding, and I wanted nothing more than to go back to sleep and pretend this wasn't my life right now.

Everett got a call from his mom last night confirming that my mother was dead. I knew that I owed it to her to be there and take care of any arrangements, but Everett and I talked about how unsafe it was for me to be in Oak Creek right now. His mom assured me that she would take care of everything and give my mother the proper burial she deserved next to my father.

"There are some restaurants close by, or we can go downstairs and see if the hotel still has breakfast," he offered, interrupting the dark thoughts creeping through my brain.

"I'm going to pee and then go back to bed."

I went into the bathroom and closed the door, hating the woman who looked back at me in the mirror. I bent down and splashed cold water on my face, hoping that it would help. But swollen eyes with dark circles beneath them stared back at me, a broken shell of the woman I used to be.

I used the restroom and then washed my hands, ready to go back to bed, when I found Everett sitting on my side of the bed.

I arched an eyebrow at him, but he simply folded his arms and held my gaze.

"What are you doing?" I asked, shifting my weight.

"I would like to go to breakfast," he said softly.

"Then go. You don't need me for that."

I took a step, hoping he would get the message and get up.

"No. I'm not doing this with you, Sloane."

He shook his head, and I noticed the tension in his shoulders.

"Doing what?"

"I'm not going to sit back and watch you waste away. I know that you've been through a lot and that you're still grieving for your family. But I can't lose you, too. I won't."

"What do you want me to do, Everett?" I threw up my hands and let them fall to my sides. "You want me to plaster on a smile and pretend that everything is alright? Because it's not. Nothing is alright!"

"I know that!"

"Then why are you pressuring me about this? Just let me be. I'm far away in God knows where New Mexico—I'll be fine. I'm not your responsibility."

He stood up and took a few steps toward me until our chests were almost touching.

"You will *always* be my responsibility, Sloane. There will never come a day when I'm not taking care of you."

"I didn't ask you to!"

"No. You didn't. I *want* to. There's a difference. So I'm sorry if you mean so much to me that I refuse to step back and allow you to waste away into nothing. I love you too much to allow that to happen!"

I blinked a few times, wondering if I heard him correctly.

His face reddened as a faint blush washed over it, and he scrubbed a hand down the scruff on his jaw.

"You love me?" I asked quietly, not sure how I felt about that admission.

He raised an eyebrow and shook his head.

"I've always loved you, Sloane. You know that."

"Yeah, but then we broke up and haven't talked in like ten years."

"That doesn't mean I ever stopped."

I rubbed my lips together, unsure of what to say.

When Everett and I dated, I was madly in love with him. He felt like the very center of my universe, the core that everything else orbited. When we broke up, I was devastated. I swore I would never find love like that again. Then I met Gabe.

My stomach turned as I thought about my husband. It had only been two months since he died, but the sadness felt like it was just yesterday.

"I'm sorry. I shouldn't have said that. I was out of line, and I apologize," he assured me, gently pinching my chin between his fingers to get me to look at him. "I would never disrespect you, your husband, or the love you shared for each other. This is nothing more than childhood friends taking care of each other like family. I don't have any ulterior motives. I promise."

Tears stung my eyes at his words. His thumb gently wiped them away as he gave me an apologetic look, knowing that I no longer had anyone. My family was gone, and I was left to live in this cruel world without them.

"My intentions are to keep you safe. To help figure out who these men are and get justice for what they did. But I need your help, Sloane. I need you to take care of yourself. I can't imagine how hard it is. I can't imagine the pain you've endured. But I know how strong you are. I wasn't lying when I said that I've got you. But you have to let me help you. You have to at least try."

I nodded as I wiped the rest of the tears away.

"Let me shower and clean up. Then we'll go to breakfast."

He nodded, his shoulders sagging in relief as I grabbed some clean clothes and headed back to the bathroom.

Truths
Everett

"Okay. I'm ready," Sloane said as she came out of the bathroom. "I just need to find my sunglasses real quick."

I stayed sitting at the small table by the window as she went through the items in her duffle bag, pulling them out and setting them on the bed. A white Colorado Rockies baseball cap caught my eye as I noticed the red blood that was splattered across the front of it.

I opened my mouth to ask about it and then stopped, unsure of how to start.

Sloane looked up and caught my eye before lowering hers to the hat.

"It was my dad's," she said quietly.

"Why does it have blood on it?" I asked, leaning forward to get a better view.

"Because it was the hat he wore the night…"

Her words trailed off as she swallowed hard to push the emotion down.

My eyebrows rose as I stared in disbelief.

"Where did you get it?" I demanded, as a million questions ran through my mind as I continued to stare at her.

She frowned and picked it up, looking at it before she answered me.

"It was with the stuff they gave me in the hospital."

"What stuff, Sloane?"

She tilted her head and studied me for a minute as if I were out of my mind.

"I don't remember," she said, throwing her hands up as the hat fell to the bed. "There was just a pile of stuff they had collected when they… You know. Whatever. It was with the stuff they collected before they sent their bodies to the morgue, I guess. Why? What does it matter?"

"It matters because you have personal property from two men who were murdered, and there's still an ongoing investigation. This is evidence," I said sternly as I stood up and approached her. "Sloane, does the sheriff's department know you have this?"

There had to be some sort of mix-up at the hospital, and they gave her the stuff that should have gone to the sheriff's department. That was the only way to explain any of this. Perhaps the small town hospital didn't have enough crime happen for them to know the proper protocol for preserving personal property and containing it in an evidence bag. Given it was a murder investigation, there was no statute of limitations, which meant these items could be kept indefinitely.

"Deputy Sheriff Anderson was the one who gave it to me," she explained with a hand on her hip.

I sucked in a breath and stared at her in disbelief.

"What?" she asked, her eyes searching mine as I shoved a hand through my hair and shook my head. "Everett, what is going on?"

I covered my mouth with my hands as the realization hit me hard.

"They shouldn't have given you any of that stuff, Sloane. They keep all personal property that is relevant to the case. This is an ongoing murder investigation. You're literally holding onto items that should have been recorded as evidence. I don't know how this even got past the cop stationed outside your hospital door—but I mean, I guess it doesn't matter if the fucking deputy sheriff was the one to give you the stuff. Who is going to call out their boss on breaking protoc—"

"I didn't have anyone stationed outside my room when I was in the hospital," Sloane interrupted.

"What the fuck? Are you sure? Maybe you didn't know they were there because you couldn't see them from your bed."

"No," she confirmed with a shake of her head. "I know for a fact there wasn't anyone outside my door because I left to go see Nicky before I pulled the pl—"

A whimper escaped her lips as she covered her mouth to keep from saying it. Tears streaked her face as her knees started to buckle. I rushed over and wrapped my arms around her, holding her as she cried.

Someone was deliberately fucking with this investigation, and it was getting painfully clear that no one could be trusted.

56

<u>Hope</u>
Sloane

When Everett and I got the call last night that they had made an arrest and needed me to ID the men who murdered my family, we got in the car and headed straight back to Oak Creek.

It was weird being back in the small town and not having my parents to visit, but I pushed those thoughts aside as I stood in the police lineup room and waited by the one-way mirror for them to enter the room. Everett stood beside me, holding my hand as I held my breath. The door opened, and a handful of men entered the room, turning to face me.

"They can't see you," Everett reminded me softly.

"Take your time. There is no pressure to make an identification," the officer in the room with us said as he stood beside me and looked straight ahead while another officer stood at the back of the room.

I let out a heavy breath and slowly began looking, starting with the man on the left. I shook my head, more for assurance to myself than anything, and kept moving down the line. When I got to the third man, my breath caught in my throat as I stared into his baby-blue eyes.

"Number three," I said, my voice shaky as I felt tears sting my eyes.

A flashback of him looking at me before chasing me up the stairs ran through my mind, transporting me back to that night at my mom's house before they murdered her.

"Are you sure?" the officer asked, turning to face me.

"Yes. Positive. Suspect number three was there the night of the shooting at the football game and again at my mother's house the night she was murdered."

"Okay. Thank you." The officer turned and said something to the other officer, and then all six of the men were led out of the room before another six came in.

"We're going to repeat the same process," the officer explained as the men lined up and faced us. "Like I stated before, there is no pressure to make an identification. The suspects may or may not be present."

I nodded and took another deep breath, squeezing Everett's hand as my eyes started scanning the guys in the lineup. I felt the hope slipping away as none of them were immediately recognizable.

The officer gave me a few more seconds before pressing the button to speak to them.

"Turn to your left," he instructed, and they all did.

My eyes traveled the lengths of their bodies, looking for anything that would click in my brain as familiar. I shook my head when I felt Everett's gaze upon me. This wasn't going well. Was it possible that they had only found and arrested one of the guys responsible for the murders of several people that night?

"Turn to your right," the officer instructed, and I sucked in a breath as they did.

The one closest to the end turned, and when he did, I noticed the snake tattoo on his hand. I pinched my eyes closed, desperate to get a clear view of that night as I watched him raise his hand and aim his gun at Gabe.

"Number six," I said, my voice shaky.

"Are you sure?" the officer questioned.

"Positive."

He turned and said something to the other officer, and then the men left the lineup room. I blew out a frustrated breath, hating that I had yet to see the guy with the black widow tattoo. Out of all of them, I wanted him to pay the most. He was the one who started all of it. He fired the first shots that killed Gabe and Nicky. He was responsible for their deaths, and I wanted to see him pay for it.

Another group of men entered the room, and before they could get lined up, I rushed to the window and pressed my hands against it, staring in disbelief.

"Number one," I said, my voice more certain than ever as the man with the black widow tattoo under his eye and the scar above his eyebrow stared directly at me. I knew he couldn't see me through the one-way mirror, but that didn't stop the chill that snaked down my spine from the ice-cold look he gave me.

<u>Corruption</u>
Sloane

I had never been inside a courtroom, but the large room was just as intimidating as the three men sitting at the table across from me. The three men who murdered my family were finally going to face justice for doing so.

The judge steepled his fingers in front of him as he waited for me to finish answering the last question. I had gone into great detail about everything that happened that night, how we went from an innocent night of attending a high school football game together as a family to suddenly burying three innocent people. My foot tapped anxiously on the witness stand as I waited for their smug attorney to finish his questioning.

"Is there anything else you'd like to ask the witness, Mr. Carrio?" the judge asked, seeming bored and uninterested.

"Yes, one final question, your honor," Mr. Carrio said as he turned to glance at the three men he was representing before turning to face me again. "Mrs. Salazar, you've said that the distinct features of each of my clients were what led you to your positive identification. Is that correct?"

"Yes."

"Could you please tell the court what exactly those items were?"

I swallowed hard and pulled my shoulders back as I felt the angry, heated looks from the three men who deserved to be behind bars.

"The first one I identified was by his eyes. They were the clearest, crystal blue eyes I had ever seen. It was impossible not to recognize them. The second person I identified had a snake tattoo on his hand that wrapped around his wrist. I saw it the night he pointed a gun at my family. The third person had a very noticeable black widow tattoo beneath his right eye and a scar above his eyebrow. He was the one who shot and killed my husband when he fired the first shot."

People in the small courtroom began whispering as the three men shifted in their seats. The judge watched, frowning, before nodding for the attorney to continue.

"I see." He stopped in front of me and rubbed his hands together as he worked his jaw back and forth. "While I understand that you feel responsible for identifying those responsible for the deaths of your family members, my concern is how well your recollection of that night is."

I opened my mouth to dispute that, but caught Everett's eye as he subtly shook his head no.

"I couldn't imagine being in your shoes, Mrs. Salazar, and having to witness the death of my husband, let alone my infant child. To add to that devastation, you witnessed your father's murder as he tried to help you. That couldn't have been easy."

"What are you getting at?" I asked through clenched teeth, even though I knew I shouldn't have responded.

"Objection," the District attorney called out from where he was sitting at the other table. "What's the relevance of this, your honor?"

"My point is," Mr. Carrio said loudly, preventing the judge from answering, "that Mrs. Salazar went through something very traumatic. Not only is she the only surviving witness from that horrific night, but she's carrying the grief of her loved ones as she seeks justice. Who is to say that her grief isn't fueling her desire to lock my clients up simply because they have similarities to those who committed the crime?"

"It was them! I swear to God. I saw them!" I objected, leaning forward in my seat as I stared bewildered at the man smirking in front of me.

"I apologize if *crystal clear blue eyes* are not enough to convince me that my client is the person whom you are accusing of murdering several innocent people. As you might have noticed, blue is a common eye color. If we're going based on that fact alone, who is to say that it wasn't Judge Curry who committed this heinous act you're accusing my client of?"

"Objection, your honor," the district attorney called out, standing from the table across from the three men. "Misleading the witness."

"Sustained," Judge Curry replied, glaring at Mr. Carrio. "Mr. Carrio, we're interested in the facts. Stop misleading the witness."

"Yes, your honor." Mr. Carrio smiled smugly before he proceeded. "While eye color may be irrelevant in this case, some physical features are not. Such as tattoos, like you mentioned those of my clients."

I nodded, feeling relieved that this was getting back on track.

"Correct," I said, even though I wasn't sure if I was supposed to respond.

"Without looking, could you close your eyes and tell me in *exact* detail what the tattoo looks like for each of my clients?" he pressed.

I opened my mouth to say something, but stopped when the DA stood up and objected again.

"Objection. Again, your honor, what is the relevance of this?"

"I'm getting there," Mr. Carrio said quickly before the judge could stop him. "You see, Mrs. Salazar made a positive identification of my clients and is accusing them of the murder of eleven people. I can't help but be a bit skeptical that her *memory* alone of their tattoos is substantial proof to convict my clients of the crime she's accused them of. If she cannot accurately describe the tattoo without looking at it, then I would question her ability to remember *any* of the fine details of that night."

"It was them!" I shouted, standing up and pointing my finger in their direction. "I would know their faces anywhere! They haunt me every single night in my sleep as I remember the night they murdered *my* family!"

"Order!" Judge Curry shouted, pounding his gavel on the wooden desk. "Mrs. Salazar, another outburst, and you will be escorted out of this courtroom," he warned.

"I understand that this is an emotional time for you, Mrs. Salazar," Mr. Carrio said with a lack of emotion once the room quieted down again. "But wrongfully convicting someone of a crime they didn't commit will not bring your family back."

"I'm not wrong! I swear to God, it was them! Look at the tattoos and compare them to the notes the police took that night in the statements from the other witnesses! I'm telling you—these are the guys!"

"You're going based on a snake tattoo on someone's hand," Mr. Carrio said softly as he pushed up the sleeve of his button-down shirt. "Anyone can have a similar tattoo and not be the one who committed the crime."

My lips trembled as I stared at the tattoo, very similar to the one on the hand of the man smirking at me from across the room.

"I will ask again, Mrs. Salazar, is it possible that your recollection of that night isn't what you thought it was?"

"No," I whispered. "It was them. I saw them. I know it was them."

"No further questions, your honor," he said as he walked back to the table and sat down beside the three men.

"This court finds that, based on the evidence presented at this preliminary hearing, a reasonable juror could not conclude that the state has met its burden of proof. Accordingly, there is no basis to bind the defendants over for trial." Judge Curry slammed his gavel down on his desk and gave me a dismissive look as I sat there, stunned and unable to move.

<u>Awakening</u>
Sloane

Time is like the slow kiss of death.

A promise of relief that never comes.

It doesn't heal wounds.

It doesn't make grief any easier.

It doesn't dull the pain you feel when you think about what has been taken away from you.

Time is not on your side.

Time is a demon that haunts your soul until there's nothing left to take.

It makes you crave the end as much as you crave revenge.

It promises you that once it's done, you'll have the peace you long for.

Because nothing can hurt you once your time runs out.

Not Over
Sloane

I jolted upright, pulling the blanket off me as sweat dripped down my brow, and I gasped for air. Their faces continued to haunt my mind as I relived the night they killed my family. I tossed the sheet off me and climbed out of bed, noting the time on the clock that sat on my nightstand. Four in the morning wasn't the earliest I had gotten up these days, but it felt worse when I hadn't been able to fall asleep until sometime after midnight. I yawned and headed to the bathroom to relieve myself.

It had been two months since the so-called trial had taken place. Everett went back to New York, and I was staying in an apartment on the outskirts of Denver because I had nowhere else to go. It wasn't that I *wanted* to return to Denver, but right now, it was the closest I had to what once felt like home. I couldn't continue to put my life on hold, waiting for justice to be served. I knew it was a risk to stay in Colorado, but so far, nothing had happened. Maybe they were done with me now that the trial was over, and none of them could be held responsible for what they did. My stomach soured at the thought.

I didn't bother turning on the lights as I walked into the bathroom and started to pull my shorts down to use the restroom. It was going to be a long night now that my nightmare had brought the memories back to the surface, not that they were ever far from it. No matter what I did or how I tried to move on with my life, I couldn't. I would never continue to be anything without my family. I was simply a shell of a person forced to live out my days on Earth until the universe took pity on me.

I flushed and washed my hands, yawning as I headed down the short hall back to my bedroom. Before I could enter the room, I heard a noise at the front door. I stared at the door separating me from whoever was on the other side, trying to force their way in. The door shook, and the wood on the side started to split as they continued to put force against it.

Knowing I only had seconds before they were in the apartment, I turned and ran to my room, grabbing the duffle bag that I never allowed myself to fully unpack. I slipped on a pair of jeans and tennis shoes, grabbed my phone from the charger, and rushed to the window with the bag slung across me.

My apartment was small, with the only other exit being the narrow fire escape located right outside my bedroom. I pushed the window up and ducked under it right as I heard the front door get kicked in. I quickly made my way down the rusty ladder, trying to focus on every step to keep from falling. If I had any chance of surviving and escaping them, I had to be quicker than they were, which meant there wasn't time to fall.

Once I was on solid ground, I slid into the shadows against the tall brick wall and walked as fast as I could around to the front of the building. There wasn't much around other than a few gas stations and a store that was open 24/7. I weighed my options and then headed into the store, hoping the clerk I usually talked to was working. I kept my head down, pulling my hair to the side to cover my face from the cameras as I approached the register.

"Hey, Carrie," Zoe said as soon as she saw me.

I hadn't given her my real name when she asked because, as far as I was concerned, Sloane Salazar died months ago.

"I need your help," I whispered, looking around to make sure no one had followed me in yet.

"Of course. What do you need?" The panic in her eyes matched that in her voice as she studied me.

"I need a place to hide."

"Follow me," she said, not asking any questions as we rushed into the back of the store through a door that said *Employees Only.*

There wasn't much back there aside from boxes of inventory that would eventually be put out in the store. She pushed a few things around and then nodded for me to move into the small space she had created in the corner of the room.

We both froze when we heard the ding sound up front as someone entered the store.

"Hurry," she urged, her voice quiet as she looked over her shoulder.

I pushed myself as tightly as I could into the corner and held my breath as Zoe quickly moved the heavy boxes, lining them up in front of me. I held my breath as I heard deep voices in the store as her footsteps faded away.

"Can I help you?" Zoe asked loud enough for me to hear. The door wasn't that far from where I was hiding, so I tried not to move so I didn't give myself away.

"We're looking for someone," a deep voice said, which sent chills down my spine.

"Well, this is a convenience store, not a bar," Zoe replied dryly.

"We think she might have come in here," he continued, ignoring her jab. "Mid-thirties, long blond hair, green eyes. Maybe you've seen her?"

"The only one who has come in here in the past hour is you guys."

"Mind if we look around and see for ourselves?"

"I don't fucking think so. I don't know who the fuck you think you are, but you have no right coming in here ask—"

Her voice cut off as a gunshot rang out in the store.

I covered my mouth with my hands to keep from screaming as the tears rushed down my cheeks, knowing that I was responsible for her death.

Trouble

Everett

"What do you fucking mean you don't know where she is?" I growled, shoving a hand through my hair.

It was a little after six in the morning, and I was getting ready for work when the guy I had watching Sloane called to tell me that her apartment had been broken into, and she was missing.

"We're looking everywhere. We'll find her."

"Find her before they do," I warned, hanging up the call.

I sat down on the edge of the couch and stared at the wall as I tried to stay calm. I knew leaving Sloane in Colorado was a terrible idea, but no matter how much I begged and pleaded, I couldn't convince her to come with me back to New York.

Leaving her there felt like a death sentence, knowing that the guys who murdered her family and my brother would keep coming back for her until they finished the job. However, trying to negotiate with Sloane after the trial was nearly impossible. I knew how frustrating it was to watch as the case fell apart at the hands of corrupt officials, but that didn't mean we could just give up.

I knew that the FBI was already involved in the case, but I quickly learned not to trust anyone, including those who were working on it. It was clear as day that there was nothing but corruption happening, which was why I was taking a step back and doing things on my own. From gathering my own intel to hiring someone to watch Sloane, I was doing what the local officials should have done from the start.

I needed her to be safe. I needed her to survive this because a world without Sloane was one I didn't want to live in.

<u>Change</u>
Sloane

"Find her," a man growled as the *Employees Only* door was shoved open and heavy footsteps rushed past me.

I pressed my lips together to keep from making a sound as I forced myself to keep breathing. Another door was slammed open, and then the familiar sound of a bathroom stall door echoed around me before they left and went toward the back. I had no idea what was back there, but I knew I had to stay put long enough for them to finish looking and give up on finding me.

My toes scrunched in my shoes as I fought the anxiety racing through me as they continued slamming doors and pushing boxes over. They were close enough now that I could smell the faint scent of tobacco mixed with cheap cologne as they started pushing the boxes around in front of me. Thankfully, there were a few rows of them before they would find me in the corner, but I wasn't counting on much right now. I had escaped them a few times already, which meant I wasn't naive enough to believe that my luck wouldn't run out.

"She's not here," one said gruffly, kicking the boxes in front of me.

I startled and jumped back, quickly covering my mouth to hide the soft gasp I let out.

I waited as I noticed the silence that fell around me.

"What?" a deep voice asked.

"Nothing. I thought I heard something."

"Well, let's get the fuck out of here. She couldn't have gone far, so let's split up and hit the two gas stations. Our job isn't done until she's dead, so find her."

"Yes, Boss," two voices replied as heavy footsteps went in the opposite direction. The sound of the employee door swinging shut reverberated around me, echoing. I waited a few minutes after I heard the familiar ding of the bell on the front door, letting me know they had left.

I let out a long, shaky breath before pushing the boxes out of the way the best I could and squeezing out of the tight space. I rolled my head on my neck and tried to find the strength I knew I needed but didn't have. I was exhausted—on many levels—and didn't have much fight left in me. But I refused to let them kill me.

I stepped quietly to the door that led to the front of the store and listened for any sign of movement. When it sounded clear, I gently pushed the door open, moving slowly as I scanned the room. The store was empty, so I rushed over and locked the front door before turning to find Zoe lying on the floor behind the register. Her lifeless eyes stared up at me as blood dripped out of her mouth, joining the puddle she was lying in.

I bent down and covered my mouth, not wanting to believe she was dead because of me. I should have found somewhere else to go. But none of that mattered now.

If I were going to escape, I had to move quickly.

I glanced out the window to the gas station across the street. I knew it wouldn't be long before they came back to the store looking for me. There was nothing else around for miles, so they knew I was hiding in one of the three buildings.

Knowing I didn't have any other choice, I reached past Zoe to the shelf beneath the register where her purse was sitting and pulled it out. I kept myself hidden beneath the register as I quickly went through it, finding her wallet with her driver's license inside. I looked down at it and noticed that we were around the same build, both 5'3 and around 135 pounds. Her hair was black and short, whereas mine was long and blonde, but we both had green eyes and fair skin.

I rubbed my lips together, hating myself for what I was about to do.

I tucked her wallet and keys in my pocket, hoping that the gray sedan parked outside was hers. I would need a way to get out of here, and this was my best bet. As I was putting her purse back, I noticed a small, black handgun lying on the shelf. I wished she had been able to reach for it and defend herself, but I knew it was too late for any of that right now.

Saying one final *thank you* to her, I gently stepped around her and made my way down the aisles, grabbing everything I needed. I had no idea how long I would be on the run or when I would find safety again, so I stuffed my bag with protein bars and energy drinks, along with some mixed nuts.

I pulled the hoodie over my head and looked out the front door for any sign of the men before I pressed the unlock button on the keys I took from Zoe's purse. The lights on the sedan flashed, confirming I had the right vehicle. I quickly turned my cell phone off so it wouldn't be traceable once I left the store. I wasn't ready to part with it just yet since it still had pictures of Gabe and Nicky on it, but at least having it turned off would buy me some time until I was ready.

Without looking back, I unlocked the door and rushed outside, getting into the car and flying out of there as fast as I could.

<u>Strength</u>
Sloane

I stared in the mirror of the dingy hotel room, studying my reflection as a woman I didn't recognize stared back at me. The dark circles under my eyes felt like a permanent part of me, but I hadn't noticed just how much weight I'd lost over the past few months. I shoved a hand through my hair, noticing how much lighter it felt now that it was cut short. I'd gone with the same cut Zoe had in her driver's license picture, matching the black color as well.

The drive to Denver was short, given how close I lived in the suburbs. As soon as I got to a populated area, I abandoned the car and then walked a few blocks to the diner I used to go to when Gabe and I first moved to Denver. It was on the opposite side of town from where we used to live, but it felt safe. I grabbed breakfast, killing some time before everything else opened for the day.

I had calculated everything perfectly on the drive to Denver, knowing exactly where I would stop and where I needed to go. The plan was to get what I needed, change my appearance, and then get on the move again before anyone realized that I wasn't really Zoe. Once word spread that she had been murdered, I wouldn't be able to keep using her ID.

While I wanted to wait and leave when it was dark, I knew I couldn't afford to waste another minute. I grabbed my duffle bag from the bed and pulled it over my shoulder before pulling the hood of my hoodie over my head. It was too hot to be wearing a hoodie, but I was desperate to be as hidden as possible right now. I looked back at the empty room, making sure I had everything I came with, then opened the door and walked out.

The parking lot was empty as I walked through it, which made sense, given how many vacancies they had. When I came in at seven this morning and asked for a room, I was shocked that they actually had one. The clerk mentioned something about how they *always* had rooms but didn't seem to care that I wouldn't need mine for more than one night. What she didn't know was that I didn't need it for more than a few hours. My goal was to change my appearance the best I could, take a shower, and then get on the move again.

The stop for the bus I needed was close by, and I had timed everything so I wouldn't have to wait more than a few minutes for it to get there. Just like clockwork, the sound of the bus approaching filled my ears as I stopped at the bench and waited for it to come to a stop. A few people got off, so I waited for them before I boarded the bus, paid my fare, and headed for a seat in the back.

I sat down and scanned the people around me, making sure there wasn't an immediate threat.

To my left was an older woman who was falling asleep on the shoulder of the guy sitting beside her. Across from them sat a woman with three small kids, two of whom were fighting over who got to play with her cell phone. Beside her sat a man who I guessed to be her husband, yet he paid no attention to the kids or the trouble they were giving her. I felt bad for the woman and would have said something to the man had I not needed to keep myself hidden. I didn't need anyone to recognize me right now or be able to say they had seen me. My goal was to blend in and stay off anyone's radar.

The bus stopped, and the mom sighed heavily as she tried to wrangle the kids together. The husband rolled his eyes and took the sleeping baby from her. They exited the bus while I tried to swallow down the anger that rose inside of me at how pathetic he was. He had a family, and yet he acted like he didn't care. I missed Gabe every second of every day and knew that if he were still here, he would be the dad holding his son on the bus while giving me a break.

A few stops later, we arrived at the Denver International Airport. I stood up and adjusted the duffle bag as I got off the bus and headed inside. The airport was busy with people rushing to their gates. I had no idea where I was going, so I scanned the area and looked for the airline that had the shortest customer service line.

"Hi, may I help you?" a petite woman with fiery red hair asked as I approached the counter.

"Hi. I was curious what your next flight out is?" I asked, chewing my lower lip as I prayed she wouldn't question why I didn't have a preset destination in mind. I could have stopped and looked at the giant display that showed all incoming and outgoing flights, but I didn't have the mental bandwidth for that right now.

She smiled and looked at her screen before answering.

"Our next flight is a direct flight to New York, arriving at La Guardia. There are eleven seats left. This flight will start boarding in about an hour."

"Perfect," I said, wearing a genuine smile. "I would like one ticket, please."

I opened Zoe's wallet and pulled out her driver's license and a credit card, handing them both over to the woman. She smiled and took them, glancing at me before checking the ID and setting it down on the counter beside her keyboard. Her fingers worked quickly as she entered the information.

My heart hammered in my chest as I watched her slide the credit card and watch the machine. I had no idea whether Zoe had enough money on it for me to use it. For all I knew, it could be maxed out. I didn't have enough cash on me to pay for the ticket myself, and I didn't want to use any of my cards in case anyone was watching them. My face flushed red with heat as I waited for it to be declined.

"All set," she said, handing me the driver's license and credit card back before retrieving the boarding pass from the printer. "Have a safe flight, and thank you for flying Skyline."

I smiled the best I could as I stuffed everything back into my duffle bag and walked away. In less than five hours, I would be safe in New York, where I could recenter and start planning my next steps.

<u>Secrets</u>
Sloane

I spent the majority of the flight memorizing Everett's address, which he had written down on a napkin for me before he went back to New York. I'd kept it in my wallet ever since, not knowing how much I would need it until now. I was thankful that I found a window seat toward the back of the plane by two men who were so busy discussing sports that they didn't notice me once I slipped past them to my seat—the fewer people who noticed me, the better.

Once we landed, I waited to stand up until most of the line of people had gotten off. I grabbed my duffle bag from the overhead storage and pulled the strap across my chest as I followed the last few people through the gate into the busy airport. It was just after six, so I hoped Everett would be home from work by the time I got to his apartment.

I headed to the bathroom, freshened up, and then purposely left Zoe's wallet in the stall with her driver's license and credit cards. I took the cash so I could get a ride to his place, but I didn't need to carry the rest. Word would get out soon that she had been murdered, and I didn't want to get caught with her stuff. I had made sure to wipe my fingerprints off everything as quickly as I could, making sure there was no trace of me left.

Traffic in New York was unlike anything I had ever seen before, and I was thankful I wasn't the one who had to drive in it as my stomach roiled. Thankfully, the drive to Everett's apartment wasn't too long, or I might have had a heart attack from the near accidents we kept almost getting into.

I pulled out the napkin and checked the apartment number one more time before lifting my fist and knocking on the door. I could have rang the doorbell, but I had so much nervous energy rushing through me that it felt better to knock and let a little bit of it out.

Heavy footsteps sounded from the other side before the door opened, and Everett stared at me in disbelief. His eyes narrowed for a second as his brow furrowed.

"Sloane?"

I nodded, chewing my lower lip. I knew I looked different, but I hadn't realized until now just *how* different I looked. Not only had I cut and colored my hair to look like Zoe's, but I'd also done my makeup the same way, with a dark, smoky eye and cat-eye eyeliner.

"Come inside," he said, pulling the door open and stepping to the side to allow me to enter.

I shifted the duffle bag as I walked in, my eyes widening at the scene in front of me.

"Sorry. I wasn't expecting company," he replied, running a hand down his jaw.

"What is all of this?" I asked quietly as I stepped forward, looking at all of the easels propped up around the living room that opened into the small kitchen.

There were dry-erase boards on all of them with pictures of the victims from the night of the massacre. I covered my mouth with a trembling hand as I stared at the image of my parents' kitchen and my mother in a body bag on the floor. I walked around, slowly taking it all in as I read the headlines on the articles printed out from the Oak Creek newspaper, as well as the handwritten notes Everett had made on the boards.

"Seriously, Everett. What is all of this?" I asked, turning to face him.

"I can't just look the other way, Sloane. My brother was murdered, and the men who killed him are running free. You lost your entire family. Oak Creek is experiencing the highest rate of crime it's ever seen, and no one is doing anything about it. My mother is constantly terrified that they're going to come for her next, and no matter how hard I try, I can't get her to leave. I'm tired of feeling helpless, so I'm doing an investigation of my own."

"Wow," I said with a soft sigh as I set my duffle bag on the couch. "You've been busy."

He nodded and folded his arms over his chest as he swallowed hard.

"I could say the same about you," he replied softly. "I almost didn't recognize you when I answered the door."

I nervously tucked a strand of hair behind my ear, noticing how hard it was now that it was short.

"What happened, Sloane? I got a call early this morning that someone broke into your apartment. Then, I couldn't reach you on your cell phone to make sure you were okay. No one has seen or heard from you, and then you suddenly show up here looking like a completely different person."

"I know," I whispered, pressing my lips together.

Then, suddenly, it clicked.

"How did you know someone broke into my apartment?" I asked, narrowing my eyes.

"I've had someone watching you," he admitted with a sheepish smile. "I'm sorry. I should have told you, but I knew you would tell me not to."

"So you did it anyway? Just behind my back?"

"I needed to know you were safe."

"You could have called and checked in anytime you wanted to."

"And yet, when I needed to today, I couldn't reach you. Do you know what a mess I've been all fucking day, Sloane? Not knowing whether you're alive or if you were one of the multiple bodies they found close to your apartment?"

"I'm sorry. I didn't mean to worry you. There wasn't time to stop and reach out to you. Unfortunately, you don't have the luxury of time when you're running for your life."

He stepped forward until he was standing right in front of me.

"I would have done anything and everything I could to help you if I knew you were in trouble. I had no idea where you were. My guy couldn't find a single trace of you. It was like you just vanished in thin air."

"I heard them trying to get into my apartment, so I grabbed my stuff and went out of the fire escape," I said with a shiver as the fear rose to the surface again. "I ran to the convenience store across the street and asked the woman who works there to help me. She hid me in the back behind some heavy boxes right before they came in and killed her. Once they left, I snuck out to the front and locked the door. I stayed hidden so they wouldn't see me as I checked on her, but she was already dead. I took her wallet and car keys, then got the hell out of there."

His eyes widened as he listened intently.

"I drove to Denver and abandoned the car. I had already turned my cell phone off before I left the store, so if anyone were tracing it, it would show my last known location at my apartment. When I got to Denver, I ran to the store to get what I needed to change my appearance and then rented a hotel room. I made myself look as close to Zoe as I could, then I took the bus to the airport and used her driver's license and credit card to get a flight to New York."

"Do you still have her stuff?"

"No," I said, shaking my head. "Once I landed, I went to the bathroom and wiped my fingerprints off of everything, then left it in the stall. I just needed it to get here. I can't keep using it because sooner or later, they're going to know she's dead."

"Word has already gotten out," Everett replied. "She was one of six people murdered in what the local authorities are calling a suspicious crime wave."

"I feel so bad that they're all dead because of me."

"They're not. They're dead because these fucking monsters should be in jail instead of out on the streets."

"We don't even know for sure that it's the same guys. I didn't see any of them. I just heard them tell Zoe they were looking for someone right before they shot her."

"They tried to break into your apartment and then went and killed everyone close by when they couldn't find you—I would say they are the same guys, Sloane."

I puffed my cheeks full of air and then slowly let it out.

"Okay. Fair point. But what do we do now? They're obviously not going to stop until they kill me. Who's to say they haven't already figured out that I came here?"

"You traveled under a deceased person's identity, so that's going to raise some flags once law enforcement figures that out. Since I believe they have connections, I'm sure that information will get back to them quickly. It would be foolish to say that they wouldn't connect your disappearance to someone using Zoe's identity after she died. But New York is a huge city, so we have that going for us."

"Yeah, but if they have connections, then they're also going to connect me to you. And then they're going to figure out that you live in New York, and they're going to know that's where I'm at."

He nodded and looked around the room.

"Then we prepare for them to come."

"And how do you expect to do that?"

"By training."

"Training? Training for what?" I looked at him with a bewildered expression.

"Training to defend yourself by any means necessary, Sloane. Starting tomorrow."

I pulled in a slow, deep breath and let it out. He was right. I needed to learn how to defend myself if I stood any chance against these monsters. But the fire burning through me at the thought of what I could do to them was a bit unnerving because I had never felt that amount of hatred for someone until now. The thought of making them suffer the way my family suffered, the way *I've* suffered their loss, was enough to get me motivated.

Adjustments
Everett

It felt weird having Sloane in my space, mainly because I hadn't expected it and didn't have time to put away the stuff I had been working on in the living room. I was thankful that she didn't judge me for it, but I knew it was hard for her to see the pictures of her family members taped to the dry-erase boards with details of their murders written beside them.

"Are you hungry?" I asked, glancing at my watch and noticing it was already after seven. My guess was that she hadn't eaten since before she boarded her flight, and since she came straight here, that left no time for her to grab something.

"Starving," she replied as she stared at the board that had images of the three men she had identified as the killers.

I walked over and stood in front of her, blocking her view as I lifted her chin to force her to look at me. Tears welled in her eyes as she tried to blink them away.

"What would you like for dinner?"

"I don't care. Whatever you want. I can cook, or we can get delivery, and I'll pay."

"You'll do no such thing," I objected, trying to hold back the growl in my throat.

"Everett, you do not have to take care of me."

"No one said I did. Maybe I *want* to."

She took a long, deep breath and slowly let it out. Sloane and I knew each other better than anyone back in the day, but I took pride in knowing that I still knew her after all of these years. Some things just never changed.

"Pizza sounds fabulous," she answered, giving me a soft smile.

"You still love Hawaiian?"

Her grin widened as she nodded her head.

"Perfect. I'll put the order in, and then we can get you set up in the guest room," I said, turning my attention to the phone to avoid looking at the slight blush that was creeping up her neck.

I could only imagine how hard it was for Sloane to be in my apartment right now, knowing she would be living with me for a while. That was always the goal when we were in high school: to graduate and then move in together and start a family. Life had other plans, but it wasn't lost on me that ten years later, we would find ourselves constantly in each other's space. Not for the reasons we would have wanted, but still.

I put the order in online through the app and then shoved my phone in my pocket as Sloane continued staring at the board.

"How did you get this picture?" Sloane asked when I joined her, pointing at the image of her mother.

I cringed and pinched my eyes shut before answering.

"A friend of mine works for the FBI in Oak Creek. He was on scene that night, and I asked him to confirm…" My throat burned as I struggled to get the words out.

"That my mom was dead?" Sloane asked, turning to look at me.

I nodded, swallowing down the emotion that threatened to come up.

"I still regret not going to her service," Sloane said softly, running her fingers over the picture. If it weren't for the kitchen confirming where it was, no one would ever know it was her mother in the body bag. Keith had asked if I needed any of the photos they'd taken at the scene of the crime, but I declined. There was no point in seeing something that my heart couldn't handle. Even if Sloane didn't have the best relationship with her mother when we were dating, I still knew Karen from when I was a little boy growing up in Oak Creek.

"I'm sorry." I didn't know what else to say because there was nothing that could take the pain or guilt away. A choice had been made to keep Sloane safe, but that came with its own consequences.

"Don't be. It's not your fault."

"It's not yours either," I said gently, facing her. "None of this is your fault, Sloane. Not the death of your family. Not the death of Zoe. You cannot control people who want to be evil. At this point, we can't even stop them. But you don't need to carry the burden of all of this."

She lowered her head as tears fell down her cheeks. I wrapped her in my arms and held her close, ignoring how it felt so right to comfort her. She pulled back and wiped her face before she locked her hands behind my neck and brought her lips to mine.

A rush of emotions washed over me as I kissed her back, allowing her to lead the way as her tongue brushed against my lips, asking for entrance. I tilted my head and obeyed, feeling like I was transported back to our senior year in high school when we would make out nonstop. Sloane was a great kisser, and I had never been able to get enough.

Slowly, she pulled away, her eyes wild as she studied my face.

I opened my mouth to speak, but then snapped it shut when I thought better of it.

She shook her head and turned away, glancing at me over her shoulder before rushing down the hall and closing the bathroom door behind her.

I let my head fall forward as I sighed in frustration. While she was the one who initiated it, I didn't want to take advantage of her right now. She was in an extremely vulnerable position, and the last thing I wanted was to make her regret something she had done. If we were going to live together for the foreseeable future, I would have to

make some adjustments to ensure things remained strictly
platonic between us.

Mistakes
Sloane

We ate the pizza in silence while a movie played on the TV for background noise. My mind had been a mess since I kissed Everett, and I hadn't been able to get out of my own head long enough to talk to him about it. But then again, he was Everett, which meant he would give me the grace of not making me talk about it. He would go on as if nothing had happened, allowing me to save my dignity and avoid embarrassment.

But that was the part that was driving me up the wall. I didn't feel embarrassed about it at all. I didn't even feel guilty for it happening—even though I should have. I was a married woman—okay, technically a widow because some madman killed my husband—but still. I wasn't single and shouldn't have acted on my instinct to kiss him. He wasn't trying to seduce me, and I needed to remember that. It was simply one friend comforting another.

"Do you want another slice?" Everett asked as he held his hand above the pizza box.

I had expected him to order his favorite, sausage and pepperoni, but I was surprised when he ordered mine instead. It only added to the confusion I was already feeling after the kiss when I came into the living room and saw everything set up. It was like being back in our senior year of high school on a typical date night. We'd always pick a house and then watch movies in the living room so our parents didn't have to worry about us doing anything else.

"I don't know what happened," I blurted out, surprising him as much as I surprised myself.

His eyebrow rose slightly as he waited for me to continue.

"With the kiss. I'm sorry. I don't know why I did that."

"You don't need to apologize, Sloane."

"I don't want to lead you on or make you think that I can be—"

He raised his hand to stop me.

"I don't think anything. I promise. It happened, and now it's in the past. We can move on from it without you obsessing over me worrying about what it meant. It's okay, Sloane."

I pushed out a deep breath and nodded my head.

"Do you want another slice?" he asked again, shifting the conversation to a safer topic.

"Yes, please."

I smiled and thanked him as he set one on my plate before we both pretended to watch the movie. An hour later, I was struggling to keep my eyes open as the movie ended, and Everett turned off the TV.

"I'm sure it's been a long day. We should get some rest," he said, standing and holding out a hand to help me up.

Maybe it was because I felt safe with Everett, but it felt like the exhaustion from the past few months was catching up to me. My body felt heavy, and my bones ached in a way I had never felt before. Between the little sleep I'd gotten and all of the rushing and planning to get to safety, it had taken a toll on my body and mind. I accepted his hand and stood up as he led me down the hallway to the guest bedroom he had set up for me earlier.

"Thanks again for letting me stay here," I said, lingering in the doorway as he took a few steps to the room at the end of the hall. His apartment was big for what I expected in New York, but I was glad he was still only a few feet away and that our bedrooms shared a wall.

"Of course. It's never a problem, Sloane."

I gave him a weird curtsey and a nod, rolling my eyes as he chuckled.

"Get me if you need anything," he said as he tapped his knuckles on the wall and then stepped inside his room.

"I will. Thank you. Goodnight, Everett."

"Goodnight, Sloane."

I closed the door and let my shoulders fall for the first time in a long time. I got changed into a pair of sleep shorts and a t-shirt, then pulled back the covers and got in. Within seconds of my head touching the pillow, I was asleep.

Demons
Sloane

"Please. Don't," I begged as I sat in a wooden chair with my wrists bound to the arms. A rag that had blood on it was shoved into my mouth, the tanginess gagging me and making me want to vomit. Then I heard the familiar sound of duct tape as a piece was ripped off and placed over my mouth and wrapped around the back of my head to hold the rag in.

I looked up and stared at the man with the blue eyes.

"Did you really think it was over?" he asked, kneeling beside me as he ran a finger down my cheek to wipe the tear that slid down it. "It will never be over. We will haunt you until your last breath."

"Why are you doing this?" I tried to ask, but my words were muffled.

"You should know the answer by now," the man with the black widow tattoo said as he stood beside Nicky.

Nicky was a man now, no longer the little boy I remembered. He looked so much like Gabe, but also different. I couldn't put my finger on what it was about him, but when he looked at me, I watched him change into a person I didn't recognize.

"We told you that night at the football game," he continued. "We were there for one reason—Hugo Sanchez."

"My husband told you he didn't know him," I countered, pushing at the rag with my tongue to try to get it out of my mouth so I could talk. I knew it was pointless, given the tape was so tight around me, but I had to try.

"And do you believe everything your husband said?"

I pinched my eyes shut to force the dream to stop, but it kept going.

When I opened them, I found my family sitting across from me, all bound to chairs similar to mine with rags in their mouths. Nicky went back to being a baby, but the more disturbing thing was that each of them sat there with pieces of their bodies missing from where they were killed.

My mother had a large open hole in the middle of her head where I'm guessing they had shot her, since I wasn't there to witness it. Gabe had a hole in between his eyes where the first bullet had struck him, then several along his chest where other bullets had hit. My dad had a gaping hole in his chest, right where his heart should have been. And Nicky. My sweet Nicky. He had a hole in his back that went straight through to his chest, barely missing his heart.

"Your husband could have saved their lives," the man with the black widow tattoo said as he pointed at each of them with his gun. "He was the only one we wanted."

"But he wasn't who you thought he was," I cried past the rag, pulling on the restraints on the chair to try to get free.

"Maybe he wasn't who you thought he was," he countered before he walked over and stood next to me. "Who should I kill first?"

I sobbed as my family stared at me with fear in their eyes. They were already dead but didn't seem to know it as they pleaded with me to spare them.

"How about the little one? Spare him from having to witness his family dying again."

"NO!!!" I screamed as I heard the sounds of gunshots as he fired repeatedly.

I counted how many shots there were, knowing the last one would be for me.

"Open your mouth," he growled as he ripped the tape off and pulled the rag out.

I clenched my jaw tightly, refusing to do it.

"Now!"

I flinched as I saw him raise the gun and bring it across the side of my face. It immediately stung as I screamed out in pain. But before I could keep screaming, he put the gun in my mouth and pulled the trigger.

"Wake up, Sloane!" someone demanded, shaking my body. My eyes flew open as I jolted up and scanned the room. My heart raced, and my skin was sticky with sweat as I focused on Everett.

I panted, trying to catch my breath as the dream flashed through my mind, and fresh tears flowed.

"Shhh," he whispered as he wrapped his arms around me and held me tightly. "It was just a dream. You're safe."

I shook my head and pulled away.

"It happens every night," I said with a sob as I finally allowed myself to break down and cry. "I relive their murders every. Single. Night. There's never a break from it. I am so tired, Everett. I'm so fucking tired."

I leaned forward and cried into my hands, finally reaching my breaking point.

"Well then, it stops now," he said matter-of-factly.

"What does?"

"These nightmares. I wasn't able to protect you or your family before, Sloane. But I will protect you now, even if it's from your subconscious."

"And how do you plan to do that?" I asked as I sniffled and accepted the tissue he handed me.

"You're going to come sleep in my bed. Every single night."

"I can't do that," I objected, remembering the kiss earlier.

"Why not? We did in the hotel in New Mexico."

"Yeah, but that was different. We didn't have any other choice since there was only one bed."

"And because there was only one bed, you had to share one with me," he pressed, raising his eyebrows so I would get the point. "You didn't have nightmares like this when you slept next to me, Sloane."

"How do you know?" I asked, though, if I were being honest, I had slept best during the time we shared that hotel and had to sleep in the same bed. If I had any nightmares back then, they hadn't been bad enough to wake me up like this one, and they definitely didn't follow me as I woke up.

"Because I watched you those nights. I had to make sure you were okay."

I tried to ignore the butterflies that took flight in my stomach because that was just a totally Everett thing to do. It didn't matter if he also needed the rest. He would always put my needs above his.

"Don't you think it might be crossing the line for me to sleep in your bed with you?" I asked nervously, squeezing the tissue in my fingers.

"The line is whatever we make it," he answered honestly. "My only goal is to take care of you and make sure you get enough rest. We both know you sleep better when you're next to me. There's nothing more than that."

I pushed away the negative thoughts that were rushing through my mind, reminding myself that I couldn't be upset when he said there was nothing more than that. That was what we needed in order for whatever this was between us to work. It would be a simple arrangement between friends who literally slept together without letting any prior feelings for each other get in the way.

The next morning, I woke up in Everett's bed with his back to me as he snored. I rubbed my eyes and looked at the clock beside me on the nightstand, surprised that I had slept through the night. I knew I was exhausted, but I honestly hadn't expected to sleep so well in Everett's bed. I wasn't sure if it was because his bed felt like heaven and I imagined I was sleeping on a cloud, or if it was because he was beside me and for the first time in a long time, I had felt safe.

I quietly got out of bed and opened the bedroom door, hoping it didn't squeak as I snuck out and headed for the bathroom. I looked in the mirror, surprised when the bags under my eyes weren't as dark as they had been. They were still there, just not as bad. It was weird what a little bit of rest could do.

I finished up and washed my hands before heading to the kitchen. I didn't want to wake Everett up since it was Saturday and he didn't have to go to work. I looked around until I found what I needed to make coffee and started a pot. The aroma was strong and made me smile. I hadn't taken the time to enjoy anything since everything happened, but there was something about the rich scent that brought a wave of happiness over me.

Once it was ready, I filled a mug and sat down on the couch, staring at the boards Everett had put together. The information was separated based on victims of the massacre and those who were believed to be involved. I leaned forward and frowned when I saw Sheriff Dowdy's name written down beside a few other police officers from Oak Creek.

My head was tilted as I tried to make the connection to the line that led to Stan Young. The name sounded familiar, but I couldn't place why I knew it.

"He had video when the massacre started, then suddenly it disappeared," Everett said, scaring the shit out of me.

I jumped and panicked when I saw the coffee slosh around the cup, nearly spilling over.

"Oh my God, I didn't know you were standing there," I said, setting my cup down on the table.

"Sorry. I thought you heard me."

"Nope. I was lost in my own little world," I admitted. "So, he had video of it, and then it just went missing?"

"Pretty much," Everett said with a shrug before folding his arms over his chest. "When the video was originally given to the Oak Creek police, they reviewed it and said it stopped seconds before the shooting. But my friend, Keith, spoke with Stan, and Stan insisted that he got the whole thing."

"So the police messed with the video? Or they just lied about what they had?"

"Both."

"Can't we go talk to him and see if he still has it? Surely we can take it to another judge and show them the proof—"

"Unfortunately, Stan was murdered a few days before the trial started. Though, if you look it up, they have reported it as a suicide."

"But you don't think it was?"

"No. Not at all. Stan was adamant when he spoke with Keith. He wanted to get justice and knew he had the key to bringing those assholes down. But the moment they knew what he had, they dealt with it."

"Why not kill him right away when it first got out that he had the video?" I asked, leaning back against the couch.

"My guess is that they thought they had it under control. The video was altered to delete the shooting, which left no record of it ever existing. If they would have killed him, then it would have drawn more attention, and they didn't want that. Stan obsessed over the missing footage, and everyone in town attributed it to him trying to cope with what happened. You know, small towns and massacres don't really go together. Everyone just assumed that he wasn't coping well and ignored it. But then, when you identified them, and it went to pretrial, Stan demanded that they put him on the witness stand so he could swear under oath that he also witnessed the shooting. That he had footage that the police had deleted."

"So they murdered him before he could say anything," I said, sadness filling my heart for Stan.

"Exactly."

"Do you really think it was the Oak Creek police who murdered him, though?"

"I don't know. At this point, I wouldn't put it past them to be working directly with the assholes who did it. They tampered with evidence to keep the truth from coming out, so I would say they would do anything at this point to keep it from coming out that they were involved."

I shook my head, trying to process all of this. I felt something tickle my brain from my dream last night, but I couldn't pull it forward. Last night's nightmare had been one of the worst ones I'd had, and it felt like my subconscious was trying to protect me by preventing me from remembering it.

"So, this goes deeper than just some random psychos who killed my family at a high school football game," I said with a sigh.

"A lot deeper. But I'm determined to figure it out and get justice one way or another."

"I want to help. Just tell me what you need from me."

Everett looked me dead in the eyes, his expression quickly sobering.

"I need you to start training and learning how to protect yourself."

I nodded, remembering the conversation we had last night when I first showed up at his apartment. We knew it was only a matter of time before someone showed up here looking for me.

"Okay. I'm on board."

I tried to smile, but my body still felt too tired.

"Good, because we start today."

Training

Everett

"Again," I growled as I stood in front of her on the mat, holding my hands up as she went through the combo we'd been working on. I ducked to avoid her hand connecting with my face and nearly lost my balance. She was learning quickly—almost too quickly.

We had been working for two weeks on hand-to-hand combat, and she was advancing her skills quickly. I knew she would be fast on her feet, but it was her strength that had caught my attention. She spent the majority of her days at the gym doing strength training with my friend, Trevor. He was vaguely aware of what was going on, and thankfully, he didn't ask questions that I didn't want to answer.

"One last combo, and then we'll finish for the day," I said, watching as she used her arm to brush her hair off her sticky forehead. "We can clean up and grab dinner on the way home."

"Chinese food?" she asked, raising an eyebrow in challenge. It had become our usual go-to these days, and I knew she was getting as tired of it as I was.

"If you complete this without letting me take you down, I'll stop for sushi," I offered, knowing it was her weakness, just like I knew this specific combo was difficult for her. No matter how many times we'd practiced it, she had yet to stay on her feet and take me down.

"Are you seriously trying to bribe her with sushi?" Trevor asked, walking in and folding his arms over his chest.

The gym was already empty, but he allowed us to stay late to train.

"She loves sushi, so it's a fair prize *if* she can take me down."

"Fuck sushi. Go for something bigger," Roman said, coming in a few seconds later and joining Trevor as they stood off to the side of the mat.

Roman worked with Trevor, and they seemed to be pretty close. They were also both terrifying as fuck, so I didn't worry about Sloane being by herself while I was at work. She had been training with both of them, which likely explained how she'd gotten so good so fast.

"I do like sushi," Sloane said, bouncing from side to side to keep her momentum. "But if I win this combo, I want steak and lobster."

She smirked as the guys laughed and cheered her on.

"It's on. Bring it." I held my hands out in front of me and jumped back the second she leaped for me.

I spun to the side and grabbed her by the waist, twisting as I lowered her to the mat. I knelt above her, locking her legs in between mine as I grabbed her hands and pinned them above her head.

"You're always so predictable," I teased, staring down at her as her chest rose and fell heavily.

"Am I?" she asked, clearly out of breath as I took pity and started climbing off of her.

I made the mistake of turning my back on her to smirk at Trevor and Roman. But before I could say anything, I felt a hard jab to my thigh as she started with the combo I'd taught her. I didn't have the time to move away before she went through each step and pinned me to the mat effortlessly.

"Never trust that they're down," Roman called as Trevor stepped forward.

"Put your full weight on him," Trevor coached as Sloane straddled my waist. "There you go. Now lean in and press your forearm across his throat."

My eyes widened as I watched Sloane's face change. A maniacal look crossed it as she did as he asked.

"More pressure," Trevor said, squatting beside her to be on her level. "Great job. If he starts to move, press even harder."

"And then what?" she asked breathlessly.

"That depends on what your end goal is. If you want to detain him until law enforcement arrives, then you continue with what you're doing."

"What if I don't care about law enforcement?" she questioned, a different tone in her voice.

"If you consider your life is in danger, then you take further action," Trevor said tightly, looking at me before returning his attention to Sloane.

There was fury in her eyes as she pressed harder, making it difficult to breathe.

"I think you're good, Sloane," he said gently, placing his hand on her shoulder to get her attention. "You can let him up."

She nodded, and I could see the mix of emotions flashing across her face as she got up and walked to the other side of the mat. Roman pulled her into a hug and whispered something in her ear.

I sat up, wondering what the fuck had been going on during their training sessions. I knew both Trevor and Roman were in deeply committed relationships, so I wasn't worried about there being any romantic feelings involved. But I also knew that they both had a past that they didn't talk about much. They'd both seen and done shit most people wouldn't understand. Because of that, they had a bond with Sloane that I couldn't relate to, and that scared me. She was changing, and I couldn't just ignore that.

"Everything okay?" I asked cautiously as I walked over to where Roman and Sloane were talking quietly.

"Yeah, I was just telling her to order a T-bone since she earned it," Roman teased.

"After that, she can order the whole restaurant, and I'll gladly treat her," I said with a smile that was directed at Sloane. I was proud of her for finally mastering the combo that had been difficult for her.

"I'm going to go clean up, and then we can get going," she said, smiling at each of us before walking out and heading to the locker room.

I waited a few minutes until she was gone before I looked at both of them and prayed they wouldn't keep anything from me.

"Is she doing alright?" I asked, unsure of how to phrase it.

"She's learning quickly and building both her strength and stamina," Trevor responded as he folded his arms over his chest.

"Yes," I said with a frustrated sigh. "I can see that. What I mean is—I don't know. Is there something I should be worried about?"

"Sloane has been through a lot," Roman said softly. "She's still working through grief that is very fresh for her. Some of that entails dealing with the anger and finding a way to expel it. I give her a lot of credit because I couldn't do what she's doing after experiencing a loss like that."

I nodded because I knew what they meant, but that didn't do anything to put my mind at ease.

"Okay. Thank you." I grabbed my stuff and then headed to the locker room to clean up so we didn't keep them any later than we had to.

Complications
Sloane

"Would you two care for any dessert?" the waiter asked as Everett gently pushed his plate away and leaned back.

"I have nowhere to put it," I replied with a laugh as Everett shook his head to decline as well.

I lifted the glass of wine to my lips and took a sip, savoring the rich taste. It had been a while since I had taken the time to sit down at a restaurant and enjoy a meal. When Everett insisted on celebrating my victory of mastering the combo, I couldn't stand the thought of hurting his feelings by saying no. Plus, the steak and lobster had been to die for.

"Thank you for asking me to join you for dinner tonight," I said to Everett once the waiter cleared our plates and left.

"Thank you for joining me. It was nice to sit down and enjoy a meal together."

My cheeks flushed with embarrassment as I fidgeted with my hair. I looked down at the table and avoided looking at him.

"I'm sorry, Sloane. I didn't mean anything by that," Everett apologized. "I just meant that it was nice to go enjoy a meal with someone. I can't tell you the last time I had dinner with anyone other than a few blind dates years ago. Work keeps me so busy that I rarely take the time to do anything anymore."

"Add in an ex-girlfriend who is living with you and relies on the comfort of delivery, and you've got yourself even more obstacles," I teased, still not risking looking at him.

"You're not an obstacle. If I wanted to go sit down in a restaurant, I would. And I would invite you every single time. We've both been busy, and it's been nice being able to order food and get stuff done."

Since the moment I showed up on his doorstep a few weeks ago, we'd spent most nights and weekends going through the information he'd gathered. At first, it was incredibly hard to talk about what happened to my family, but when I pushed the emotion out of it and focused solely on the facts, it got easier. Not only that, but I had also been learning how to work off some of the built-up anger I felt during my training sessions with Trevor and Roman. I was also still sleeping in Everett's bed, which had helped to keep the nightmares to a minimum. They hadn't stopped completely, but lately, when they would start, he would wrap me in his arms and hold me until they went away.

"So, I've been thinking about the information we've been going over lately," I said quietly, leaning in so he could hear me. More so, I wanted to change the subject, but given that we were consumed with figuring out why Gabe was targeted, to begin with, I didn't have anything else to talk about. "I think we need to look up Hug—"

"Stop," Everett interrupted, holding his hand up. "I agree. But let's talk about that when we get home."

I nodded, forgetting that even though we were in a big city and no one had tried to kill me yet, that didn't mean we weren't being watched. We'd found several inconsistencies that showed the corruption spread deeper than the Oak Creek law enforcement. There appeared to be several FBI agents that Everett was suspicious of, and rightfully so.

Everett paid our bill and rolled his eyes when I offered to pay. It was nice to be treated, but at the same time, I couldn't help but feel guilty that I had allowed him to, given our history. Everett was such a huge part of my life growing up, and it was unnerving how easily I fell back into the comfort of being with him. Allowing him to pay for such an expensive meal at an upscale restaurant felt a bit like being on a date, and my brain was having a hard time with that.

Once we got back to his apartment, my body was tired, and my stomach fuller than it had been in months. Celebrating something as simple as mastering a combo he had taught me brought me a sliver of happiness I hadn't expected. I couldn't remember the last time I did something for myself, let alone had been happy about it.

"Did you want more wine?" Everett asked as he opened the fridge to pull out a bottle of wine and looked at me.

We'd only had a glass each at the restaurant, so one more glass couldn't hurt anything. I didn't have any plans to train tomorrow since it was a Sunday and I needed a break.

"Sure. Thank you," I replied, stepping around him to get the wine glasses while he worked on getting the bottle open.

I set them down on the counter and then turned to go to the living room at the same time he turned toward me. Our bodies brushed against each other as his hand protectively wrapped around my waist.

Without giving it a second thought, I leaned in and brushed my lips over his.

He pushed the bottle of wine to the side and then brought his other hand around and pulled me tighter against him as I deepened the kiss.

I knew I shouldn't be doing this, but I felt alive, and I didn't want that to stop. Perhaps it was the idea of doing something I shouldn't, or maybe it was because there was still an undeniable chemistry between Everett and me. Either way, I forced logic out of my mind as I wrapped my arms around his neck and parted my lips to grant his tongue access.

His hands slid down my waist, squeezing my ass as he lifted me to his hips. I wrapped my legs around him and locked my arms behind his neck as we continued to kiss. My body was on fire, begging to be touched and kissed with every promise his lips left as they trailed over my skin. He walked us down the hallway to his bedroom and lowered me to the bed.

I lifted my shirt and tossed it to the floor as I watched him study me. I could see the apprehension in his eyes, unsure of whether to cross the line with me. But I didn't want to worry about any of that right now. I just wanted to feel. I wanted to be careless and reckless for once, only worrying about the pleasure we could give each other.

"Sloane," he whispered as I got up and stood in front of him, pressing a finger to his lips.

"Everett, don't," I begged, shaking my head. "I know what I am doing, and trust me when I say that I want this. And based on the bulge in your pants, I know that you do, too."

The corner of his mouth curved up into a playful smirk as he grabbed my hand and pressed it against his erection.

"See, I told you." I grinned at him as I gripped his cock tighter through the fabric.

He shook his head and then pulled me into him again as his mouth crashed down over mine. I parted my lips, loving the way he made me feel as his hands roamed my body and spread goosebumps in their wake.

Everett was slow and gentle, taking his time as he undressed me, savoring each moment as he explored my body with his tongue and hands. I was so needy, wanting to be touched in all of the places he had yet to touch me.

He reached behind me and unclasped my bra, taking his time as he pulled it down my arms and tossed it to the floor. I stood before him, wearing nothing but my panties, as he shamelessly looked me up and down, licking his lips as he caressed my full breasts.

I leaned forward and grabbed the bottom of his shirt, pulling it up and over his head. His body was immaculate, sculpted, and chiseled with muscles that I had never seen before in real life. I knew he worked out often at the gym, but I had no idea he was this toned.

My fingers trailed each dip and curve until they hovered above the button of his jeans. I looked up and caught him watching me, never taking his eyes off mine as I worked on undoing them. The sound of the fabric hitting the floor was almost as satisfying as when he hooked his thumbs into his boxer briefs and slowly lowered them. I licked my lips as the head of his cock poked out first, then opened my mouth as his full length emerged. I knew Everett was always well-endowed; I just forgot how big he really was.

He kicked his boxer briefs off and then stood there, stroking his cock while I watched. I was beyond turned on and wanted nothing more than to feel that thing deep inside of me. But as always, Everett had other plans.

He dropped to his knees, lowering his head until it was lined up with my pussy as he gripped my thighs and held me in place before lifting my leg over his shoulder.

"I got you. I won't let you fall," he assured me before pressing his face against my pussy.

My fingers tangled in his hair, trying to find something to hold onto as he swiped his tongue along my slit, making me shudder.

I was already wet and fully aroused as he teased me with his tongue before sliding it inside. My head tipped back as a low moan rolled past my lips. I closed my eyes and tried to stay focused on standing as he squeezed my ass and began sucking my clit.

Fireworks exploded behind my eyes as he sucked harder, bordering on pain. But it was so much more than that. He was teasing my body in a way only he could, and it was responding the way it used to, as if those memories would never end. He held one hand on my ass, pressing my pussy tighter against his face as he brought his other hand up and inserted a finger while he continued sucking my clit.

Within seconds I felt the first wave of pleasure wash over me as my pussy spasmed and I came on his face.

Once I was done, he slowly stood up and wiped his lips as a satisfied smirk graced them.

"Everett," I whispered, nearly panting as I tried to come down from the high I was on. "That was…"

"Nothing because I'm just getting started," he said, leaning forward and nipping my earlobe before lowering me to the bed.

I got situated, adjusting the pillow so it wasn't in the way while Everett retrieved a condom from the nightstand. I wanted to suck his cock and take him deep into the back of my throat, but I also just needed him to fuck me. It had been so long that I didn't want to wait anymore.

I reached down and stroked his cock as he positioned himself above me with his knees bracing my thighs. He ripped the condom wrapper with his teeth and spat the little piece of foil on the floor as he waited for me to stop touching him so he could put it on.

"Are you sure this is what you want?" he asked, genuine sincerity in his voice.

I nodded, hating the well of emotion that was rising inside of me.

I knew how significant this moment was, but I didn't want to think about that right now. Nothing I said or did would bring Gabe back. Right now, I was with Everett, and I owed it to him to be focused, and in the moment we were about to share.

"I want this," I said, giving him my verbal consent so he knew I meant it. "I want you inside of me, Everett. I want to feel you as you come."

He pulled his lower lip between his teeth as he leaned forward and braced himself with one hand above my head while he used the other to guide himself in.

I gasped at the sensation, not because it was painful but because he was so thick. He went slowly as he stretched me, my pussy fully wrapped around his cock.

"Fuck, Sloane," he breathed, closing his eyes as he took his time sliding in the rest of the way. "God, you feel so good."

"Mmmm." I couldn't get any real words out as I scratched my nails down his back and moaned.

I lifted my hips, allowing him to sink a little deeper before I began grinding them, hoping he would fuck me the way I needed to be fucked. Hard and fast was what always got me off, and he used to know that.

He grabbed my hips and held me steady as he pulled out and then slammed back into me.

"Yes!!" I screamed, letting my head fall back as pleasure jolted through me. He did remember.

"Fuck, yes, Everett. Fuck me just like that."

He chuckled as he repeated the motion three more times before changing position. He dropped my legs and braced both hands above my head, laying his body flat over mine as he ground his pelvis, lining his cock up perfectly to stimulate my clit.

"Shit. Shit. Shit!" I screamed as he went faster, keeping the pressure where I needed it as he sent me over the edge.

My pussy spasmed around him, tightening as it gripped him for dear life as he pulled out.

"No," I pleaded. "I want more."

I knew he hadn't come yet, and honestly, I was just getting started, even though I had already come twice.

"And you're going to get more. Now turn over. Face down, ass up."

I grinned and did as he said, loving the way his hands felt as they rubbed my ass. I braced myself and popped my ass up, knowing it was giving him the perfect view of my wet pussy. He dug his fingers into my hips as he lined himself up at my entrance and slammed into me.

A gargled mess of moans and incoherent words floated out, but I ignored them as he pounded into me from behind, nearly making me see stars with each thrust. He had way more stamina than I did, which was impressive as he kept going until he grunted and came a few minutes later.

He slowly pulled out of me as I collapsed on the bed, falling asleep before he could get back from dealing with the condom.

<u>Revelation</u>

Everett

Last night with Sloane was amazing. While I hadn't intended to sleep with her, I knew that it was bound to happen, given our history and how much time we were spending together. It wasn't like we were random people who met in a bar and decided to fuck. Sloane had always been one of my best friends, and I loved her more than she would ever know.

By the time I got cleaned up and made it back to the bed, Sloane was already asleep. I climbed in beside her and wrapped my arms around her, knowing we both slept better when I held her. The night was calm and peaceful as we got some of the best sleep we'd had in a long time.

The next morning, I got up and started breakfast while Sloane took a shower. Needing something to distract me from my thoughts of last night and how great the sex had been, I turned on the TV and let it play, not intending to pay attention.

Sloane came down the hall right as I was pulling the bacon from the pan and setting it on the plate I'd made for her. She stopped suddenly, pulling my attention to her and then immediately to the TV as she stared at it with her hands covering her face.

I grabbed the remote and turned up the volume as we both stared in silence. A picture of Sloane looking over her shoulder as she entered a convenience store popped up.

"While local police in Denver have yet to call this a serial killer, they are encouraging anyone who knows the whereabouts of Sloane Salazar to contact them immediately. She is wanted for questioning in the murder of convenience store clerk Zoe Wilton, as well as five other individuals whose identities have not been released. Salazar was caught on camera leaving the store and taking Wilton's vehicle before using her stolen ID to board a flight to New York. Salazar is considered armed and extremely dangerous. If you see her, please call the police immediately," the female news anchor said before the screen changed to the local weatherman.

"Oh my God," Sloane whispered, looking at me with complete shock on her face. "I have to leave. I have to get out of here."

I checked to make sure the stove was turned off before rushing to her and pulling her into my arms.

"It's going to be okay," I said softly, hating how her body trembled with fear.

"It's not going to be okay, Everett. They think that *I* murdered Zoe. They believe that I am armed and dangerous. You know what that means. The second a police officer sees me, they're going to kill me because they think I'm a threat. Or it will be someone involved in all of this, and they will kill me after saying that I attacked them. It's all a game to—"

She stopped talking as her shoulders slumped, and she looked up at me.

"A game to what?"

"A game to get me back to Colorado so they can finish what they started."

I closed my eyes and lowered my head, resting my forehead against hers. As much as I didn't want to admit it, she was right.

Broken

<u>Run</u>
Sloane

Everett and I spent the day erasing the information from the dry-erase boards, knowing it would only be a matter of time before someone showed up looking for me. It was easy to connect me to him, given our past, so we didn't want to jeopardize all of the work we had done by someone else getting hold of it.

We had talked about different options and what the next steps would be, but there weren't any that would keep him safe. It was me they wanted, and I knew they would do whatever it took to get to me. I couldn't risk him when he'd been so selflessly going out of his way to take care of me. I loved him too much to let them take him from me.

He left half an hour ago to do his grocery shopping, trying to keep to his normal habits in case anyone was watching. While he was gone, I erased any sign that I had been there. I cleaned and wiped everything down with bleach to erase as much as I could in what little time I had. Then I grabbed my duffle bag and snuck out, locking the door behind me.

I knew it would kill him to return to the apartment and not know where I was. I hoped that with there being no sign of a break-in, he would know I left willingly and that no one had come to kidnap me. It was among the hardest things I had ever done, but I knew I had to do it.

Manhattan was a large, busy city, but I couldn't take a chance that someone would see me and recognize me. I kept my hoodie on with the hood pulled low over my head as I made my way into a tourist shop. The bell chimed when I entered, immediately reminding me of the night Zoe was killed. I took a deep breath and forced myself to do what I needed to.

I had a small amount of cash left on me since I didn't need to buy much while staying with Everett. I quickly browsed the aisles, grabbing a plain black backpack, sunglasses with dark lenses, a large bottle of water, and some energy bars. I paid quickly, not bothering to make eye contact with the man who rang me up before I rushed out of the store and headed across the street.

It was busy, which I appreciated as I made my way across the street and then darted behind a run-down-looking building. I looked around, scanning every inch to make sure there weren't any cameras before I sat down and stuffed what I needed from my duffle bag into the backpack. I pulled my hoodie off and changed into a clean, plain black t-shirt. There wasn't anything I could do at this point to alter my appearance any further, so I grabbed my dad's baseball cap and pulled it on, tucking my hair underneath it so it wasn't easy to tell what color or how long it was. I pushed the sunglasses up my nose and then looked around to make sure I was still alone.

There wasn't enough time to plan anything, so I scarfed down an energy bar and chugged the bottle of water, tossing both into the dumpster along with my duffle bag and the stuff I was leaving behind. The only things I needed were tucked safely in the backpack that I adjusted on my back.

I walked the length of the alley, trying to find the right spot to make my way back into a crowd of people, when I noticed a man wearing a baseball cap heading toward me. He looked around as if he was trying to avoid being seen just as much as I was.

"Sloane," he said, my name urgent on his lips as he got closer. "I've been looking all over for you. You're not safe out here."

I narrowed my eyes as I studied him, knowing he couldn't see them easily with how dark the sunglasses were.

"I'm Everett's friend, Keith," he added, extending his hand to me. "We have to go. Now. It's not safe fo—"

I gasped as a red dot suddenly appeared on his forehead, his body bouncing back before he stumbled to the ground. Blood splattered on my face, stunning me as I processed what had just happened. I spun around, looking for the threat as a puddle of blood quickly pooled around him. I hadn't heard a gunshot, but it was clear as day with the bullet hole in the middle of his head.

I stepped to the side, making sure not to get it on my shoes, when a man with tattoos on his face stepped out of the shadows and approached.

"We've been looking for you," he growled, stalking toward me as he lowered the gun to his side.

I tried to move, but I was frozen in fear, my feet rooted to the bloody ground beneath me.

I opened my mouth to speak, but the words wouldn't come out.

"I had direct orders to shoot you and get it over with," he said as he tucked the gun into the back of his jeans and grabbed me by the neck, dragging me to the side of the building and into the shadows. "But I think I'd rather take my time and make you suffer. Watch you bleed, just like your husband and baby."

Fire roiled through my veins as my body stiffened. I took a shuddered breath, trying to force oxygen in as he shoved me against the hard brick wall. He stood in front of me, his eyes taunting me as I stared into them.

"Watching the video where that bullet went through your husband's brain was so satisfying. I won't lie, I was a little saddened about the baby, but you know, shit like that happens when you fuck with the wrong people. And man, did your husband fuck with the wrong person." He whistled through his teeth as I listened, plotting my next move.

"None of this had to happen. If it weren't for your husband stealing from my boss, we never would have crossed paths. But now that he's taken something that wasn't his, we won't stop until we get it back."

"I don't know what you're talking about," I admitted quietly.

He scoffed and looked down at the ground with a smirk on his face before his features hardened as his fist made contact with the side of my head. I heard the sound of the sunglasses breaking as they flew off my head.

I wanted to reach up and touch my face to see how bad the damage was, but the fire that was burning inside refused to let me. He grinned menacingly as he struck again, only this time I was faster and jumped out of the way before he could hit me. He cursed as his hand made contact with the brick wall, and blood poured down his fist.

"You stupid fucking bitch," he cursed as I threw a punch that landed against his jaw. He spat a mouthful of blood to the ground before he growled and came at me again.

I moved quickly, thankful that Trevor had been so patient with teaching me how to be fast on my feet. He had said that if I didn't have weight to use to my advantage, then I needed to use what I did have—speed.

I ducked as he tried to punch me, missing again as he stumbled to the side. I hit him hard in the ribs twice before lifting myself and going in for an uppercut. I knew that all it would take was one slip on my end, and he would kill me, so I couldn't let that happen. I had to fight hard if I had any chance at surviving this.

The harder I fought, the angrier he got. But he was alone, and right now, that was all I needed.

I waited him out for a few seconds, letting him get situated while allowing him to believe that I was already wearing myself out. I needed him to think I was weak so he would make another move. I leaned forward, resting my hands on my knees while I pretended to pant. I was just out of reach for him as he lunged forward, grabbing my arm. I spun quickly, slamming my fist into the side of his head and hitting his temple.

He let go as he tried to catch his balance, stumbling again in an effort to stay upright.

I stood tall, pulled my shoulders back, and looked him in the eye as I grabbed him by the throat and shoved him against the wall. A thrilling sensation washed over me as I noted the fear in his eyes. Fear that *I* put there.

"What's the matter? A big, strong guy is afraid of little ol' me?" I asked in a mocking tone, tilting my head to the side as I pressed my hand tighter against his throat. He was pinned between me and the wall, but his strength seemed to have subsided after that last blow to the temple. I reached back and forced my hand between the brick and his body to retrieve the gun.

"You know, maybe you should have shot me when you had the chance," I said, holding his gun up for him to see.

His eyes narrowed as his nostrils flared.

"You won't fucking kill me," he spit out, along with some blood.

I took a deep breath before leaning in to whisper in his ear while still maintaining my grip on his throat.

"Are you sure about that? Because, unlike you, I have *nothing* to live for."

"They'll find you and kill you. You can't hide forever."

"Who said anything about hiding?" I asked as a maniacal laugh spilled out of me. "I gotta admit—this is kind of fun. Almost therapeutic in a way." I shrugged, making sure I didn't accidentally pull the trigger before I was ready, as I pressed the gun against the side of his head.

I maintained my grip on his throat as I used my feet to kick his legs apart.

"Your first mistake was not killing me when you had the chance. Your second mistake was bringing up my family. Now I'm pissed off, and you know what happens when you piss a woman off?" My voice got louder as the anger threatened to overcome me.

I had no idea if anyone was around, but I didn't care. I felt alive, and I was going to live in this moment for as long as I could. It wouldn't bring my family back, but I could at least feel better about eliminating this asshole from the face of the earth.

He didn't answer me as his cold, hard eyes stared into mine.

"When you piss a woman off, they kick you where it hurts," I said proudly as I brought my knee up with such force that I imagined his balls were probably lodged into his throat.

He groaned and tried to bend over as the pain spread through him, but I held my grip on his throat tightly.

"Please," he begged, barely able to get the words out as his face turned purple.

"I'm sorry. I think you've mistaken me for someone who has a heart and cares," I replied, my voice void of emotion as I pulled the trigger and let go of him.

His lifeless body slid down the length of the wall as I adjusted my dad's baseball cap on my head and walked away.

Beautiful Monster

Sloane

People say '*monster*' like it's a bad thing. Like monsters are only faceless creatures who haunt our sleep when we're little.

They never realize just how many monsters they come into contact with every single day. How easy it can be to allow yourself to love one without even knowing it.

But no one truly understands what makes a person a *monster* until they become one themselves.

When the world has robbed you of everything you love and you have nothing left to live for.

When the darkness is so welcoming that you would sell your soul to the devil if it meant you had a reprieve from the pain you suffered daily.

I might be a monster, but I'm not here to haunt those who haven't done anything wrong.

I'm here to take care of those who unleash their demons on the innocent.

I rid the world of the people who make it a worse place.

I take care of the things most people wouldn't have the courage to do.

I look death in the eye and flirt with it, knowing nothing worse can happen to me at this point.

Killing is easy.

It's a beautiful escape from the world that threatens to consume us.

Feeling someone's heartbeat racing beneath your fingertips as they beg to be spared, only to have it stop moments later, is a thing of beauty. It's poetry.

Knowing that you're righting the world of its wrongs is a rare gift that's been bestowed upon me.

It's not murdering people that I'm obsessed with.

It's balancing the universe by getting rid of those who threaten it.

I'm not a monster.

I'm a daughter who lost her father.

A wife who lost her husband.

A mother who lost her child.

There's no greater pain than being a parent who watches their child suffer, knowing there's nothing they can do.

I'm not a killer.

I'm an eliminator.

<u>Help</u>

Sloane

"I'm sorry. I didn't know where else to go," I said, shivering as I stood off to the side of the door, hiding in the shadows.

I knew it was risky to show up at the gym, but aside from Everett's apartment, I didn't have anywhere else to go. The sun had set a little while ago, so I had kept to the shadows, trying to make myself as invisible as possible.

"You never need to apologize," Trevor replied quickly, pulling me inside before looking around and locking the door. "What's going on?"

I inhaled deeply and shook my head as tears filled my eyes. I wanted to tell him everything, but struggled with where to start. The look on his face when he saw the fresh blood splattered on my skin said enough. Thankfully, my shirt and hoodie were black, which hid most of it.

"I killed a man," I blurted out, surprising him as much as I did myself when the words came out.

"What's up?" Roman said, coming around the corner and stopping when he noticed me. He started out smiling, but then his features changed as he noticed the look on our faces. He folded his arms over his chest and studied me as I started talking again.

"He tried to kill me first. But something in me snapped, and then I—" I took a shuddered breath as I lowered my head and cried harder.

Roman got to me first, wrapping his arms around me in a tight hug while I tried to pull myself together.

"Let's go somewhere private," Trevor said, nodding at Roman.

I pulled away and looked around, knowing that the gym was already closed for the night.

"Our office doesn't have any windows, and we can watch the cameras from the monitors," Roman explained as he guided me down the hallway to the office.

Trevor pulled out a chair for me while Roman pulled up the screen that had all of the camera views in a grid. I took the backpack off and sat down, feeling nervous about telling them what had happened. But out of everyone, aside from Everett, I trusted them the most.

I felt stupid for not realizing that I had just put them in danger by coming here. If anyone were watching me, they would know where I was, which was why they were both intently studying the screen and looking for any sign of movement.

"Okay, tell us what happened," Trevor said as he sat down and faced me.

"I… I don't know. Everything was fine until this morning when we saw a story on the news that said I was a possible serial killer, and they were blaming me for the murder of Zoe. Everett and I didn't know what to do, so we started clearing the dry-erase boards in his apartment since it would be easy for someone to link me to him in New York. After that, I waited until he left to do his weekly grocery shopping, and I left."

I paused for a moment, running my now sweaty palms down the front of my jeans.

"I went to a store and grabbed a backpack so I could get rid of my duffle bag. I didn't want anyone to be able to identify me with it. I was in the alley sorting my stuff and tossing what I didn't need when I ran into a guy that Everett knew. I hadn't met him before, but I had been on a few video calls with him and Everett, but he never showed his face. His camera was always directed at his computer, so we could see what he was looking at. He worked in the FBI with him."

"Worked?" Trevor asked with a single eyebrow raised.

"He said I wasn't safe. He knew me by name. As he approached me, I saw this red light on his forehead, and, um…" My nose scrunched as the sting of new tears burned it.

"I didn't hear the gunshot like I did when they killed Gabe. It wasn't loud. I saw him die, but it took me a few moments to realize what happened. Then there was this other guy, and he said he'd been instructed to kill me. I don't even know how they found me," I said as I pressed my lips together to stop the crying. "Everything I have is in that backpack. I don't have much, so it's not like it was easy for them to plant a tracking device in something without me noticing."

"May I?" Roman asked as he pointed to the backpack.

I nodded, watching as he slowly took each item out and set it on his desk. I had tossed my dad's baseball cap into the bag before I left the alley to make it less likely someone would be able to say they saw me.

He didn't say anything as he looked at it before setting it down next to Nicky's baby book and a change of clothes I had packed away. Aside from a handful of snacks and an empty water bottle, there wasn't anything else in the bag.

"Do you see anything?" Trevor asked Roman, steepling his fingers in front of his face as he rested his elbows on his knees.

"Not yet. But there has to be something."

Roman opened each of the pockets of the backpack, not finding much until he pulled out my cell phone.

"I haven't turned it on since I left Colorado and came to New York," I said quickly, knowing they must be thinking I was an idiot for having it still. "I couldn't part with it because it's the only thing that has pictures and video of my family. But I swear I haven't turned it on once. I keep it charged just so I have it, but they can't track it if it's not on. Right?"

"Not likely, no. There have been advances in technology, but I don't think that's what we're dealing with here," Roman said. "You said the guy who got shot was a friend of Everett's who was in the FBI?"

"Yeah. I think his name was Keith. Why?"

"It just seems odd to me that he's a friend of Everett's, yet he somehow knows where you are and approaches you by himself without Everett," Roman replied, cutting his glance to Trevor.

"You think Keith was one of the bad guys?" I asked as a million thoughts raced through my mind when I thought about all of our conversations with him. "Oh my God."

I covered my mouth with my hands as the blood drained from my face.

"What is it?" Trevor asked, gently touching my elbow.

"We told him everything. All of the research Everett was doing, everyone he suspected was corrupt. Everett showed him the boards with all of the information he had gathered. He trusted him."

"So he knew all along where you were and what information you guys had," Trevor said, shaking his head.

"But he said he wanted to help me. That I wasn't safe," I objected, refusing to believe someone could be so cruel.

Just then, Trevor's phone started ringing. He tipped his head in frustration before lifting it to his ear and pressing a finger to his lips, asking me to be quiet.

"Hey, Everett. What's up?"

My heart dropped in my chest, hating that I had left without saying anything.

"No, I haven't seen her. Is everything okay?"

Trevor nodded, locking eyes with me.

"Yeah. Of course. We were getting ready to head out for the night, but I'll let you know if we see her." He paused as Everett spoke, and it killed me not knowing what he was saying. "You too."

Trevor hung up the phone and gave me a look I never wanted to see again in my life. Sadness filled his eyes as he stared at me and shook his head.

"You need to leave."

Trust No One

Sloane

I shook my head, trying to process his words.

"Now. You need to leave now, Sloane," he said firmly, standing up and lifting me by my elbow.

"I'm so sorry. I should never have come here. I didn't mean to bother you guys with my problems."

Roman quickly shoved everything back into my backpack before handing it to me, and I refused to look at him because I didn't want to cry. I knew that I shouldn't have expected them to help me, given how bad things had gotten. They had their own lives, and I wasn't trying to ruin them by bringing them into this mess.

"You are always welcome here," Trevor said, grabbing my shoulders and forcing me to look at him. "Everett is looking for you, but he didn't say anything about Keith being dead, which means he doesn't know."

"What are you talking about?"

"If he knew that his friend died, he would have been more of a mess when I talked to him. Right now, he's a mess because you're gone, and he doesn't know where you are. If he doesn't know that Keith is dead, then that means someone else cleaned it up before the FBI found out. There's no way they would be quiet about it unless they were involved in his murder. Everett doesn't know just how much danger you are in. They're going to keep following him, hoping they can get to you. You have to go now before he shows up and finds you here."

"I don't—" I started to say before Roman interrupted.

"I have a place you can go. I'll take you. Your phone stays here."

"But—"

"No buts, Sloane. It makes sense for you to have forgotten it here since you've been training here. We can find it and turn it on to see whose phone it is. That way, I can save the photos and videos for you on a hard drive without anyone knowing where you are. But we gotta go. Now."

I looked between the two of them and blew out a heavy breath as blood rushed through my ears, and my heart thundered in my chest.

"Okay. Tell me what you need me to do," I said.

"Take her out the back," Trevor said to Roman. "I'm going to lock up and head out as if it's a normal day."

"Got it."

Roman nodded his head, and I followed, giving Trevor a final glance over my shoulder as he rushed to turn everything off before turning off the light in the office.

Roman's footsteps were loud, which made it easy to follow him down the dark corridor to a door I didn't know existed. He paused for a moment before opening it, peeking his head out to make sure it was clear before stepping outside.

We were behind the gym in a long, dark alley. He grabbed my hand and pulled gently as he used his other hand to send a text message. We got closer to the street, which made me nervous because it wouldn't be as easy to hide. I considered pulling away and making a run for it, even though I had no money and nowhere to go. But I also couldn't keep putting people I cared about in danger, which was what I was doing the longer I stayed with him.

Before we stepped onto the street, Roman pulled his hoodie over his head and handed it to me, waiting until I put it on. It covered my backpack, which thankfully didn't stick out too much since I didn't have a lot in it. He pulled the hood over my head, then grabbed my hand and led me across the street and into a parking garage.

He pulled keys out of his pocket and pressed the button to unlock a truck with lifted wheels. He opened the back door and nodded for me to get in.

"Lie down as flat as you can," he instructed before closing the door and getting in the driver's seat. He glanced back to make sure I was how he wanted me before grabbing a blanket from the back seat and handing it to me. I grabbed it and covered myself with it as he reversed out of the parking spot and drove off.

"I need to make a phone call, but I need you to stay quiet, okay?" he asked.

"You got it."

"I don't want any cameras to pick you up, so I also need you to stay lying down back there until I can get us out of the city. I'll let you know when it's safe to get up."

I took a couple of deep breaths as I tried to get comfortable while the phone rang on the speaker in the car.

"Hello," a man answered gruffly.

"Hey, Rob. It's Roman. I was wondering if I could use the cabin for a week, maybe two."

"Go for it."

"Thanks, man."

The call disconnected, but I remained silent as he made another call.

"Hey, baby. Are you on your way home?" a female voice asked.

"Not quite. I need to head to the cabin for a few days."

"Oh. Okay."

"Can you—"

"I'm already on it. I'll see if my mom can take Rosie for a few days and meet you there."

"Thanks, baby. Don't forget to bring the essentials."

"Dr. Pepper and sunflower seeds. Got it."

The line disconnected again, and I laid there, confused as to what was happening.

"My friend, Rob, has a cabin in the middle of nowhere. That's where we're headed. It's a few hours outside of the city, but you'll be safe there. Once we get off the main highway, I'll have you sit up. So far, I think we've done well with hiding you if anyone was watching, but I'll feel better once we get to the cabin."

"Was the woman your girlfriend?" I asked, lifting the blanket slightly so I could breathe.

"Yeah. That's Quinn. She'll meet us up there shortly."

"Does she know?"

"Not all of it. But she knows that Trevor and I have been helping out a friend of Everett's, as well as the general stuff about your family. She works in the FBI, so I'm hoping I can pick her brain later about what happened with Keith."

"Are you sure it's safe?" I asked, immediately regretting asking.

It was rude of me to ask it, but it also felt impossible to know who I could and couldn't trust these days.

"Quinn has been through her share of shit, including corruption and someone trying to take her daughter. If anyone can help right now, it will be her."

I took a deep breath and slowly let it out, trusting that everything would be alright.

<u>Desperation</u>
Everett

I raked a hand through my hair and kicked the side of the wall when I got to the gym, and it was already closed for the night. Trevor had said they were closing up soon; I just thought I would make it there before they did. I was half tempted to break in, just to make sure Sloane wasn't there.

I knew she had left willingly because the house was cleaned thoroughly before she left and smelled strongly of bleach when I got home. I didn't even bother putting away the groceries as I desperately searched for her and found every trace of her gone.

It was getting late, and I was running out of places to look. I didn't want to draw any attention to her by filing a missing person report, but I was at that point of needing to know where she was and if she was safe.

Having Sloane gone felt like my world ended, and I couldn't stand the thought of this being what my life would be like. I had gotten so used to having her around me all the time that now that she was gone, I was beside myself.

I walked down the street, pressing my cell phone to my ear as I tried calling her cell phone again. I knew she wouldn't answer it because she always kept it turned off, but this time, it went to voicemail.

I stopped dead in my tracks and listened to her voice as the recorded greeting played before a long beep for me to leave my message.

I knew that the only way her phone would be turned on was if someone found her, and she knew she needed help.

I raced home, running as fast as I could. I needed to trace her phone and find out where she was before it was too late.

Pieces
Sloane

"The men you identified in the police lineup are all part of a highly dangerous drug cartel that has recently taken over parts of Colorado. Juan Rodriguez, the man with the black widow tattoo on his face, is the leader of the Lagrimas Rojas, though he reports to higher-ups in Mexico," Quinn said as she showed me the computer screen with his picture and the information about him.

I felt the heat spread through me as anger radiated in my veins as I stared at his face.

We got to the cabin a few hours ago and had been sitting in the living room, going through all of the information we had so far. Quinn had done some quick research before she came, primarily on the men who killed my family. It was obvious they were the ones still trying to kill me. Now, we needed to figure out why.

"As far as the man who approached you in the alley, we have confirmed that it was not Agent Keith Montes. NYPD is currently investigating, but I have a trusted contact who works in the same office as Keith and has confirmed that he is alive and well."

"Someone pretended to be him?" I asked in disbelief.

"Yes. I don't know much at this point, but my guess is that whatever information Keith was getting from Everett was somehow intercepted, and someone used it to find you. Until we know the identity of the man who was killed, I can't do anything other than make random guesses about what is happening. Once we know who he is, we can look at how he's related to the Lagrimas Rojas."

I leaned back against the high back of the chair and let out a long, shaky sigh as she and Roman sat across from me on the couch.

"Never in my life would I have thought I would somehow be involved with a drug cartel. This is wild," I replied, shaking my head.

"There's a lot going on," Quinn said empathetically. "But the important thing is that we keep you safe."

"I haven't been safe since the night three men showed up to a small-town high school football game and asked my husband if he was Hugo Sanchez."

Quinn's eyes widened in surprise as she leaned forward and stared at me.

"I'm sorry. What did you just say?"

"I said that I haven't been safe—"

"No. What was the name you just said?" she rushed out, cutting me off.

"Hugo Sanchez."

"You've got to be fucking kidding me."

I knew she wasn't angry with me, but I still flinched from her reaction as she leaned forward and started doing something on her computer.

A few seconds later, she turned the screen to face me again, and I gasped. My hands flew to my mouth as I stared, tears rolling down my cheeks.

"Have you seen him around?" Quinn asked cautiously.

I forced myself to look away from the screen and meet her eyes.

"That… That's… That's Gabe. That's my husband," I sobbed, returning my attention to his photo before it disappeared.

Quinn glanced nervously at Roman and then reached over and gently placed her hand over mine.

"According to our records, that is Hugo Sanchez, the leader of the Dark Rebels cartel. They primarily operate on the East Coast and have huge ties to Cuba. According to our intel, they started taking over parts of the Midwest, including dropping down into Colorado around the same time your family was murdered."

"That's not possible," I objected, pointing to the screen. "That is my husband. That is Gabe Salazar, not Hugo Sanchez. There's been a mix-up."

"I know that these questions are hard, but we need all of the information we can get to figure this out," Roman said gently. "Is it possible your husband was living a life you weren't aware of? Was he maybe gone often for business? Or did he go visit family out of town without you?"

"No," I practically shrieked. "Gabe would never do that. He worked at a car dealership, and when he wasn't there, he was at home with me and Nicky."

"What about family?" Quinn pressed. "Did he have visits with anyone when you weren't included?"

"Gabe didn't have a family," I said, my stomach turning sour. "He was adopted when he was a baby after being abandoned in a park. His parents didn't have any other children and passed a few years before we met."

"Is it possible he had siblings from his birth parents that he didn't tell you about?" Roman asked.

"I mean, I guess anything is possible at this point. And since he's dead, I can't ask him any of the million questions I've had since he died." I threw my hands in the air in frustration, knowing it wasn't their fault. This was bringing up a lot of emotions I had purposely chosen not to deal with.

"Do you mind if I ask what Gabe's date of birth was?" Quinn asked, her voice soft.

"January 17th, 1997," I replied as I watched her fingers move over the keyboard.

She pressed her lips together and then looked at me before showing me the screen again.

The image had changed to a mugshot of Hugo Sanchez, and the information listed beside it showed his date of birth as being the same as Gabe's.

"That's impossible," I sobbed. "You really think that my husband had some secret identity he never told me about and did time in prison?"

"No," Quinn replied quietly. "But given your husband was adopted and didn't know much about his biological family, I think it's possible that he had a twin he never knew about. They share the same birthday, and pulling their images up side by side, you can hardly tell the difference." She pointed to the screen, where an image of Gabe was displayed beside Hugo's picture.

"According to our intel, he was also wanted in Colombia for drug trafficking two years ago. So, unless Gabe was sneaking out of the country and traveling abroad, I would say they are twins," Quinn added.

I leaned back and let out a heavy sigh as I considered that.

<u>Helpless</u>
Everett

I paced outside of the gym, waiting for Trevor or Roman to get there. It was early in the morning, but I was awake and wired on the excessive amounts of coffee I'd had throughout the night as I worked on trying to find Sloane. Tracing her phone showed that it was at the gym, which meant she had come here at one point after she ran away from my apartment.

Twenty minutes later, I was sitting on the sidewalk, trying not to fall asleep as Trevor walked up and started unlocking the building.

"She's not here," he said as his way of greeting me.

"Her phone says otherwise," I replied sourly as I stood up and shook my head. I needed food and sleep, but all of that could wait until I knew Sloane was safe.

He opened the door and waited for me to go inside before heading down the hallway to his office.

"She left her phone here," Trevor said, walking behind his desk and turning on his computer. I looked down at the phone sitting on the desk and wondered how long it had been there.

"Was she here last night?" I asked, hoping our friendship was solid enough that he wouldn't lie to me.

He leaned back in his chair, folded his hands over his stomach, and looked at me.

"Yes."

"When I called you, was she here?"

"Yes."

"Why the fuck didn't you tell me?" I demanded, shoving a hand through my hair as I turned and paced in front of him. "I spent the entire night trying to find her. I've been worried out of my mind, and this whole time you knew where she was."

"I didn't tell you because Sloane needed to be safe."

"And you think she wouldn't be safe with me? Or that I would somehow put her in danger if I knew where she was?"

"Yes."

"Oh, for fucks sake, can you please give me complete answers instead of this yes bullshit?"

Trevor didn't move, but that didn't mean I missed the way his lips curled into a slight smirk, knowing he was getting to me.

"The reason I didn't tell you that she was here is because she came here after she got attacked in an alley. A man approached her, claiming to be your friend, Keith. He insisted that she go with him because she wasn't safe, but before she could ask any questions, he was shot in the head. Want to know who shot him?"

"Sloane?" I asked, my stomach curdling as I thought about how she would have gotten access to a gun. We had spent a lot of time at the indoor shooting range, so I knew how accurate her aim was these days. Not only that, she grew up hunting with her dad and had been around firearms most of her life.

"No. One of the assholes that has been trying to kill her. Want to know how they found her?"

A rush of air whooshed out of me as I sat down in the empty chair in front of his desk.

"They found her the same way your so-called friend found her. Someone has been watching you two and knew exactly where she would be."

"Keith would never do that," I said, dumbfounded.

"You're right. He wouldn't. Roman confirmed last night that Keith is fine and still in Colorado. Which means someone knew she would know who he was, and they counted on her to trust them."

"What are you saying?" My brain tried to keep up but I was so fucking tired none of this was making sense.

"It means that the information you've been sharing with Keith has somehow gotten into the wrong hands. Someone has been taking that information and using it to get close to Sloane."

"Where is she now?" I asked, hoping he wouldn't lie to me again. I didn't care if I couldn't see her; I just needed to know that she was safe.

"She's with Roman and Quinn."

"Where?"

"An undisclosed location."

I tilted my head and arched an eyebrow.

"I like you, Everett, but let me make myself very clear. While we might be friends, Sloane is my top priority right now. My loyalty lies with her. I will do everything in my power to make sure she is safe. Same with Roman."

"I would never hurt her," I whispered, hating the feeling that was settling deep inside my chest.

"Then step back and let us help her. It is still unknown who has access to the information you were sharing and how they got it, so that makes you a huge liability. The best thing you can do for Sloane right now is to leave her alone and stay far away from her. Forget any of this ever happened and go back to your life as it used to be."

"I can't do that," I said, my voice hitching in the back of my throat. "You don't know what she means to me, Trevor. She's the only thing that gives me a reason to wake up in the morning. I love her more than I have loved anyone. She is the one who got away, so I'm not willing to lose her when I just got her back. I want justice for her family as much as I want it for my little brother. Asking me to walk away isn't something I can do."

"I'm sorry, Everett. But I wasn't asking. I'm telling you that you need to walk away. If you want Sloane to live through this and have any chance at a future with her, walk away."

I got up and shook my head, not bothering to say anything as I walked out and headed back to my apartment.

Broken

<u>Stronger</u>
Sloane

"Aim higher," Roman said, gently lifting my elbow as he stood behind me.

We were out in the middle of nowhere with a dozen targets set up in the forest for me to practice shooting. Some were easy to find, while some were purposely harder to make sure I could quickly identify any threats.

We'd spent the morning going over the information Quinn had acquired before Trevor called to let Roman know that Everett had been by the gym. He was pissed—and rightfully so. I hated that I was creating so much worry for him, but this was what I needed to do if I wanted to keep both of us safe. Staying with Everett would lead the bad guys to him, and I wasn't willing to risk his life right now.

I lifted my hand slightly and then pulled the trigger, grinning when I hit the can perfectly.

"I wouldn't want to be on the receiving end of that," Quinn said, speaking loud enough we could hear her. "Nice shot."

"Thank you," I said, looking around at where the other cans were lying on the ground, imagining how satisfying it would be to see the lifeless bodies of the Lagrimas Rojas cartel instead.

"Lunch is ready if you guys want to take a break and come eat," Quinn offered, smiling warmly at me.

"That sounds great. Thank you."

I secured the gun behind my back and then started collecting the cans when Roman reached a hand out to stop me. I was about to ask what was wrong, but kept my mouth shut when his eyes quickly scanned the woods. Whatever he heard had him on high alert as he didn't move.

Quinn lingered by the front door, standing completely still as we waited for Roman to give us the all-clear. Instead, he slowly let go of my arm and reached behind him for his gun. Quinn pulled hers and took a few quick steps, shielding me with her body as she watched in the other direction.

"Get her inside," Roman growled, his tone sending goosebumps along my skin.

I fought the urge to pull my gun and instead allowed Quinn to usher me inside, never taking her eyes off the woods around us.

"Get on the floor and stay there until I tell you it's okay," she ordered, still keeping her gun aimed at the front door.

"I have a gun, too," I said, stopping when I noticed the motherly look she gave me over her shoulder. Deciding it was better not to piss her off when she was trying to protect me, I got down on the rug.

The front door closed, and I knew she had gone outside to join Roman. I hated that they were in danger because they were protecting me. I hadn't known either of them very long, but they already felt like friends, and I didn't want any harm to come to them.

It felt like forever before the door opened, and I heard footsteps.

"It's clear. You can get up," Quinn said as Roman stepped into view and offered me his hand to help me up.

"What was it?' I asked, knowing that the likelihood of someone finding us up here was slim but not impossible, given how easily they had been tracking me before.

"I'm not sure. It could have been an animal, but I'll watch the cameras to make sure whatever it was doesn't come back."

I nodded and took a seat at the kitchen table while Quinn grabbed a pitcher of iced tea from the fridge and set it down. Lunch was simple, but the meal was packed with lots of protein, which I appreciated. I needed to build up my strength so I could do what needed to be done.

A few hours later, we were all relieved that there had been no activity on the cameras. Quinn spent some time on her computer, though she didn't say what she was working on. I took the time to make a list using an empty notebook I had found lying beneath the coffee table.

"What are you working on?" Roman asked as he sat down beside me on the couch, giving me plenty of space.

I had been so lost in thought that I hadn't noticed him and immediately clutched the notepad to my chest. His eyebrows rose in response, giving me a curious look.

"It's just a list," I said, not giving any additional information.

"A hit list?" he teased, though he had no idea how spot-on he was.

"No," I replied with a laugh so nervous it grabbed Quinn's attention from the kitchen table. Not that it was hard for us to see and hear everything, given that the kitchen and living room were all one small space combined.

"Sloane," he warned, giving me a look that made me immediately want to trust him.

"I wouldn't call it a *hit list*," I explained as I lowered it and looked down at the names I had written. "It's more of a *people I don't trust* list."

"Can I see it?"

My grip on it tightened as I felt vulnerable. But if Roman had taught me anything, it was that I could trust him more than anyone else right now. He'd put his life on the line to help get me somewhere safe and taught me how to defend myself.

I handed over the notepad and waited for him to say something as he looked at the list.

"Am I on it?" Quinn teased, more so to remind us that she was there in case I didn't want her to know something. But I trusted Quinn as much as I trusted Roman.

"No, but there is a lot of law enforcement on here," Roman answered as if he were reading a grocery list. "A couple of people I don't know and a judge."

His eyes cut to mine, and he raised his eyebrow again in silent question. I shrugged, not knowing what to say. How was I supposed to trust anyone who was involved in the trial that set those monsters free?

"If you tell me who they are, I can look into them and see if we find any connections. That way, we'll have a better idea of how deep all of this goes," Quinn replied.

Roman looked at me, and I nodded, giving him permission to do so.

"We have Sheriff Dowdy, Deputy Sheriff Anderson, Judge Curry, Antonio Carria, who is the criminal defense lawyer, Officer Butchkins, Officer Contreras, Officer Ozwald, and Agent Keith Montes," Roman said, his voice changing with the last name.

"Is that it?" Quinn asked as she wrote down the names on her notepad.

"That's it for law enforcement and the judge," Roman replied. "The rest of the list appears to be members of the Lagrimas Rojas cartel?"

"I don't know their names," I admitted. "I just know them by what I remember about them. The one with the blue eyes, the one with the snake tattoo around his wrist, and the one with the black widow tattoo beneath his eye."

"The one with the black widow tattoo is—" Quinn started, but then stopped when I turned to look at her. My expression must have given me away because her face changed as she rubbed her lips together.

"The less I know about them, the better," I replied, feeling the flush in my body as the blood raced through my veins with the excitement of what I was going to do to them.

Trouble

Everett

I glanced down at my phone vibrating on the coffee table. I had called in sick today, which meant I wasn't required to take any calls, especially from someone I no longer trusted. I pressed the button to ignore Keith's phone call and returned my attention to the TV.

The news was on, and I was waiting to see if they said anything more about Sloane being wanted for questioning in the murder of Zoe. I imagined it would come up again if any street cameras caught the incident in the alley yesterday. I knew they would cut whatever they had to before giving it to the news channel so they could spin the story how they wanted to. Anything to make Sloane look like the bad guy so they could get people to turn on her and give her up to the authorities.

My phone rang two more times, back-to-back, but no voicemails were left. I didn't feel like dealing with Keith right now, but I knew that if I didn't answer, he would just keep calling, *if* it was even him. Who knew at this point if they had gotten to him, too? I didn't trust anyone and hated that I had no one I could talk to about all of this. I was alone in the world, and the only person I wanted to be with was running for her life.

By the fourth time he called, I grabbed the phone from the coffee table and answered it.

"What?" I bit out, allowing my irritation and frustration to seep through.

"We have a problem."

"You fucking think?" I asked bitterly. He obviously had no idea what I was talking about, but that didn't dull my anger any when I thought about what Trevor said regarding Sloane and the attack in the alley.

"You already know?"

"About someone pretending to be you so they could take Sloane? Yeah. I know."

"What the fuck are you talking about?" Keith said, his voice sounding muffled as papers shuffled in the background.

"Someone approached her in an alley and claimed to be you. Told her she wasn't safe and that you were my friend and wanted to help her."

"When did this happen?"

"Last night," I replied, scrubbing my hand down my face in frustration. I hated that I didn't have more information and that I had to rely on whatever Trevor was willing to tell me.

"Fuck," Keith muttered.

"Wait—if you didn't know about that, then what problem were you calling to tell me about?"

"When I came into my office this morning, my computer was turned on, and the spreadsheet with all of the info we discussed was open. To make matters worse, the files for Juan Rodriguez, Tomas Cortez, and Ricky Santos are all missing."

I furrowed my brow as I tried to figure out why those names sounded familiar.

"They're the three suspects Sloane identified," he continued.

"Shit."

None of this was good. Without those files, we had nothing, and whoever took them wanted to send us a message by ransacking his office.

"How did someone get into your office without anyone noticing?"

"I have no fucking idea. We have security cameras outside, but they were conveniently offline this morning and didn't capture anyone coming or going."

"Even without the cameras, it should have been impossible for anyone to get through security without a badge," I said, thinking through it.

"Exactly."

"Which means this wasn't someone outside of the agency."

"Nope. This happened within," Keith agreed. "Trust no one. I don't know who did this, but I assure you that I will find out."

"Either way, we have a leak and need to figure out who it is."

"Agreed." He sighed heavily. "Where is Sloane?"

I opened my mouth and then stopped because that was a strange question to answer since I hadn't told him that I didn't know where she was. I had only mentioned the situation in the alley, not that she had left my apartment and never returned.

"She's with me," I lied, suddenly feeling very uneasy.

"Good. Keep her safe until we can figure out what is going on," he replied, but his tone felt off.

"I agree. It's probably best for her to stay in my apartment until we know it's safe for her to leave."

"Yeah…" His voice trailed off, and I could tell he was distracted by something, but didn't know what.

I ended the call and then went to the window. I had no idea who I was looking for, but I knew someone was out there watching me, waiting for Sloane.

<u>Framed</u>
Sloane

I spent a few days with Roman and Quinn at the cabin, trying to figure out my next steps. The list I made continued to get longer the more we dove into everything, and everyone started to look like a suspect. The additional names were added to Quinn's master list while I kept the piece of paper with my names on it tucked inside my pocket at all times. Something about knowing they would soon be dealt with gave me an alarming sense of tranquility.

We had just finished dinner when the evening news came on. I was lost in thought when the screen cut to a man doing a live broadcast in the alley. In the corner of the screen, an image of me appeared as I walked into the convenience store where I bought the new backpack before getting rid of my duffle bag.

"Authorities say that Sloane Salazar was last seen entering the convenience store a little after six o'clock. The two men who were found in the alley behind the store were pronounced dead on the scene from a fatal gunshot. Police confirmed they found a duffle bag belonging to Salazar in the dumpster by where their bodies were found. She is still wanted in Colorado for questioning in the case of a convenience store clerk who was murdered before Salazar stole her vehicle and used her identification to purchase a plane ticket to New York. If you see Salazar, the police ask that you do not approach her as she is considered armed and extremely dangerous. You can either call the tip line shown at the bottom of the screen or call 911 if you feel it's an emergency. Back to you, Kim."

I shook my head but didn't cry like I wanted to. It shouldn't surprise me that another murder was being pinned on me. That just meant there was only one thing left for me to do.

Get even.

****

After we saw the news story about my so-called murder streak, we decided to act quickly and get me out of town before it was too late. Roman drove me to the bus station and paid my fare with cash, so we didn't have any paper trail. I knew it would be a long drive and would take a few days to get there, but I planned to spend that time resting the best I could because what I had planned meant I needed all of the strength and energy I had.

Once I made it back to Denver, I used the extra cash they gave me to get a ride to Oak Creek. It was a few hours' drive, but for the right price, I was able to get a ride without anyone asking questions. I sat in the back seat with my backpack between my feet, easily accessible if I needed it. I pretended to be asleep the majority of the drive, with the baseball cap Roman gave me pulled low over my face to hide my eyes. But I wasn't sleeping.

I was plotting my revenge.

Fuck Around and Find Out

Sloane

Everyone has their breaking point.

A time when enough finally becomes enough.

But for me, I was just getting started.

I used to hate scary movies because I couldn't stand horror.

Now, I was the scariest thing alive.

That was what happened when life stripped away everything that once protected you and left you raw and vulnerable.

You found yourself in the worst way.

You became the very thing that used to haunt you.

They fucked around, and now, they were about to find out.

Watch It Burn

Sloane

I walked around my parents' backyard, staring at what used to be my childhood home. The crime scene tape was gone, but the house was still eerily empty. The nice thing about living in a small town was that no one bothered the house. The people in Oak Creek knew whose house it was and what had happened, so no one bothered with it. I figured most of them expected that I would come back one day and take it over. It was already paid off, so there was no mortgage to keep up with.

It was late, which meant it was easy for me to hide in the shadows. I opened the back door and walked inside, stopping in the kitchen and staring at the floor that was still stained red with my mother's blood. The mess had been cleaned, but apparently, the blood had seeped into the wood flooring, leaving a faint stain behind that even the strongest cleaner couldn't remove. Or maybe fate left it there for me to see so it could fuel my anger at what they had done to her—a reminder of what was taken from me.

I knelt down and ran my fingers over it as tears slid down my face. I didn't get to say goodbye to my mother or tell her that I loved her. We had just started figuring out how to have a better relationship with each other, only for it to be cut short.

I stood up and wiped my cheeks with my hands. I didn't have time to stop and fall apart. I had people to visit and hell to make them pay.

I grabbed the backpack and headed upstairs to my bedroom as if nothing had happened. I couldn't afford to be emotional right now because if I allowed myself to feel even an ounce of the anger that was coursing through me, the entire house would burst into flames.

I didn't turn any of the lights on because I didn't want anyone to know that I was there. Besides, I was more comfortable in the darkness these days, anyway. I set my backpack down and began unpacking it now that I was going to be here for a while. I was done running.

I pulled out the framed picture of me, Gabe, and Nicky and kissed it before setting it on my nightstand. Then I grabbed my dad's baseball cap and set it beside it. I didn't have much with me since I had left most of it here when I left the first time. I hadn't expected to ever come back to this house, but it seemed like the perfect way to end things where they all started.

I set my backpack on the floor and then changed into comfortable clothes. I no longer had the luxury of sleeping in pajamas, just in case someone came in and tried to kill me in my sleep tonight. But tomorrow, I would work on setting things up the way I wanted them so no one would have the opportunity to surprise me again.

Traitor

Everett

The past week at work had been hell with my lack of sleep and frustration over not knowing where Sloane was. I knew that Trevor and Roman were taking care of her the best they could, but when Roman showed up at the gym and refused to tell me anything, I was about to lose my mind. He assured me that Sloane was fine and that she would handle things the way she needed to, as if I were supposed to find any comfort in that.

I had seen the news story that broke out about her being a person of interest in the murders that happened in the alley where she had been attacked. Someone was actively framing her, and I hated that we didn't know who it was. My contact with Keith had gone from constant updates on my theories to absolute radio silence. I trusted him as much as I trusted myself these days.

I knew it was reckless to be so consumed by someone, but I couldn't stand the thought of something happening to her. I'd spoken to my mother a few times to make sure she was okay, but she hadn't seen or heard anything about Sloane, which meant she hadn't gone home. I had no idea where she was or what she was doing, which infuriated me. How was I supposed to protect her if I didn't know where she was?

I got home a little past six and tossed my keys on the kitchen table. I hadn't stopped to grab dinner, even though I knew there was nothing in the fridge. My depression was getting the best of me, but I couldn't pull myself out of it.

Just as I was about to head to my bedroom to change clothes, the doorbell rang.

I rushed over to answer it, hopeful that it was Sloane.

"Keith? What are you doing here?" I asked as he stood on the other side, a strange darkness in his eyes.

"I'm here for Sloane."

"Sloane? She's not here."

"That's funny because you told me she was with you. And when we traced her cell phone, the last location it tracked was New York City."

I worked my jaw back and forth before shaking my head. This mother fucker.

"Yeah, well, she's not here. See yourself out." I slammed the door shut, startled when he shoved it open, and two guys I hadn't noticed before stepped out from behind him.

"You wouldn't mind if we had a look ourselves, would you?" Keith asked with a condescending tone.

"Do I really have a choice?" I cocked my head to the side and stared at him as the two guys pulled their guns out and pushed their way into my apartment.

I listened as they rummaged through every room, trying to find Sloane while Keith stood there with me.

"What are you fucking doing?" I asked him, the anger making my jaw clench so tight it was hard to get the words out.

"Taking care of what needs to be taken care of."

"You fucking asshole. I should have known you were dirty."

"No one said I'm dirty. I'm simply doing the job that was assigned to me."

"By who?"

"None of your fucking business," he sneered as the guys came back to the living room.

"No sign of her," the one with the facial tattoos said.

Keith sighed heavily and locked his hands together in front of him as he stared at me.

"Tell me where she is," he demanded.

"I don't fucking know. She left. I haven't seen or heard from her since."

"Where is her phone?"

"I. Don't. Fucking. Know."

I barely had a chance to blink before I felt the sharp sting as his fist collided with my cheek.

"I will ask one more time. Where is her phone?"

"Even if I knew, I wouldn't tell you. Fuck you," I said, spitting out a small amount of blood as I rubbed my face.

Keith stepped back as one of the guys punched me in the stomach, forcing me to bend over from the pain. A fist flew up, hitting me in the jaw as another fist collided with my ribs. I dropped to my knees as the pain radiated through my body with every punch and kick they delivered before I felt the sting of a knife plunging into my back.

A few minutes later, they backed off as I lay bleeding on the floor.

"We'll be back. I suggest you find out where she is before then," Keith warned before the door shut behind them.

I rolled over and groaned in extreme pain as I struggled to pull my cell phone out of my pocket. My eye was swollen from one of the hits they landed catching me straight in the eye, but I squinted until I saw Trevor's name. I pressed send and then hit the button for the speakerphone so I didn't have to hold it to my ear.

He answered on the third ring.

"Hey, I still haven't—" he started, but stopped when I interrupted him.

"Keith was here looking for Sloane and tracking her phone. Get rid of it. Now."

I heard him ask questions, but I lost consciousness before I could process what he was saying.

Planning

Sloane

I woke up feeling rested and ready for the day after a peaceful night of dreams filled with the brutal deaths of everyone who had ever wronged me. Okay, so maybe not everyone. But the list was rather long these days.

The sky was cloudy and overcast, giving me the perfect opportunity to sneak out to the detached garage without anyone seeing me. It was a typical cold day in Oak Creek, with fall quickly removing any evidence that summer had ever existed.

I pulled the hoodie over my head and stayed close to the tree line so I could duck in and hide if needed. It was helpful that there was a lot of space in between houses, so unless someone was outside today, they weren't likely to know I was out there. I went to the side of the garage and pulled the door open, satisfied that it didn't give me any trouble.

Memories of hiding in there the night they murdered my mother rushed through me, but I quickly forced them away as I walked over to the gun safe in the corner and entered the code to unlock it. My dad and I used to hunt a lot over the years, which meant I was familiar with guns and how to use them. Not only that, but he also taught me everything I needed to know about how to handle them.

I took off my backpack and began loading it with ammunition before checking the handguns to make sure they weren't loaded before adding them in. I glanced at the rifle we used so many times when we went hunting, but left it on the rack, knowing I wouldn't need it. Instead, I grabbed the AR-15, knowing it would come in handy with the thirty-round mag.

Once I had everything I needed, including my dad's buck knife, I took it back to the house and up to my room. I needed to secure the house, which meant I needed to head into town for supplies. I knew it was risky to be seen, but at the same time, I wanted them to know I was back.

I hid everything in the closet and then pushed the dresser in front of it before grabbing my wallet and climbing out the window. I knew I could easily go through the front door, but I didn't want anyone to know I was staying at the house. Even if they knew I was back in town, I didn't need them knowing where I was living right now.

The streets were quiet as I made my way down to Main Street, keeping my head down with the hood pulled over it as it started drizzling. I was about to open the door to the convenience store when it flung open. I stopped and stepped back so I was out of the way as a woman came out.

"Sloane? Is that you?"

I looked up to find Everett's mother leaning down to see my face better.

"Hi, Nancy," I said softly, moving to the side as people walked past us.

"Oh, good heavens," she whispered, pulling me in tightly for a hug. "I didn't think I would ever see you again. Everett said you left, and I thought it was for good."

"I just needed a little time before I came back to deal with things," I replied gently, forcing a smile so she didn't catch on to what I had just said.

"Right. With your parents' house. I'm so sorry, dear."

I pressed my lips into what was supposed to be a smile, but they fell flat.

"Will you be in town for a while? I would love to spend time with you and catch up, but I have a flight to catch."

"For a little while," I said, nodding my head.

"Oh, wonderful. I'll let Everett know, and maybe once he's doing better, he can come down to see you. I know he's been worried sick about you. At least now I can tell him that you're safe and okay."

My mind tried grabbing onto what she said, but it was stuck on one part.

"I'm sorry, what do you mean, *once he's doing better*? What's wrong with Everett?"

She let out a soft gasp as if she realized what she was about to say.

"He's in the hospital. Someone broke into his apartment last night and stabbed him. The police think it was a robbery gone wrong, but he hasn't been awake to tell them what happened. A friend of his found him and called an ambulance. They barely got him to the hospital in time…"

I covered my mouth with my hand and shook my head.

"Did they say who the friend was that called for the ambulance?" I asked.

"I don't think they said. I honestly can't remember. I was so shocked by it that my brain must not have heard it. But speaking of friends, I see Keith." She stopped and waved her fingers, looking at someone across the street. "They both went to school—"

"I'm sorry. I really have to run," I interrupted, hating the look of disappointment on her face as I rushed into the store and made my way to the section I needed as quickly as possible.

Death

Everett

The monitors continued to beep around me, but I couldn't open my eyes. My body was weak, and I felt restrained, though I didn't know where I was. Last I knew, I had been stabbed and left for dead in my apartment.

My head throbbed, which was a sure sign I hadn't died yet. Or at least I assumed I hadn't.

You weren't supposed to feel anything once you died, were you? Wasn't that the promise they preached to you at Sunday school, that once you died and went to heaven, all of your troubles would be gone? You would no longer feel pain, no longer suffer.

One thing was for sure—I was both feeling pain and suffering.

Maybe I didn't deserve to go to Heaven.

Maybe I was just sitting in hell, waiting to be welcomed by Satan himself.

Broken

Be Prepared
Sloane

I made it in and out of the store without running into anyone I knew, including Keith. Not that I knew what he looked like, given that he never showed his face in any of the video calls we'd done when I was staying with Everett. I might know what his voice sounded like, but I could come face-to-face with him and have no idea it was him.

By the time I got home, I regretted not taking my mother's car instead of walking. My arms were sore from the bags of groceries I carried, and my back hurt from the amount of stuff I had crammed into my backpack. But I had what I needed, and that was all that mattered.

I made a quick sandwich while I got to work in the kitchen. The goal was to make it impossible for anyone to enter the house without my hearing them. I went out to my father's woodworking shed and brought in whatever he had, using it to secure the doors. After they were taken care of, I used the few pieces of particleboard I found and boarded up the windows.

I didn't plan to spend any time in this portion of the house other than to make food and use the refrigerator.

Thankfully, the utilities were still on since they were set up on an automatic payment and my mother had plenty of funds in her account to pay them. I knew they wouldn't come to turn them off until I asked them to, given that I would now be responsible for everything. As their only child, I knew the house and everything they owned were left to me in their estate, with no one to contest it.

I looked around at my work, pleased with how quickly I was able to get it done. For good measure, I pushed the couch in front of the front door and then moved the bookshelf to block the window. The back door was harder to barricade, so I stacked the kitchen chairs sideways, forcing them to wedge between the door and the wall. It wasn't much, but it would definitely make it harder for someone to get in.

My mind was still spinning about the news of Everett being stabbed. I wanted to reach out to Trevor and Roman to see if they knew anything, but I couldn't since I didn't have a phone and never bothered to get their phone numbers. It was better that I didn't try because if they were watching me and attacked Everett, there was a good chance someone was watching Roman and Trevor as well. I hated the thought of it, but hoped that they would find they were a dead end and leave them alone when they found that they didn't know anything about where I was.

I sat on my bed with the ammunition spread out to the side of me as I cleaned the AR-15. I grabbed a bullet, and an image of Nicky flashed through my mind. His poor little body as the bullet pierced it. His screaming cries as the pain overtook his body. His tiny hand that I held onto when the doctor turned off the life support that was keeping him alive and didn't let go until he took his last breath.

"This bullet is for you, black widow man," I said to myself as I loaded it into the gun.

I picked up another bullet, studying it as I thought about whose life I wanted to take with it. One by one, I loaded the bullets, saying each victim's name out loud as I did.

I didn't know who was responsible for hurting Everett, but I knew that I had plenty of extra bullets, and they all had their name on them.

No Regrets
Sloane

I had the TV on while I was going over the list of notes I had made when I was staying in the cabin with Roman and Quinn, when a news story interrupted my train of thought. I dropped the paper and turned the volume up as I stared at the screen.

"Joe, I'm reporting live outside of the Oak Creek FBI office, where we just received confirmation that one of our own was viciously murdered in New York City. Agent Everett Reid grew up in Oak Creek before moving to New York to study criminal law. As many of you may remember, Agent Reid was the older brother of Frankie Reid, who was shot last year in the unspeakable massacre that took several lives."

My heart raced as the emotion flooded through me.

Everett was dead.

Because of me.

I got up and ran to the bathroom in time to throw up in the toilet. I hadn't eaten much, but what little I had quickly came up. My body shook each time until it finally gave up.

I grabbed a piece of tissue and wiped my mouth as I stood up and flushed the toilet. I looked at my reflection in the mirror, looking for that glimmer of hope I had been holding onto for so long. But now that Everett was dead, I had nothing left to live for.

I splashed cold water on my face, then changed into a black hoodie and black jeans. I grabbed my backpack and opened it, making sure I had what I needed. It was already dark outside, which meant it was time to play. I opened the window and climbed down, making sure I was as invisible as possible.

By the time I got to the house, I had a split second where I second-guessed what I was doing. But then something washed over me and I pictured Everett as he made love to me. No one had ever loved me as unconditionally as he had. He was my soulmate, and now he was gone.

I pulled the hood down over my head as I walked around the side of the house, making sure to stay hidden and away from the cameras so they couldn't see my face. I knew the area well and knew there weren't any houses close enough to hear what I was about to do. That was the nice thing about growing up in a small town where things never changed and people rarely moved. It made it easy to know exactly which house was his. I made my way to the front door and took a deep breath as I pulled the sleeve over my hand and knocked.

I was worried he hadn't heard me and was getting ready to knock again when it opened.

"Whatever you're selling, I'm not interested," he grumbled, getting ready to shut the door.

"You don't remember me, do you?" I asked, tilting my head as I studied him.

"Should I?"

I lifted my head so he could see my face as I smiled.

"No. But you're about to."

~~Judge Curry~~
Sloane

"Do you see what I did there?" I asked, sitting on the edge of Judge Curry's desk as he sat bound to his chair with a piece of duct tape across his mouth.

I pushed the hood off my head, revealing the blood-stained Colorado Rockies baseball cap my dad had been wearing the night he was murdered. I knew everything suddenly dawned on Judge Curry when he saw it by the way his eyes widened.

"This is called a Fisherman's Knot. My dad taught it to me when I was a little girl, and he would take me fishing. As you can tell, it's a very secure knot and not easy to get out of," I continued, pulling on it to make my point.

He attempted to say something that sounded like *why are you doing this,* but it was so muffled that I couldn't tell what he said.

"My dad taught me a lot about fishing and hunting…" I smiled wistfully as I stared off into the distance, reliving the memories before I returned my focus to him. "You wanna know a secret?"

I leaned close to his ear and looked around to make sure no one was listening—totally for dramatic effect because I enjoyed torturing the piece of shit.

"He never told me that someday I would grow up and be quite the hunter myself." I hopped off the desk and smiled proudly at him. "But, then again, I also never imagined that it would be disgusting *humans* that I hunted."

I let my voice drop from the cheery, happy tone to one of malice, along with my features, as I bent down and stared at him.

"Do you remember me now, Judge Curry?"

He didn't answer, so I pulled my dad's hunting knife from the sheath attached to my pocket and plunged it into his shoulder. His head tipped back as he cried out in pain, the sound stifled by the tape as his fingers turned white from clenching them so tightly into fists.

He nodded his head as tears filled his eyes.

I reached forward and pulled the tape from his mouth, tossing it to the floor so he could speak.

I raised my eyebrows as I stared at him, telling him to answer me.

"Yes," he stammered. "I remember you."

"Good. Now we're getting somewhere," I said, sitting on the edge of his desk again as I slowly wiped the blood on the collar of his shirt.

"I'm sorry. I don't know what you want from me," he sobbed, pulling against the rope as if that would free him.

"You don't know what I want from you?" I asked, standing as I stared at him in disbelief. "What I wanted from you was for you to do your job. I wanted justice! I wanted to see those men rot in prison for what they did!"

"I—I –I—"

"It's a little too late for your pathetic excuses, Judge Curry. You took an oath, and you failed us. You failed the families of every single person who was murdered that night. You have continued to fail us by allowing those monsters to run free. So you know what I'm going to do?"

He shook his head, too afraid to speak.

"I'm going to serve justice myself."

He continued to shake his head as I pulled the gun from behind my back.

"Say their names," I instructed, aiming it right between his eyes.

"Who—whose names?" he rushed out, his body visibly trembling.

I leaned forward and stared at him with a vengeance in my eyes.

"My family. Say. Their. Names."

"I don't… I don't remember… Off the top of my head… I can—"

I shook my head as I fired the first shot, hitting him in the shoulder after adjusting my aim at the last second. I wanted him to be as afraid for his life as my family had been.

"That bullet was for Gabe, my husband."

I took a deep breath and smiled as his white dress shirt turned red from the blood. Then I fired another shot.

"That bullet was for my father."

I didn't want him to die before I could get through my list, so I aimed for the other shoulder and fired again.

"That bullet was for my mother."

"Please, stop. I'm so sorry."

"Sorry doesn't bring them back, now does it?"

I lowered my gun and aimed for his stomach.

"Did you know that my baby fought for his life after the man you allowed to go free shot him in the back?" I asked, my hands tightening around the gun as my finger pulled the trigger. "That one is for my son, Nicky."

There was so much blood, but it didn't bother me. If anything, I felt more alive seeing all of it combined with his sobbing. I wanted him to be in pain, and if I had the time, I would drag this out even longer. But I had other people to visit, which meant I needed to keep this short and sweet.

"This is for Everett, you low-life fucking piece of shit," I growled as I lifted my hand and shot him between the eyes.

His head immediately fell forward as the life drained out of his body.

Faking

Everett

"I still can't believe I allowed you guys to talk me into this," I groaned as I shifted on the couch in some cabin.

"It was the only way," Roman assured me as he sat across from me in a chair.

"How did you even know…" My words cut off as I hissed in pain and shifted again.

"Quinn and I were with Trevor when you called about the phone. It was her idea to fake your death to see if we could put pressure on Keith and whoever he was working with."

"I get it, but you have no idea the trauma you've caused my mother by making me pretend to be dead in that hospital bed. She won't recover from this."

"She knew about it beforehand," Quinn said, coming into the living room and sitting beside me. "I spoke to her privately in the women's restroom and explained what was happening. She knew you were alive and that the nurses had messed with the monitors to make it look like you were dead. She is currently heading back to Oak Creek to plan a service for you once she receives your ashes."

"Wow," I replied, shaking my head. This was still so unreal. "Has anyone heard from Sloane?"

"Unfortunately, no. We expect that she is in Denver based on the bus ticket we purchased for her, but that doesn't mean she didn't get off at another stop. Without her having a cell phone, we don't have any way to track her," Roman said.

"I want to go look for her," I replied, knowing their answer as soon as I saw their faces. "Look, I know I'm supposed to be dead and everything, but I can't stand the thought of someone hurting her. It's driving me mad. Keith came to my apartment looking for her. What's to stop him from killing her the moment he finds her?"

"I know you don't want to hear this, but Sloane is capable of protecting herself." Quinn's eyes were soft as she spoke. "I watched her train while she was here, and I'm not the least bit worried about her. She is stronger than anyone I've ever seen, especially with what she's been through."

"Stronger than a bullet that strikes an organ and instantly kills her?" I bit out, knowing it wasn't Quinn's fault I was in a bad mood.

"None of us are. But she's strong, Everett. She has survived every attempt they've made on her life so far. We have to trust that she will do what she needs to survive."

I didn't miss the underlying message in Quinn's words, but chose to ignore them because the thought of Sloane hurting anyone wasn't something I could handle. It wasn't that I didn't see her being a total badass and beating the shit out of someone because I knew how good she had gotten with her training. I didn't want it to go any further than that because I knew she could never live with herself if she took someone's life.

~~Antonio Carrio, Criminal Defense Attorney~~

Sloane

I took a sip of my coffee, gripping the to-go cup in my hand as I watched Mr. Carrio leave the courthouse, rushing to get to the car that was waiting for him as he pressed a phone against his ear. It was the middle of the day, so I wasn't going to murder him in front of all of these witnesses—but there was something thrilling about openly stalking him, knowing he would be my next victim.

I made a note of the car he got into and memorized the license plate number as it drove off. The research I did this morning at the small public library confirmed that he was a partner at Hughson, Carrio, and Valles Law Firm. I tossed my cup into the trash and pulled the hood down to keep the rain off my face as I walked the short distance to his office. I had no idea where he was going, but given that the car was heading in the opposite direction, I was betting that it wasn't back to the office.

When I got to the brick building, I stood outside and gathered myself for a few minutes before I pushed the hood off my face and walked inside with my shoulders pulled back. I glanced at the giant sign on the wall above the receptionist's desk, confirming it was the right place.

"Hello. May I help you?" She was young, maybe in her early twenties, and looked like she would rather be anywhere but there.

"Hi. I'm supposed to deliver Mr. Carrio's dry cleaning to his house, but he was in a rush this morning and didn't give me the address," I said, scrunching my face as I held my hands in front of me, hoping she would take pity on me.

"I thought Susan handled his dry cleaning?" she questioned, pulling her brows together.

"She does, but she's out sick today and asked if I could help. I was supposed to get the address from Mr. Carrio, but he ended the call before I could get it. I didn't want to call and bother Susan since she's so sick. I was hoping you might be able to help me. I would really hate to make Mr. Carrio mad, given how he seemed so bothered by my call this morning," I lied.

Her shoulders slumped, and I knew that I had struck a nerve. Apparently, he wasn't just a dick who represented the scum of the earth; he was an asshole to her as well.

"I totally get it. He can be *difficult*." She turned to the computer, typed something in, then grabbed a pen and scribbled the information down on a Post-it note. "Try to deliver it before two. He goes home for lunch around that time and doesn't like to be bothered. Susan usually has everything done by one o'clock, just in case he comes home early."

"Everything?" I asked, wondering if I was going to interrupt whatever it was Susan was likely doing for him, as I glanced at the clock on the wall and noticed it was already after eleven.

"The cleaning and other errands. She goes back around five so she can start preparing dinner. Since she's sick, I'll check with him when he gets back to see if he wants me to have food delivered this evening. Thanks for letting me know."

"Thank you for your help as well," I said, holding the sticky note in between my fingers.

I turned and walked out the door, quickly stuffing the note in my back pocket as I pulled the hood over my head and got the hell out of there.

By the time I got to the address that was written down, I found a red sedan in the driveway, and from the kitchen window, an older woman inside cleaning. I was thankful that the receptionist warned me about Susan because the last thing I needed was to walk in and surprise her, then turn around and kill her because she would know who murdered her boss. I didn't have time for things to get messy like that.

I went across the street to the park Everett and I used to hang out at and sat beneath our favorite tree since I had time to kill. Well, that wasn't the only thing… But since I had to wait for the right time, I couldn't jump the gun on this one.

I leaned back against the stump and closed my eyes, allowing the sun that had finally decided to shine through to warm my face. Memories of Everett and me sitting here, holding hands and sharing kisses, flooded my mind, bringing fresh tears to the surface.

Last night, I cried myself to sleep once I got home and washed the sins I had committed away. I knew that losing Everett would be hard, but I hadn't expected it to almost kill me. I allowed my anger and rage to guide me to Judge Curry's house last night because if I hadn't, I might have done something stupid. I wasn't afraid to die—I just wanted to get revenge first.

I had no idea what time it was since I didn't have a watch or a phone, but once I saw the red car pull out of the driveway and leave, I knew it was time for me to move. The receptionist had said that Susan would leave for a few hours while he came home for lunch before she came back to prepare his dinner. I didn't need that much time, but I also wanted to get inside the house before he came in and startled me.

I got to my feet and wiped the wet leaves off my pants as I pulled the hood tighter around my face and crossed the street. I hated doing stuff in the middle of the day, but this was my only chance.

Making sure no one was looking, I walked around to the back of the house and found a back door. I didn't want to make loud noises, but I had no other choice but to kick it in. Just then, I looked down and noticed a dog door to the left. It wasn't huge, but I was small enough that I could fit through it. I pushed my hand against it to make sure it was open before committing to anything. I also had no clue what kind of dog would be waiting for me on the other side, given that it was big enough for a human to fit through.

The thick plastic flap moved easily, allowing me to bend down and crawl through it. I pulled my backpack off and set it on the ground beside me since it was too big to fit if I tried to wear it. As soon as my head was through the hole and inside the house, I stopped and froze as a pit bull stared directly at me.

"Hey, puppy," I said nervously, immediately reconsidering my choice.

It would take me longer to get out of the hole than it would for the dog to rip my face off.

It sat down and cocked its head as if confused by what I was doing. Yeah, me too, dog. I slowly pushed inside, a little bit at a time, fully committing to my plan now that the dog didn't appear to want to kill me. The closer I moved in, the closer the dog got.

Then it happened.

Just as I pushed myself all the way in, the dog came over and licked my eyeball. Not even giving me time to close my eyes first, just one big wet tongue scratching right across my eyeball.

I crawled the rest of the way inside and laughed as the dog was immediately on me, showering me in kisses.

"Oh my!" I laughed, noting how strange it felt to do so. I couldn't remember the last time I had laughed. "You're such a good boy!"

The dog stopped licking me and slowly backed away, sitting in front of me. I stood up and looked down as the dog rolled onto its back and stared at me.

"Ohhh… you're such a good *girl,*" I cooed, realizing my mistake.

I reached down and rubbed her tummy for a few minutes, enjoying the interaction as much as she did.

"I'm sorry. I would love to stay and give you tummy rubs, but I have work to do. You see, your dad is a very bad man, and I'm here to make him pay." She got up and licked my face repeatedly, almost knocking me off balance. "Yes, he is. He's a very bad man."

I reached through the dog door and retrieved my backpack before wandering through the house while she followed. I had no idea where the perfect spot to kill him was, but I wanted it to be something that would make a statement when they found his body.

The clock on the wall showed it was just after two when I heard the familiar sound of a car pulling up outside.

"It's showtime," I whispered to the dog who was still standing next to me as I adjusted my dad's Colorado Rockies baseball cap on my head. It made me proud to wear his hat as I took care of things.

The front door opened and then slammed shut as heavy footsteps stormed over the tile floor into the kitchen. His head was down as his fingers flew across his phone, barely looking up in time to keep from tripping over the dog.

"What the fuck are you doing here?" he growled as I aimed the gun at him.

"I've come to have a quick chat with you," I replied, lowering it and pulling the trigger as a bullet went straight to his thigh.

He dropped his phone as he bent over, clutching his leg.

"You fucking bitch," he yelled, making the dog flinch.

My eyes narrowed as anger flooded through me. It was apparent how he treated her if his voice alone could elicit that response. He was still bent over as he tried to hobble to the chair, which was quite perfect, actually, as it saved me the energy of having to get him there myself.

Once he was seated, I opened my backpack and pulled out the rope.

"I don't fucking think so," he warned, pulling away as I reached for him.

I held the rope in one hand and the gun in the other as I stared him down.

"You know what's funny?" I asked, letting my lips curl up slightly into a grin.

"What?"

"That you think you actually have a say in any of this. It's kind of like when we went to trial, and you silenced me so no one could hear the truth about what your clients did to my family."

He opened his mouth to speak, but my fist landed on his jaw first, forcing his head to the side from the impact. Knowing he was as weak as he was going to be, I quickly put the gun behind my back and began tying him to the chair. I used the same knots I had used last night on Judge Curry, enjoying that there was now a common theme we were building on.

"I didn't silence you," he bit out. "You had your say."

"Yeah, and you changed the story and questioned everything I said so you could get the trial dismissed. You knew what you were doing and didn't have a single regret for the pain you caused the families of every single victim that died at the hands of those monsters."

I glared at him as I dug through the backpack and found what I was looking for. I lifted the meat mallet and studied it in my hands. It was my mother's, and it gave me a great sense of joy to use it this way.

His hands were bound to the wooden chair, his palms facing down, and his ankles bound to the chair's legs. He wasn't going anywhere.

"Do you know what pisses me off the most?" I asked as the dog whined and lay down behind me. She made no effort to go to him or protect him from me, which warmed my heart.

He gave me a dirty look but didn't answer.

"That you got paid to represent those assholes. That you would sell your soul to the devil for the right price." I shook my head as I gently smacked the steel mallet against my hand before swooping it down and crushing the bone in his.

"FUCK!" he screamed, his face contorting in pain. "You crazy, fucking bitch."

"Do you know why I'm a crazy, fucking bitch?" I asked as I stood over him, glaring down at him. "Because *you* made a huge mistake. And guess what? I'm here to fix that!" I roared as I brought the mallet down again, this time on the other hand.

He screamed again, which was irritating, but I hadn't thought to gag him first.

"You had one job, and you failed at it, just like Judge Curry. But don't worry. I'm here to make the world right again, starting with eliminating those who wish to do our world harm." I lifted my arm and swung, making direct contact with his kneecap, but this time, I didn't wait to hear him scream as I shattered the other kneecap seconds later.

His head fell forward as tears ran down his face. The dog lay there, completely unbothered by the entire thing as she closed her eyes and fell asleep. Either this was a regular occurrence, or she couldn't give two shits about what was happening to her owner.

I waited a few seconds, tapping my foot impatiently as he struggled to catch his breath and sit upright. I pulled my dad's knife out and flipped it open, smiling at the reminder of last night when I'd used it on Judge Curry.

Once he was sitting somewhat upright, I knelt down and touched my fingers to his hand, loving how he winced and tried to pull away.

"Do you know what my mom used to sing to me when I was little that used to help when I was upset?" I asked, totally lying because my mom never bothered to do anything to cheer me up when I was little. But he didn't need to know that. I really just wanted an excuse to sing the song.

"This little piggy went to the market," I said, tapping my knife against his pinky. "I mean, I know this is supposed to be done with toes, but feet kinda gross me out, and I'm not about to make any exceptions for you. Anyway, this little piggy went to the market. This little piggy stayed home. This little piggy ate roast beef, and this little piggy had none," I continued, digging my knife a little deeper into his skin with each poke on the finger I was talking about.

"But this little piggy… Oh, this little piggy really fucked up." I pointed to his thumb and grinned when I saw him watching me with so much hate and disgust. At least we felt the same way about each other.

"This little piggy was a crooked defense attorney who cared more about money than doing the right thing," I growled, lifting the knife and bringing it straight down over his thumb, immediately severing it.

I gasped and let out a giggle as I looked at the digit sitting on the edge of the chair before it rolled to the floor and blood poured from his hand. He screamed in pain, but I was more concerned with the dog, who got up to come check it out. She was timid as she looked at the thumb before looking up at me.

"Do you want a treat, sweet girl?" I asked, kneeling as I picked it up and placed it in the palm of my hand. "Here you go."

She licked it a few times before putting it between her teeth and carrying it over to where she was lying a few moments ago.

"You're never going to get away with this," he growled, pulling against the rope as he tried to free himself.

I grabbed his chair and turned it the best I could, given how heavy it was with him sitting in it. I put my hands over his and tightened my grip, knowing I had easily broken the bones in both hands with the meat mallet.

"It's too bad I don't have an attorney like you to help me," I said as sweetly as I could before I stepped back and pulled the gun from behind my back. "But thankfully for my family, they have me. You might not have given them the justice they deserved, but I will."

Following what I did last night with Judge Curry, I aimed the gun at his thigh.

"This bullet is for my father," I said, pulling the trigger.

"This bullet is for my mother." Another shot, this time his foot.

"This bullet is for my husband, Gabe." I moved the gun around, trying to decide where I wanted to shoot him. "Since you signed away any chance of those families getting justice for their loved ones, it seems fitting that you should never have that privilege again." I didn't know if he was right-handed or left-handed, so I shot both hands and added, "That other shot was for my son, Nicky. He wasn't even a year old when his life was taken. I hope that haunts you for all of eternity."

I could see him losing strength as the floor beneath him was covered in a puddle of blood. I needed to be quick and finish this before any of his neighbors reported the gunshots. While nobody was right beside him, they were closer than the neighbors who bordered Judge Curry's house.

"And this final shot is for Everett," I said, my voice cracking as I said his name. I aimed for his heart and pulled the trigger. If I were dying of a broken heart, he needed to be as well.

I put the gun away and wiped my cheeks as I gathered what I needed and stuffed it back into my backpack. I covered my hand with the sleeve of my hoodie as I unlocked the back door and opened it, but was surprised when I looked down and saw the dog standing beside me, ready to go.

I looked at Mr. Carrio one final time, knowing he was dead and could never harm anyone else again as I walked out the door, feeling a huge sense of relief.

Meditation

Sloane

I was upstairs making notes in the notebook I had when I heard banging downstairs. The dog popped up from the bed and started growling. I walked to the window and looked down, not seeing anyone. The knocking continued, so I headed downstairs with the dog by my side.

The front door and window were still boarded up, but there was a small sliver I could see through to who was standing there. Everett's mom looked like she was shivering from the cold. She wore a heavy coat and held a foil-covered pan in her hands.

I rushed to the back door and opened it, heading around to the front. I had no choice but to sneak in through the window earlier and unbarricade the back door since the dog was too heavy to try to carry.

"Nancy? What are you doing here?" I asked, lifting my hand to shield the rain from my eyes.

"I brought you dinner," she replied, lifting the pan. "I thought you might want some company?"

"Come around the back," I said, nodding for her to follow me.

I led the way, but continued to check behind me to make sure she was okay, since the ground was slippery and wet. I held the back door open and waited for her and the dog to come inside before closing it.

"You got a dog?" she asked, setting the dish down on the counter as she looked at the pitbull.

"It's a long story, but yeah, I guess so." I looked down at her and smiled, knowing no one would ever know the story.

"Did you bring her back with you from… wherever you were?" Nancy asked, pulling her coat off and setting it on the back of the kitchen chair.

That was a better story, and it wouldn't give away that she was actually someone else's pet until a few hours ago.

"Yeah. She has been such a great friend and keeps me company," I replied, scratching the top of her head as she sat beside me.

"What's her name?" Nancy walked through the kitchen and grabbed some plates from the cabinet, having been here often enough to know where everything was.

I swallowed hard, trying to get past the lump in my throat as I realized she wanted to have dinner with me at the kitchen table. I hadn't done that since my dad was alive, and the thought made me want to crawl out of my skin. I felt her eyes on me as she waited for an answer.

"Justice," I blurted out, trying not to frown when I realized how that would give me away with what I was doing.

"Oh my gosh, I totally forgot how much you and Everett loved those comic books," she gushed, putting a hand to her heart. "You were obsessed with the Justice League."

"Still am," I said with an awkward laugh. But what was more concerning was how she had just mentioned his name without breaking down. Her last living son was dead, and it seemed like she didn't even care. But then again, who was I to judge someone for how they dealt with their grief? Everett died, and I went on a murdering spree. To each their own…

"How is Everett?" I asked, testing the waters as she dished a large portion of lasagna onto each plate and brought them over to the table.

Her face fell, and I noticed the tears in her eyes as she shook her head and turned away.

"I'm so sorry," I whispered, pressing my lips together to keep from losing it. The last thing she needed was to take care of me while dealing with her own grief. I knew I was wrong for asking when I had already seen it on the news, but part of me felt like it wasn't real until I heard her say it.

She grabbed two forks and sat down at the table, smiling as I joined her. I hated the feeling that washed over me as I desperately wanted to crawl out of my skin. I didn't want to be rude, but sitting at the table felt so wrong when my parents weren't there to join us.

"He's being cremated," she said, gripping the edge of the table as she stared down at her plate of food. "I'm going to do a celebration of life for him in a few weeks after I get his…"

I reached over and squeezed her hand tightly, letting her know she wasn't alone as the tears washed down both of our faces. A few minutes later, I let go, and we both picked up our forks and began eating.

"How did you know I was here?" I asked.

"Lucky hunch." She shrugged. "It's like a mother's ins—" She pressed her lips together and stopped talking.

I set my fork down and turned to look at her.

"All of this sucks," I said, my voice catching in my throat. "But you are literally the last friend I have in this world, and I don't want us to walk on eggshells to keep from hurting each other. The truth is that we are both hurting so much, but this isn't a pain that we've caused each other. It's okay to talk about them. To talk about what we lost."

She nodded, and her eyes filled with tears as she looked at me.

"I cry every time I drive by this house, and I see your car in the driveway. I cry knowing that your son's toys and blanket are still in the backseat and that you haven't been inside that car since the last time you got out of it with your family. My heart hurts for you so much because now that I've lost two sons, I can't compare that to what you feel losing yours. My boys lived what life they were given. They had experiences. They had their first kisses and made friends at school. Your sweet boy never got any of that, and I can't stop crying over it, Sloane."

She let her head drop as I cried with her, letting out tears I had been holding for far too long. But she wasn't wrong. I hadn't gotten into the car or even looked at it since they died. We had taken my dad's truck to the game that night, and then my mother brought it home shortly after I had been released from the hospital.

"My heart aches for you, too, Nancy. No mother should know the pain of losing their child."

She nodded and wiped the tears from her face as she gave me a soft smile.

"If only our justice system worked the way it was supposed to," she replied with a heavy sigh before picking up her fork and taking a bite.

I chewed the inside of my cheek to keep from responding to that. Justice *would* be served, one way or another.

Broken

Missing Pieces
Everett

"So, you're telling me that Sloane's husband has an evil twin?" I asked in disbelief as Quinn stood in front of the TV, pointing to the large paper propped up on an easel. It reminded me of the work I had been doing before Sloane left.

"I wouldn't say *evil*," Quinn replied, scrunching her face.

"He's a drug lord who runs a cartel," Roman pushed back with a frown on his face. "I wouldn't call him a saint."

"True. But from what I found, Hugo Sanchez hasn't been doing this for long. Or at least, he hasn't been showing up on our radar until recently. His father, Diego Sanchez, on the other hand, has been wanted for years, and no one has seen him since Hugo took over. Rumor on the street is that Hugo murdered his father to take over the family business."

"So this Hugo Sanchez guy is the one the Lagrimas Rojas cartel wanted, but instead, they killed Sloane's husband, thinking it was him?"

"That's what it looks like. Unfortunately, we don't have any insider information from either cartel, so it's a guessing game. My source said that the Lagrimas Rojas were spreading quickly in Colorado and made a statement by taking over that territory." Quinn set the marker on the table and then sat on the arm of Roman's chair, where he wrapped a protective hand around her legs.

"Well, we know that they have local law enforcement on their payroll," I said with a heavy sigh, thinking back to my encounter with Keith. "Do we know how deep that goes?"

"Not yet." Quinn's eyes softened as she looked at me. "Your mother scheduled your memorial service for this Saturday and confirmed she received the package with your ashes. I have a few friends who will be around and monitor things there."

"I should be there."

"You will," Roman replied with a hint of a smirk on his face.

"Not as a dead person, you fucker. I should be there to make sure nothing happens."

"You can't be there without exposing the lie we told. It's imperative that you stay here and continue to hide until we know what's going on. Trevor and Roman will be flying out for your service, so they'll keep an eye out for Sloane."

"You think Sloane will be there?" I asked, leaning forward as I hung onto the hope that was blossoming in my chest.

"I know she will," Quinn replied softly.

"How? Have you talked to her? I thought you said you didn't know where she was?"

"I don't. But Sloane hears everything, and if she thinks you're dead, she's going to show up to your service."

"Fucking great," I groaned, tossing my head back in frustration. "You're going to get her killed by leading the bad guys right to her."

"Do you honestly think that Sloane is going to live the rest of her life just hiding in the shadows?" Roman asked, pinning me with a look. "She killed a man, Everett. Did you know that?"

My eyes widened as I processed his words. I opened my mouth and then snapped it shut, struggling with what to say.

"When they cornered her in that alley, she killed a man to protect herself. It was her life or his. She chose wisely. But if you honestly think that Sloane is some weak, grief-stricken person who is going to live her life in the shadows and constantly on the run—you're mistaken."

"She killed someone?" I whispered, tears stinging the back of my eyes.

Roman nodded as he watched the mixed reactions play out on my face based on what he had said.

"Do you think she's going to keep… killing people?" I asked, hating the words as they floated onto my tongue.

"It's not like a hobby or anything," Quinn offered. "But Sloane will do whatever she has to do to survive this."

I scrubbed a hand down my face and struggled with how to take all of this. While I didn't love that she would have to live with murdering someone sitting on her subconscious,

I was proud as fuck that she had been strong and brave enough to protect herself. Something I had failed to do while she was with me.

Anniversaries
Sloane

I sat on my bed, looking at my notepad as the local news played in the background. Nancy had mentioned to me that the memorial service for Everett would be on Saturday if I wanted to attend. While I wanted to say goodbye to him, I never imagined it would be like this. I hadn't been able to stop obsessing over how I left things with him when I took off without telling him where I was going. I thought I was protecting him, but it seemed I sucked at doing that for anyone. My mother died because of me. Zoe had died because of me. Everett had died because of me. I found myself wanting to push Nancy away so that she wouldn't have the same fate.

The commercial that was playing ended, and a breaking story appeared on the screen with Sheriff Dowdy standing outside of Judge Curry's house. I set the notepad down and turned up the volume as I listened. Justice sat up from where she was lying beside me on the bed and growled at the screen. I gave her a curious glance, wondering what she knew about Sheriff Dowdy, before scratching the top of her head and returning my focus to the TV.

"The people of Oak Creek demand justice, and I will see to it that whoever is responsible for the gruesome and horrifying murder of Judge Joseph Curry will be prosecuted to the full extent of the law," Sheriff Dowdy said, his eyes narrowed at the camera.

I rolled my eyes, finding it comical that he was determined to seek justice for this murder but never once gave a shit about the victims who were murdered in the massacre almost a—

My jaw dropped as I realized the date. I shook my head and grabbed the burner phone I bought last night, opening it to the calendar.

Tears ran down my face as my finger trembled as it slid across the days until Everett's memorial service. How was it fair that I would have to say goodbye to Everett on the one-year anniversary of the murder of my family?

I exited the calendar and tossed it on the bed. I had purposely avoided every anniversary and birthday since they died, but this one I couldn't forget. It was like the date was a bad omen for losing people I loved.

I picked up the notepad and looked down at the list of names still on it as a new rage filled my body, turning my blood to lava.

They would pay for what they took from me.

Each and every single one of them.

~~Ricky Santos (AKA Blue Eyes), Tomas Cortez (AKA Snake Tattoo), Random Dude #1, Random Dude #2~~

Sloane

It was easier than I thought to locate the piece of shit men who murdered my family. I sat outside the gym where they were working out as I contemplated how I wanted to approach this. The sun had already set, allowing me to hide in the shadows for a little while longer.

I didn't know much about this gym or who owned it, but I could tell that the four men inside were all part of the Lagrimas Rojas cartel that Quinn had told me about. I immediately recognized the one with the snake tattoo on his wrist as he lunged for the one with the blue eyes that continued to haunt my dreams.

I adjusted my dad's Rockies baseball cap and touched the gun tucked into the back of my jeans, making sure it was still there. I made sure it was fully loaded and ready before

I left the house. It felt weird not having my backpack or multiple weapons to choose from, but these guys weren't ones that I had the luxury of tying to a chair and dragging out their suffering. I would have to be quick and effective before they ganged up on me and I was outnumbered.

Taking a deep breath in, I slowly let it out as I pulled the door open and stepped inside.

At first, they didn't hear or notice me as two of them continued boxing in the middle of the ring, off to the side of the room. The two who saw me first weren't anyone that I recognized. I gave them two seconds to alert the others to my presence as I pulled my gun out and shot them both in the head.

My pulse hammered in my ears as adrenaline raced through me. I was fucking impressed with my aim as they both fell to the floor, their lifeless bodies lying in pools of blood.

"What the fuck?" the one with the snake tattoo growled as he threw down the boxing gloves and stalked my way.

"Na ah," I warned, raising my gun and aiming it between his eyes as the one with the blue eyes slowly took his gloves off as he watched me. "Come rushing at me, and you'll be dead as quickly as your friends down there."

"You have no fucking idea what you're doing, you crazy bitch," the snake guy snarled.

I locked eyes with him while still keeping an eye on the other guy, who took his time walking over to us.

"What do you want?" the blue-eyed guy asked.

The memory of him chasing after me in my house the night they killed my mother tried pushing through, but I quickly forced it away and focused my attention on the other guy. I couldn't risk allowing myself any distractions right now.

"Justice," I said tightly, keeping my hand steady as the guy with the snake tattoo took a step toward me.

I could feel the strength in how his body moved and loved the way his eyes widened as a bullet ripped through his shoulder.

"I said—don't fucking move," I bit out, shaking my head at him as he dropped to his knees and tried to apply pressure to the wound. "You'll die when *I* say you will."

"No one has to die," Blue Eyes said, raising his hands in front of him. "You said you want justice. Justice for what?"

My mouth opened in disbelief as he stared at me, pretending he didn't know who I was or what they had taken from me. The guy with the snake tattoo turned his head and rattled off a bunch of stuff in Spanish to the guy with the blue eyes, but his attention was still on me.

"What do you think, Ricky?" I asked, grinning when I saw the way his facial features hardened when I used his name. While I preferred calling them by their identifiers, I had spent the evening last night memorizing the names I had written down when Quinn and I went over the information she had on the cartel and the guys I had identified.

"What's the matter? Cat got your tongue? Or did you think that I wouldn't figure out who you are?"

"Doesn't matter if you know my name," he said easily. "Dead people can't talk anyway."

A split second passed before he lunged at me, catching me off guard. His arm came down on top of mine, knocking the gun out of my hand as we tumbled to the floor. I landed on my back with such force that the air rushed out of my lungs as he straddled me and wrapped his hand tightly around my throat.

"You think you can come in here and take us down?" he growled, leaning closer so his lips were next to my ear. "You should have stayed away. Stayed the fuck away."

I tried to take a deep breath as he pressed tighter on my throat. Off to the side, the other guy was still bleeding but had lost a lot of blood. I knew a gunshot could be fatal regardless of where it was if there was a significant amount of blood lost and no way to stop it. At least I didn't have to worry about him right now while his friend tried to choke me.

Thoughts of Everett flooded my brain as I tried to calm myself. Ricky continued speaking, but I couldn't hear what he was saying as the ringing in my ears got louder. I reached down beside me, trying not to draw attention to myself as I tried to feel for my dad's knife.

"Isn't this the hat your dad was wearing the night we killed him?" Ricky said, letting go of my throat as he plucked it off of my head and looked at it.

I sucked in a deep breath, immediately coughing as I tried to get oxygen flowing through my body again. I turned slightly to the side, pretending to still be coughing as I grabbed the knife and flipped it open.

"I think I might keep it and wear it once we add some of your blood to it," he continued. "It'll be a nice little trophy of what we did to you and your family."

His words pierced a piece of my heart and sent a rush of anger flooding through me. With what strength I had left, I pulled my arm to the side and then plunged the knife directly into his side, piercing the spot between his ribs.

His eyes widened as he looked down right as I pulled the knife out, and blood began pouring out of him. I didn't wait as I shoved him off of me before kicking him in the balls and taking a step back. My hand shook as I held the knife, ready to stab him again.

He pressed his hand tighter against the wound, frowning when more blood soaked his shirt.

"Say their names," I demanded as I picked my gun up off the floor and put the knife away.

"Fuck. You."

I cocked my head to the side and glared at him.

"Say. Their. Fucking. Names."

"I ain't saying shit, you stupid bitch."

I shook my head and knew that I needed to wrap this up quickly. Just then, a cell phone started ringing, but I couldn't tell which dead guy it belonged to.

"Fine. We'll do it the hard way," I said, raising my gun and staring at him. I turned to the side and aimed at one of the guys I had shot right away. "This bullet is for my father."

He was already dead, but it still felt good to shoot him again, just to be sure.

"This bullet is for my mother." I fired a shot at the other dead guy, hitting him in the chest.

I walked over and stood in front of the guy with the snake tattoo. He hadn't died yet, but I could tell he was close. He didn't bother lifting his head as his cold eyes stared at me.

"This bullet is for my husband, Gabe. Rot in hell, Tomas Cortez." I pulled the trigger and didn't flinch as the bullet pierced his brain.

"And this bullet is for my son."

I locked eyes with him as he stared deep into my soul, making me question who and what I had turned into.

I didn't give it a second thought as I pulled the trigger, shooting him in the stomach.

"This one is for Everett," I added, firing another bullet into his heart.

The phone began ringing again, so I secured my gun and then searched each of the guys until I found it. I knew it wouldn't be long until someone called in the gunshots, which meant I needed to get the hell out of there.

I lifted the dead guy's finger and swiped it across the screen to answer the call that came in from someone stored as *Boss*.

"What the fuck is happening," a deep voice growled on the other line.

"What the fuck is happening is that I just killed four of your men," I said cheerfully.

"Who the fuck is this?"

"You can call me Karma. See you soon!"

I hung up the phone and wiped my prints off of it before tossing it to the floor as I stepped over the dead bodies and walked away.

<u>Updates</u>
Everett

"What the fuck does that mean?" I asked, staring in disbelief as Roman held his cell phone in front of him while Quinn spoke on the speakerphone.

"It means that someone is taking care of business in Colorado," Quinn replied tightly.

I knew she wasn't in a place where she could talk freely like she could when she was with us at the cabin. Between her and Roman constantly keeping an eye on me there, I was surprised no one had questioned where they were or what they were doing. Thankfully, Trevor knew what was going on, so it allowed Roman to be gone as long as needed without having to report to anyone. Quinn, on the other hand, needed to report to work as usual and maintain as much of a normal, everyday life façade as possible to keep from drawing any unwanted attention.

After they found out that Keith was in New York City and looking for Sloane's phone, Trevor transferred everything to a new phone for her and wiped her old one clean. Then he turned it on and tossed it into a trash can in Central Park.

Whether or not Keith had sent anyone to retrieve it after that was unknown.

I leaned forward and lowered my head as I processed the news she had just called to share. Her contact in Colorado had sent her links to news reports of a recent killing spree happening in Oak Creek, with the judge and criminal defense attorney among the victims.

Roman finished the call and hung up as a heavy silence fell between us.

"Please tell me that you don't think all of this involves Sloane," I begged.

"We don't know anything at this point. Whoever is doing this is making a statement."

"Yeah, a very clear, deliberate one. It's almost like they have a hit list—"

 I stopped when I noticed the look on Roman's face as he got up and stalked across the room to the table. He picked up a stack of papers and began thumbing through them until he found the one he was looking for.

"Son of a bitch," he muttered, dragging his hand down the scruff on his jaw.

"What? What is it?" I asked, getting up and joining him.

"It's the list Sloane made of people she didn't trust. She kept the original, but this is the list that Quinn made so she could start looking into everyone."

I took the paper from him and began scanning it.

1. *Judge Curry*
2. *Antonio Carrio—criminal defense attorney*
3. *Sheriff Dowdy*
4. *Deputy Sheriff Anderson*
5. *Officer Butchkins*
6. *Officer Contreras*
7. *Officer Ozwald*
8. *Agent Keith Montes*
9. *Juan Rodriguez—Lagrimas Rojas Cartel*
10. *Tomas Cortez—Lagrimas Rojas Cartel*
11. *Ricky Santos—Lagrimas Rojas Cartel*

I shook my head and pushed out a heavy breath.

"Four out of eleven of these people have been murdered in the past twenty-four hours?" I asked, though it was more of a statement than a question.

"Well, longer than that. It took them a few days before they found the bodies of Judge Curry and Antonio Carrio. It wasn't until they were noticeably absent at work and a wellness check was requested that anyone found them."

"This cannot be Sloane. There's no fucking way."

"Have you ever been pushed to a breaking point?" Roman asked, watching me carefully.

"I—Well—No. I can't say that I have. But I've been through my fair share of shit."

"Until you've reached your breaking point, you don't know what you're capable of."

"So you're saying Sloane reached hers, and now she's out terrorizing the town she grew up in?"

"No. I'm saying that she reached hers, and she's doing the only thing she can right now to stay alive. None of us knows what is going through her head right now. She has lost every single thing she has ever loved. If that doesn't break someone, I don't know what will."

"Sloane is grieving. She isn't broken," I objected, not wanting to believe him.

"Are you sure about that? Because none of this started until she found out you were dead."

No News Is Good News—Unless It Is Fake News

Sloane

I woke up Saturday morning in the worst mood ever. My dreams had been haunted by my family and memories of them, which seemed fitting given that today was the one-year anniversary of their deaths, aside from my mother.

I turned on the TV, wondering if there would be news coverage of Everett's service today, given how things like this were a big deal in small towns. Not only that, but the news had been focused on remembering his life and the impact he left on Oak Creek. I hadn't seen Nancy since the night she brought me dinner, which was for the best. I couldn't look at her right now and not fall apart as I thought about her laying her last family member to rest. She and I were a lot alike at this point, with neither of us having anyone to live for anymore.

The volume on the TV was turned down as I blow-dried my hair, but when I glanced at it, I immediately stopped and turned it up. On the screen was Sheriff Dowdy standing at a podium with Deputy Sheriff Anderson and a man I didn't recognize as they did a live broadcast.

"The Oak Creek Sheriff's Department wouldn't have been able to take down part of the Lagrimas Rojas Cartel without the assistance of Agent Keith Montes. Agent Montes has worked tirelessly to bring justice to our town after the devastating massacre that took the lives of eleven people one year ago today," Sheriff Dowdy said as he smiled smugly at the two men.

In the corner of the screen, an image appeared with the mugshots of the four men I killed last night. I clenched my fist and shook my head, staring in disbelief as the sheriff tried to pretend they were responsible for taking those thugs off the streets.

I picked up the remote and turned the TV off, too pissed off to listen to another word. It was clear as day that I had been right about Sheriff Dowdy all along. He was just as dirty as the rest of them, and now, I had the privilege of knowing what Keith looked like.

****

I dressed in black jeans and a black turtleneck sweater, not having anything nice to wear. But when I saw Nancy, she pulled me in for a hug and cried into my shoulder, and I remembered that it didn't matter what I was wearing. I needed to be there for her and help her say goodbye to Everett.

The church was packed with people I recognized and several that I didn't, likely colleagues of Everett's. I took a seat beside Nancy and folded my hands in my lap to keep from fidgeting as Reverend Blue began speaking. I could feel eyes on me, but I didn't acknowledge them as I stared at the urn sitting on the small table in front of us with a picture of Everett behind it.

The tears ran down my face as a fresh wave of grief washed over me. One year ago today, I woke up in Gabe's arms, happy and loved, with a sweet baby boy in the crib beside us. Today, I woke up, forced myself to get ready, and made my presence in Oak Creek known as I said goodbye to my best friend.

The service was quick and wrapped up with a few people taking the podium to share memories of Everett. I knew I should honor him by doing the same, but every time I considered it, I felt the weight of losing him crush my chest and make it so I couldn't breathe. Thankfully, the turtleneck hid the bruises on my neck from where I had been strangled last night.

Once the service ended, I got up and walked to the bathroom, needing a moment to myself before anyone stopped me. I had gotten plenty of curious glances and excited waves when they realized I was there. The problem was that I didn't want anyone to know I was there. I wanted to be invisible and go back to no one knowing where I was or what I had been doing.

I used the restroom and then walked to the sink, studying my face in the mirror after washing my hands. My eyes had dark circles beneath them again, and my face had thinned out from the weight I had lost since leaving Everett's apartment.

The bathroom door opened, and a woman wearing a black tailored suit and dark sunglasses entered, turning to lock the door behind her.

I opened my mouth to say something, but stopped when she removed her sunglasses.

"Quinn," I whispered, more thankful to see her than I would have imagined.

"How are you holding up?" she asked, studying my face.

I felt my neck flush with heat as I imagined her eyes uncovering the evidence of everything I had been doing.

"I'm okay," I said, only partly lying because there would never be a time in my life when I was okay. But I was alive and, for the most part, sane, which made me somewhat okay.

"No one can know that I am here," she said quickly as she slid her glasses back up her face. "I just wanted to check on you."

"Thank you. I appreciate that," I replied as we both heard someone try to open the door. "I got it."

She nodded and went into one of the stalls, closing it behind her as I unlocked the door and smiled at the little old lady on the other side.

"I'm so sorry," I offered with a laugh as I held the door open for her. "I didn't mean to lock it. I don't know where my head is these days." I pressed the palm of my hand to my forehead.

"Oh, dear. It's okay," she assured me, squeezing my hand in between hers before patting it.

She had lived in Oak Creek for as long as I could remember, but I couldn't recall her name at the time.

"Well, it's all yours." I smiled and gently pulled my hand away as she walked inside. I pulled the door open and stepped out into the hallway, looking around desperately for an exit so I could get some fresh air.

"Follow me," Roman said, grabbing my hand and tugging until I followed him down a hall and through a door that was marked as *emergency exit.*

I stepped into the cold air and tilted my face to the sun, hoping it would dry up the tears that were about to spill over. I had completely forgotten about the bruises on my neck until I felt his fingers pulling the fabric down for a better look.

My head snapped forward as I took a step back and nervously rubbed my lips together.

"Sloane…" he groaned, tipping his head back with a sigh.

"I can explain," I replied softly, hoping I could come up with a lie quicker than he would realize I was lying.

"I sure as fuck hope you can," another voice said as a man stepped out from behind the trees with a hoodie covering his face. He stopped and looked up, the light catching the features that I had always admired.

"Everett," I gasped, covering my mouth as a sob escaped my lips.

A Pissed-Off Woman Is A Dangerous Woman
Everett

"What the actual fuck, Everett?" Sloane grit out as she shoved my chest, nearly knocking me off balance.

I planted my feet, making sure the hoodie still covered my face the best it could and allowed her to take out her frustration on me. I deserved it—though it wasn't like it was *my* idea to fake my death. I knew why we needed to do it, but that didn't mean that I wanted to. I knew how hard this would be on Sloane once she learned the truth.

"I'm sorry," I said, not able to say anything else because I truly was sorry. Not just for faking my death and allowing her to grieve for me, but for not protecting her the way I should have from the start.

"Who the fuck does something like this? Do you think I haven't been through enough already without adding your *fake* death to the list? Did you even stop to think about how this would affect your mother? God, Everett! What were you thinking?" Sloane stepped away from me and shook her head as a fire blazed in her eyes.

"If you guys are going to do this, I recommend moving it somewhere private," Roman warned, looking around to make sure no one was close enough to hear us.

"And you fucking knew about this?" Sloane asked, turning her fury on him as she spun to face him.

"I did. And I'm sorry that we hurt you, but we had our reasons for doing this. However, *he* wasn't supposed to be here. *He* was supposed to stay in the fucking cabin like we told him to," Roman said, nearly snarling.

"I had to make sure she was okay. I was going crazy in that cabin, not knowing what was happening with her. I didn't have a choice."

"Didn't have a choice?" Sloane shrieked, causing Roman to wince as he moved around and checked the area to make sure we weren't drawing attention to ourselves. We were in a thick wooded area away from where everyone should be, but that didn't mean someone wouldn't come around to the back of the church and find us.

"Do you actually know what it means to *not* have a choice?" she continued, tilting her head to the side as she glared at me. "My son didn't have a choice. My husband didn't have a choice. My father didn't have a choice. My mother didn't have a choice. Frankie didn't have a choice. Don't you dare fucking stand before me and go on about how *you* didn't have a choice. You've been doing whatever the fuck you want without having to worry about who it impacts, and I'm tired of it."

"What is that supposed to mean?" I asked, clenching my jaw, even though I knew better than to keep aggravating her right now. Sloane needed time and space to calm herself, and I wasn't giving it to her.

"You know what the fuck it means, Everett. Don't play stupid. It doesn't look good on you."

"We gotta wrap this up," Roman said, interrupting. "You two can kill each other later, but we have to go *now*."

He pushed me toward the car, and while I knew I needed to talk things out with Sloane, I couldn't continue to put her in danger.

"What about—" My words cut off when I saw Trevor come around the corner and grab Sloane. He tucked her under his arm and whispered something in her ear as I took a few steps back to the car. Whatever he said had Sloane leaning into his side as she cried harder than I had ever seen before.

"Get him out of here. Now," Roman instructed the driver as he shoved me into the back seat of the sedan and slammed the door. The windows were tinted so dark you couldn't see inside, which allowed me a few more minutes to watch Sloane as Roman ran over and joined them right as a few people came around the corner to find them.

My jaw clenched when I noticed Keith was with them, watching Sloane with an intensity that nearly killed me. After what he did to me in New York, I didn't want him anywhere near her. Rage and fear warred inside me, and it was all I could do to keep from jumping from the car to end him myself.

Tread Lightly,
Or You Might Sink
Sloane

"There you are, dear," Nancy said as she found me coming around the corner of the church, tucked under Trevor's arm. "I got worried when I couldn't find you."

"I'm sorry, Nancy. I just needed a minute to collect myself."

"I completely understand." She reached forward and squeezed my hand while I forced myself not to look at the man standing beside her.

I recognized him immediately from the news and remembered that Nancy had mentioned Keith being a friend of Everett's, so it made sense that he would be there. My mind raced as I wondered if she knew that Everett was still alive and, better yet, if she had been in on the entire thing.

She had been stronger than I had anticipated during the service, though she cried often, especially when people shared their memories of Everett. Part of me wondered if she was just going through the motions of it because the grief was still so fresh from her losing Frankie, or if she was trying to make it as believable as possible for anyone who was watching. I had a million questions, but couldn't ask any of them right now.

"Sloane, I wanted to introduce you to Everett's friend, Keith. They went to school together, and Keith has been helping to keep an eye on things here after what…"

I nodded, knowing what the end of that sentence was without her having to say it.

"It's nice to meet you," I lied, forcing a smile when I felt Trevor's fingers slightly dig into my side in a gentle warning. "Or I guess I should say *officially* meet you since we did have a few phone calls together when I was staying with Everett."

"The pleasure is mine," Keith said, his voice smooth and laced with poison as he extended his hand for me to shake.

Okay—maybe I was being dramatic, but there was absolutely nothing about this guy that I trusted.

I quickly pulled my hand away from his and tucked it by my side as Trevor continued to hold me protectively against his side.

"Well, I guess we should get back to everyone," Nancy said, folding her hands in front of the floral dress she was wearing.

I nodded and allowed Trevor and Roman to guide me back to where people were still lingering around and talking. It was weird now that I knew that Everett *wasn't* dead. Thankfully, my anger toward him helped keep me grounded. I pressed my sunglasses up my nose to cover my eyes and pretended to be numb to keep from losing my shit. While I was incredibly grateful that he was alive, I couldn't push past the anger and frustration I felt over being duped into thinking he was dead.

We fell in line behind Nancy, and I immediately tensed when I noticed Keith slow his steps so he was right beside me.

"I wasn't aware you were back in town," he said quietly, though I could swear I saw Nancy's shoulders tense in response.

"Temporarily," I lied, taking comfort in Trevor's embrace.

"Oh? So, are you heading back to New York with your *boyfriend*?" he asked, leaning forward as he gave Trevor a once-over.

"I'm not sure where I'm heading, and he's not my boyfriend."

I expected Trevor to pull away and give us distance so as not to give the wrong impression, but he didn't. I had met his girlfriend several times and knew she would kick Keith's ass if he pissed her off, so I wasn't worried about Trevor having to explain anything to her. She knew what was going on and had been supportive from the start.

"Where are you staying while you're back?" Keith asked, causing Trevor's body to tense as quickly as mine.

I tilted my head and looked up at him, making sure he saw that there was no fear in my eyes.

"She's staying with me," Nancy said over her shoulder. "Is there a problem?"

"No. None at all," Keith replied, shoving his hands into the pockets of his dress slacks. "I just wanted to make sure I knew where she would be so I could help keep an eye on her. Make sure she's safe."

I took a deep breath and tilted my head further to the side, smirking when his eyes went to the bruise on my neck.

"I'm not the one you need to be worried about."

I pinned him with a look before I gently pushed away from Trevor and caught up to Nancy, giving her a warm smile as she glanced at me. Something about the look she gave me made me feel like she knew Everett was still alive.

Twenty Questions

Sloane

By the time everything was done with Everett's fake service, I was exhausted. Trevor and Roman escorted me to Nancy's house, where I was supposed to be staying. I noticed the sedan parked across the street and purposely waved at whoever was inside watching us.

Once we went inside and closed the door, Trevor locked it while Roman quickly cleared each room in the house, checking for any wires or recording devices.

"I already did that," Everett said as he came into the living room.

It was the first time I had seen him without his hoodie. The short hair that I used to run my fingers through was now gone and replaced with a buzz cut. While I would recognize him in an instant, even with the new look, I couldn't deny that it would probably be easy for him to blend into a crowd with a pair of sunglasses, given the new, thick beard that seemed to have come out of nowhere.

"We cleared the house a few hours ago," Quinn said as she came into the room and joined us. "We left immediately and came straight to the house. The sedan showed up about twenty minutes later and hasn't left."

"They're watching Sloane," Roman confirmed as he stepped in and placed a quick kiss on Quinn's cheek. "Keith was asking her about where she was staying, and Nancy told him that Sloane was staying here."

"How long ago was that?" Everett asked.

"About an hour ago?" I replied, though I couldn't stop scowling at him.

"That tracks," Quinn said with a heavy sigh. "I can put someone on them, but I would hate to spread resources too thin when I already have them watching Keith. We secured the house, so for now, I think we're good. No one is coming in here without one of us stopping them."

"We do need to know where you're staying so we can secure it as well," Roman added, giving me a gentle smile.

"It's taken care of," I replied, still not able to pull my attention away from Everett.

My face flushed with heat as the anger spread through me. I pressed my lips together as I clenched and unclenched my fists, needing a way to expel some of the energy that was rushing over me before I exploded.

"We'll be back. Do not come looking for us," Everett said as he grabbed my hand and started to pull me toward the hallway.

"I'm not going anywhere with you," I shrieked, pulling my hand free. "I am still so fucking pissed at you that I could punch a hole in the wall and then shove your stupid head through it."

I didn't mean to embarrass him, but I couldn't be trusted to be alone with him right now. I was furious with him and needed more than just a few minutes to cool off.

"I am well the fuck aware that you're pissed off, Sloane," he said tightly before tossing me over his shoulder. "And guess what? I am equally fucking pissed at you."

"What?" I said, turning my body the best I could as I glared at him.

His hands firmly gripped my thighs, holding me in place as he stormed off down the hallway and slammed his bedroom door shut once we were inside. He slowly put me down, but blocked the door so I couldn't escape.

"You have no right to be pissed at me," I yelled, placing my hands on my hips as I stared at him. "YOU fucking FAKED your death, you stupid, selfish, pri—"

Before I could finish the word, his mouth was on mine, smothering it as his hands wrapped around my waist and held me in place.

I wanted to push him away and continue yelling at him, but at the same time, I couldn't bring myself to step out of his embrace. I kissed him back, parting my lips as he deepened the kiss. I wrapped my arms around his neck, blinded by the desire as he touched me, only to be let down when he stepped back a few seconds later and stared at me.

There was a fire behind his eyes, and I knew he was actually pissed off. I had seen that look on him several times, but this was the first time it was ever directed at me.

"Where did you get the bruise on your neck?" he demanded, pointing to where the turtleneck had shifted.

I quickly pulled the fabric up, but knew it was too late. He had already seen it.

"That's none of your business," I bit back.

"YOU are my fucking business, Sloane. Don't you get that?"

"That's really funny, given how you've allowed me to grieve for you all this time. Everyone, including your mother, knew that you were alive, yet you all let me believe you were dead!"

"We never wanted you to get hurt. That wasn't our intention."

"Oh. I'm sorry. I must have been overreacting. Silly me, why would anyone think that your death *wouldn't* have an impact on me or that it wouldn't be the one that fucking *killed* me, Everett? Out of everyone and everything that I've already lost, losing you was—"

I stopped and covered my mouth with a trembling hand as tears ran down my face. I looked away because looking at him only broke my heart even more. Going through the emotions of losing him, only to find out he was still alive, was exhausting, and I didn't have it in me to continue on this rollercoaster ride.

He stepped forward and opened his arms as he tried to hug me, but I stepped back and held my hand up.

"You don't get to be the hero who steps in to fix this. You don't get to be the one who offers me comfort from the pain you created."

"I know that you are pissed, Sloane, and rightfully so. But I didn't do any of this. I didn't come up with the idea to fake my death, but I went along with it because I was told that it was the best way to protect *you*. If you seriously think that a single day goes by where you are not my utmost concern, you are mistaken. Everything I do these days is for you, Sloane. Don't you see that?"

The weight of his words sat heavily on my heart as I struggled to hold onto the anger that I needed to keep from giving in to all of these emotions.

"Okay, so why the whole fake death thing?" I asked, keeping my distance from him as my heart started to slow down to a normal speed again. I sat on the edge of his bed and watched his eyes as they studied me.

He leaned against the dresser and folded his arms over his chest without saying anything. His eyes went back to my neck, and I knew he wasn't going to let that go. He wanted answers about what happened to me as much as I wanted answers on why they needed to fake his death.

"How about we make a deal? I answer one question of yours, and you answer one of mine. No bullshit. Just the truth. We keep going until we're both satisfied."

I hated the way my body betrayed me with a flush of color that went straight to my cheeks at the word *satisfied*.

"We'll deal with that later," he commented with a knowing smirk. "What do you say, Sloane? Are you in?"

"Fine. But only because I want answers, and you better not lie to me."

"Same. I'll even let you go first."

I sighed heavily and let my shoulders fall, trying to force myself to relax.

"What happened in New York? When I ran into your mom, she said you had been attacked and that they thought it was a robbery gone wrong."

"Keith showed up at my apartment looking for you. When I didn't tell him where you were, he had two guys search for you before they attacked me. They stabbed me in the back and left me for dead when I wouldn't tell them where your phone was."

A soft gasp escaped my lips as I imagined the pain he had been in because of me.

"Oh my God, Everett. How did they find you to get you to the hospital?"

"That's two questions," he warned. "First, you answer one of mine."

"Alright." I took in a deep breath and held it before scrunching my face. "But before I do, is there like a no-judgment clause or something?"

He raised an eyebrow but said nothing as he pushed off the dresser and walked over to me.

"What happened?"

His question was simple, as his fingers tugged at the fabric of my turtleneck and revealed the bruise.

"I was strangled," I replied cautiously, looking up and noticing the fury etched on his face.

He pulled the rest of the fabric down as he checked for more bruises, and I shivered as his fingers trailed over my skin.

"Who the fuck put their hands on you, Sloane?"

"I think that counts as two questions since you're keeping track of the rules and all."

"We will come back to this," he warned, pointing a finger at me as he took a few steps back. It was as if he didn't trust himself not to touch me as much as I wanted him to touch me.

"Alright, my second question was how did they find you to get you to the hospital, but I think I want to change it."

He nodded his head once in agreement.

"Why did you have to fake your death?"

"Because Quinn and Roman felt it was the best way to figure out who was putting your life in danger. We knew that Keith was dirty, but we wanted to see who else."

"And you dying was the way to do that?"

"It was more to see who came to the service and why. More so, who was focused on *you* at the service."

"You guys used me as bait?"

"No. Yes." He sighed heavily and rubbed a hand down his face. "The goal was only ever to protect you, Sloane. We can't keep protecting you from unknown threats if we don't know what they are. This was our chance to see if they would slip up and make a move now that they knew where you were."

"Are you disappointed that they didn't?"

"The night is still young, and that's more than one question."

He pinned me with a look as he rubbed his lips and studied me.

"Who tried to strangle you, Sloane?"

I looked down at the floor, avoiding his eyes.

"I don't remember his name," I lied.

"This was a random attack? Where? Why didn't you report it?"

"That's three questions, and no, it wasn't random."

"What do you mean it wasn't random?"

I stood up and took a few steps toward him until our bodies were only inches apart.

"It wasn't random because I went looking for them."

He pulled his head back in disbelief as his eyes widened.

"Wait. What do you mean *them*?"

"I paid a visit to the guys who murdered my family."

"Are you out of your fucking mind?"

"Umm… Yeah. Probably." I laughed, though he didn't find it funny. But seriously, I hadn't been in the right mindset for over a year now.

"You think this is funny? Sloane, they could have killed you. You're lucky that they—"

"Luck had nothing to do with it," I interrupted, pulling my shoulders back. "I knew exactly what I was doing when I went there."

He dragged a hand down his face in frustration and shook his head.

"Did you happen to pay a visit to the judge, too?" he asked, his voice softer.

I wanted to look away and get out from under the harsh look he was giving me, but I didn't. I knew it was risky telling Everett about what I had done because I was as much a criminal as they were. But oddly enough, I wasn't ashamed of any of it. I wanted Everett to know that I had been more than capable of taking care of myself. Not only that, but I was getting justice for those who had been taken from us at the hands of these monsters.

"He didn't do his job," I whispered, not fully admitting that I was the one who murdered him.

He closed his eyes as my words sank in.

"Antonio Carrio?"

I took a deep breath and slowly let it out as he opened his eyes and looked at me. I simply nodded, not bothering to say anything.

"I don't even know what to do with all of this information, Sloane. I can't fucking protect you when you're running around playing vigilante and killing people. I work for the FBI—"

I stepped forward and pressed a finger to his lips, silencing him.

"Well, then, I guess it's a good thing that *dead* people can't talk."

Comfort

Everett

I said goodbye to my mother before I left out the back door with Sloane. We knew the sedan was watching, so Quinn and Sloane swapped clothes so they would think it was Sloane who left with Roman and Trevor. Sure enough, we watched from inside the house as the sedan slowly pulled out and began to follow their car.

It was a quick walk to Sloane's house from my mom's, one that we both memorized over the years as we grew up. I knew that she wanted her space to process everything, but I wasn't ready to leave her just yet.

We walked to the back door, and I frowned when I noticed she had paused.

"What's wrong?" I asked and then paused when I heard growling on the other side. "Umm… what the fuck was that?"

Sloane turned and looked at me nervously as she kept her hand on the doorknob.

"I… um. I got a dog…"

"A dog? Since when?"

She shrugged and winced as if the memory of it pained her.

I arched an eyebrow at her and folded my arms over my chest while I waited.

"Okay. Fine. I didn't *technically* get a dog. The dog just decided to come with me when I was leaving."

"Leaving where, Sloane?"

"Mr. Carrio's house," she replied as she scrunched her face and looked away.

"Let me get this straight—first, you murdered the guy, then you stole his dog?"

"Shhh," she hissed, looking around as if anyone could hear us. "I didn't *steal* his dog."

"You know what I love the most about this?" I asked teasingly. "The fact that you didn't even try to deny that you *murdered* him."

"Eh. He had it coming." She shrugged as if this was no big deal whatsoever, which left me genuinely concerned as my balls threatened to shrivel up and die inside of me.

"I don't know how she's going to react to you, so no sudden movements, okay?" Sloane warned as she slowly turned the knob and pushed the door open.

A gray-colored pit bull sat on the other side, snarling until it saw Sloane.

"Hey, Justice, this is my friend, Everett," Sloane said softly, reaching down to scratch the top of the dog's head. "Let's try not to eat this one, okay?"

I stepped inside and closed the door behind me as the dog continued to sit there and stare at me. At least she hadn't lunged for me, but still, that didn't make her any less intimidating.

"Has she eaten someone before?" I asked nervously, trying not to make eye contact with her.

"Not like a *whole* human or anything," Sloane replied as she went to the fridge and pulled two bottles of water out, handing me one.

"I have so many questions," I said as I shook my head and followed her upstairs to her room.

I tried not to be nosy, but it was impossible as I stared at the guns spread out on her dresser and the piles of ammunition sitting beside them. Without saying a word, Sloane walked over and pulled a knife from her pocket, adding it to the collection.

"I don't use the rest of the house, except for the bathroom and occasionally the kitchen," she explained as she kicked off her shoes. "You can either sit on the bed, or I can get you a chair from the kitchen. But I am tired. It's been a long day with people coming back from the dead and whatnot."

"Do you mind if I share the bed with you?" I asked softly, not wanting to push my luck.

"You'll have to get Justice's permission since you'll be taking her spot."

I looked down at the dog who was sitting in front of me, just staring.

"Is it okay if I sleep in the bed tonight?" I felt stupid talking to a dog, but then she nudged my hand with her head, and I found myself grinning. I scratched the top of her head as she closed her eyes and leaned into it. "You really are a good girl, aren't you?"

She whimpered, then lay on her back and waited for me. I glanced at Sloane, who was watching with a full smile spread across her face.

"You know the drill. Gotta pay that tax of belly rubs before she lets you take her spot tonight."

"I am more than happy to do that."

I bent down and gave her belly a good scratch, laughing every time her leg would start going. After a few minutes, I stood up and smiled when she went over and lay down by the door. I didn't love Sloane being on her own in this house, but seeing how protective this dog was of her made me feel a lot better that no one was getting to Sloane without Justice warning her first.

We both took a few minutes to get ready for bed before climbing in. It felt nice being with Sloane again, and I hoped it comforted her as much as it did me. The world could come crashing down on us, and I wouldn't care as long as she was next to me.

I waited until she was situated and under the blankets before I reached over and wrapped my arm around her waist, pulling her to me. She giggled but didn't fight me as she arched her back so that her ass was lined up against my cock. I stifled a groan as memories of our last night together surfaced and made me hard.

"Everett," she whispered with a laugh. "What are you doing?"

"I'm not doing anything but trying to hold you. You're the one who pressed your ass into me, making him hard."

"Is it a little creepy that you're supposed to be *dead*?" she teased, looking at me over her shoulder, pulling her lip between her teeth.

I reached over and freed it as she shifted, making my eyes roll when I thought about how good she would feel right now.

"Hey, even dead guys need love, Sloane. You can't blame him for remembering how good she felt last time."

"Trust me, she hasn't forgotten either."

I leaned in and kissed her shoulder, taking my time trailing kisses over her skin as I brushed her hair to the side and saw the bruise. I hated the thought of someone hurting her, but I knew better than to keep pushing her for details on it. She shut me down earlier when I tried asking more questions, but that didn't mean I was going to give up on it. I would hunt them down and kill them for what they tried to do to her, but she had already beaten me to it.

"You're thinking too much," she whispered as her hand slid between us, rubbing my cock.

I slipped out from behind her and rolled her onto her back as I held myself over her with my hands next to her head.

"It's funny because I was just thinking you're wearing too many clothes. Mind if I help you out of them?"

"Nope. Not at all."

She grinned as she leaned up and allowed me to pull the t-shirt up and over her head, my breath catching when I found she wasn't wearing a bra underneath. She lifted her hips as her eyes stayed locked onto mine, allowing me to remove the shorts and panties she was wearing.

"Now you're the one who's wearing too much," she teased.

I reached behind me and grabbed the back of my shirt, pulling it up and over my head before tossing it to the floor. She reached for the waistband of my joggers, desperate to free my cock, but I reached out and stopped her as I grabbed her wrists and pinned them above her head. I lowered myself on top of her, kissing her neck while grinding against her with nothing but the fabric of my joggers separating us.

"Fuck," she whimpered, arching her body against mine for more friction. "Everett. Please."

I lowered myself the best I could while keeping her wrists pinned to the pillow, lining my face up with her breasts. I pulled her nipple in between my teeth and began sucking, knowing how much it drove her crazy. She moaned, the sound deep and throaty and making me want to plow into that beautiful pussy of hers.

I ground harder, making sure she could feel my erection as I dry-humped her, taking myself right to the edge before stopping so I didn't come right away.

"If you don't give me your cock in the next thirty seconds, I'm gonna—"

"You're gonna what?" I asked, pulling back and thrusting my hips hard so she could feel how it would feel if I slammed into her right now.

"Don't fuck with me, Everett," she warned, though I could feel her body melting against mine. "Just because you're in my bed doesn't mean I have forgiven you for everything."

I continued holding her wrists with one hand while I slid the other down between us, allowing it to tease her as it grazed her pussy.

"Ahh," she cried out, hips lifting as she chased the touch she craved.

"You want to talk about being pissed at someone, Sloane? How do you think I feel when I know you're out there by yourself with someone who wants you dead?" I slipped a finger inside, loving the way her pussy immediately clenched around me. She was so fucking wet it glided right in.

"I can handle myself," she breathed, eyes closed as her head tipped back. Her back arched, bringing her full tits right into view as I leaned in and sucked the other one.

I slipped a second finger inside and fucked her hard, not touching her clit even though I knew she wanted it.

"That's fine, but the thought I can't stand is what happens when they get to you when you're not expecting it? I'm not okay with you constantly putting your life on the line because living without you isn't something I am willing to do." I fucked her harder as she panted, her hands trying to break free from the hold I had on her wrists.

"You mean like you did to me with faking your death?"

I pulled my hand out and looked at her. Her face was beautiful with color flushing it from her arousal, but I hated the sadness I saw in her eyes.

"Fuck. I'm sorry, Sloane."

"I'm sorry, too, Everett. But you're going to be sorrier if you don't fuck me. I swear to God," she moaned.

I let go of her wrists so I could use my hands to strip off the rest of my clothes before I climbed on top of her.

"I don't have a condom," I said, the frustration thick in my voice as I realized it.

"I don't care. I have an IUD."

"I get tested every year." I looked deep into her eyes, needing confirmation from her that she really wanted to do this without any protection.

She nodded and reached for me, wrapping her arms around my neck as she practically tried to climb me from beneath me. I chuckled and pressed a kiss to her forehead before placing another on her wrist, promising her that I would always take care of her.

I lined myself up at her entrance and pushed inside slowly. I gritted my teeth to keep from coming right away because being inside Sloane without a condom was pure heaven, and I wanted to spend all of my days right there.

She locked her legs around my waist and pulled me in deeper before lifting her hips to thrust against me.

"I got you, baby," I promised as I adjusted myself, then lifted her legs and rested them against my chest as I began fucking her hard and deep, just like she liked.

"Oh my God," she moaned, her body so receptive to my touch. "Fuck, Everett."

"You feel amazing, baby."

I reached my hand down between us and began rubbing her clit, grinning when I felt the first spasm as her pussy clenched around my cock. She cried out as the pleasure washed over her, but I didn't stop until I knew she had given me every single bit.

I gripped her hips and held her steady as I thrust inside her, fucking her like my life depended on it until I came so hard I saw stars.

Goodbyes Are Always Hard
Sloane

I forgot how well I slept when I was with Everett when Justice came over and licked my face, letting me know she needed to be let outside. I laughed and scratched her head before climbing out of bed and getting dressed. It was still early, so I tiptoed out of the room and went downstairs to let her do her thing.

When I got back to the bedroom, Everett was already up and dressed.

"What's this?" he asked, looking up from the notepad he was holding in his hand.

I swallowed hard, not wanting to have this conversation with him right now.

"It's just a list of people whom I don't trust," I said cautiously, folding my arms over my chest.

"And the ones with a line through their names?"

I pressed my lips together and stayed quiet.

"Where are you going?" I asked, hoping to change the subject.

He had mentioned last night that he couldn't stay long because it would be too risky if someone in town saw him. But then we had sex, and I got distracted and forgot to ask him what was next for him. Obviously, he couldn't just go back to work and resume his life as if nothing had happened. But he couldn't stay here either.

"I'm heading to a friend's place for a while," he replied, setting the notepad down on my nightstand where he found it.

"Where at? Or are you not allowed to tell me?"

I hated how awkward things had gotten between us, mainly from the secrets we had been keeping from each other.

"It's a small town in Colorado, not too far from here."

I nodded and looked away, hoping he wouldn't see the emotion that was trying to take over my face. I needed to be strong, just as I had been before he showed up yesterday. If I allowed myself to feel any emotions right now, it would make me weak, and I couldn't afford that.

"It's a town called Haven Brook. My friend is going on work travel for a few months, so I'll have the place to myself."

"Oh. That's nice."

He stalked toward me, wrapped his arm around my waist, and pulled me against his chest.

"I will find a way for us to be together, Sloane. This distance that we have to put between us is just temporary. Okay?"

I nodded, swallowing hard to keep from crying.

"Try to be good and not murder too many people while I'm gone?"

"I will try my best," I answered, holding my hands behind my back as I crossed my fingers.

I could tell he was teasing and trying to make light of the list he found, but I couldn't promise him anything. As far as I was concerned, there was more work that needed to be done.

~~Officer Butchkins~~

Sloane

It was a weird feeling to feel someone's life slip away in the palm of your hand, but that was exactly what happened when I pressed my hand against his throat. His eyes bulged dramatically as they pleaded with me to spare his life as I pinned him against the cold brick wall. His face was already swollen and turning shades of red and purple from the beating he'd endured before we got to the fun part. I was surprised he could still stand at this point, though I was technically doing all of the work by holding him against the wall.

I smirked as I lifted my hand slightly, teasing him with the thought that I might, in fact, have a tiny bit of pity in this dark soul of mine and let him live. His lips parted as he tried to speak but quickly snapped shut as my features hardened, just like my grip on his throat.

"Please," he croaked, attempting to get his final word out.

"Aww, you say that as if you think I care about you or your pathetic fucking life. You know, I actually care as much as you did the night of the shooting. You know, when you heard all of those gunshots, but you were too scared to do your job—the one where you *protect* and serve. Instead, you hid—like a coward. You let all of those innocent people die while the monsters who did it got away."

I tilted my head and stared at him, my glare ice cold.

"I didn't," he coughed out, trying to speak as his eyes widened in horror. "Please. Please don't kill me. I have a family."

His words immediately made me see red as I glared at him. *I had a family, too, asshole.*

"Please don't kill me. I didn't mean to hurt anyone. I'm really a nice person. I'll do better," I mocked as I reached behind me and pulled out a knife.

"I'm sorry—"

His words were cut off as I released my grip and plunged the knife into the divot at the base of his throat. Blood began spurting out as he coughed, his hands flying to his throat to try to stop the bleeding.

His eyes widened as he took me in, utter disbelief etched onto his face.

I was *not* the same woman he had once met.

No, this time, our roles were reversed.

I wasn't the one begging for a life to be spared.

"You know, you really shouldn't say sorry if you don't mean it," I scolded, kicking his leg away from me as his body collapsed to the floor. Blood quickly pooled around my feet as his lifeless eyes stared up at me.

I knew I had told Everett that I wouldn't kill too many people, but sometimes, things needed to be dealt with the right way. If we couldn't count on our local law enforcement to do their jobs, I would gladly step up and rid the world of the people who made it a terrible place.

I adjusted the white Colorado Rockies ballcap on my head, then reached into my back pocket and pulled out the piece of paper with my list written on it.

"Another down, a few more to go," I muttered as I pulled out a pen and crossed through his name.

Broken

Unexpected Gifts
Sloane

I sat at the back of the café, trying to focus on the news story on the TV that was mounted on the wall across the room from me. I didn't bother trying to stay hidden after everyone had seen me at Everett's memorial service. Whether I was still wanted or not, I stopped worrying about it since I had plans for most of their law enforcement. I hadn't wanted any attention, but that didn't stop people from coming over to say hi and let me know they were glad I was home. Maybe that was the thing with small towns, they didn't care what the news said about someone if they thought they knew them better? Or maybe they were just as fed up with what was happening in Oak Creek that they didn't mind someone stepping in and getting justice for them.

The funny thing was that I didn't have a home. I was stuck in this eternal state of being with nowhere to go until my work was finished. I wasn't the person who was going to have the long, healthy life with the husband and family that I always longed for. Those days were over. And even though Everett was still alive, he technically had to stay dead until we figured out who all was involved—which might not ever happen.

I was tired on every level, my body aching from the physical altercation I got into last night with Officer Butchkins. I hadn't planned to attack him, but when I saw him standing behind the school gym taking video of the cheerleaders, I decided to help the world by getting rid of him. I hadn't bothered to see what he had recorded because I was still pissed off that he had been there the night of the massacre and hadn't done anything. Videoing high school girls was just the cherry on top that I needed to justify the slow and very painful death he endured.

I knew leaving him there would mean someone found him sooner rather than later, which was apparent by the crime scene displayed on the TV. The reporter shivered as she held the microphone, glancing over her shoulder to where the area was taped off and surrounded by police.

A waitress grabbed the remote and turned up the TV, glancing around the nearly empty café before returning her focus to Sheriff Dowdy, who was now speaking.

"Our hearts are heavy this morning as we mourn the loss of one of our own. The murder of Officer Butchkins comes as a shock to many in our community, but I assure you, I will find who is responsible for this. Justice *will* be served."

His eyes were dark as he clasped his hands tightly in front of him, refusing to say anything more as the reporter shifted gears and took over again. She quickly summarized what had happened before the camera cut back to the news anchors in the studio, and the screen changed to show the weather forecast.

"Such a terrible thing, isn't it?" the waitress said as she stopped beside my table and refilled my coffee.

It took me a second to realize she was talking about the news. I nodded my head and lifted my cup to my lips to keep from having to answer her. She gave me a soft smile and then headed to the front desk to speak with the other waitress.

"Since it's slow this morning, I'm going to start working on the order for Sheriff Dowdy," she said to the other waitress.

"What time are they coming to pick it up?"

"Around eleven. I think Rusty said he'd come grab it since he is setting everything up with Officer Contreras and Officer Ozwald. Sheriff Dowdy is supposed to be out in the field for a few hours, so they're going to set up while he's gone."

"You mean *Deputy Sheriff*," the other waitress said with a laugh, correcting her friend.

"Hey, he grew up with my son. He'll always be *Rusty* to me."

"Just don't let him hear you call him that. You know how upset he gets when people don't respect his title." She wiggled her finger at the waitress who had been helping me as I climbed out of the booth and pulled a few dollars from my wallet to leave as a tip on the table.

"You all set?" my waitress asked, giving me a warm smile.

"I am. Thank you."

"Can I get you a pastry or anything for later?"

I shook my head, trying to keep the smile off my face.

"No, thank you. I have everything I need." I handed her my money and returned her smile as I walked outside, pulling the hood over my head.

It was windy but not too bad. I would much rather have some wind than the downpour we had the other night. I crossed the street and headed to the pet store to get food for Justice. I had been sharing some of my leftovers, but I knew it wasn't healthy for her, and she probably wasn't getting enough to eat. I pulled the door open, the bell chiming over my head.

"Hello. Welcome to Oak Creek Pets. Let me know if you need anything," a woman's monotone-sounding voice greeted me as I walked past the register and headed toward the sign that had a picture of a dog on it.

The girl looked to be in her early twenties with jet-black hair and tattoos covering her arms. Her head was down, which was nice because I didn't feel like having anyone notice my presence more than she had already.

I walked to the back aisle and scanned the options, unsure of what to get. I never had a dog growing up, so I had no idea what was good and what wasn't. I scanned the options, noticing the difference between each brand. Some claimed to be free of this or that, but I just wanted something basic that would keep her healthy and fill her belly.

"What kind of dog do you have?" a woman wearing a T-shirt with the Oak Creek Pets logo asked as she stood next to me.

"A pit bull," I answered, chewing the inside of my lip.

I had no idea whether anyone had reported Antonio Carrio's dog as missing, so I was a little reckless by saying I had the same kind of dog he had, especially since I hadn't been back to Oak Creek long enough to take ownership of a pet.

"I always recommend this one," she said, pointing to a giant bag on the floor. "I have two myself, and this one works well. It's high protein, which they need."

"Sounds great. I'll take that one then," I replied, bending to grab it.

"Let me." She picked it up, hoisted it on her hip, and then carried it to the cash register, where the other girl was now gone. "Did you need anything else?"

"Nope. That should do it." I opened my crossbody bag and pulled out my wallet when movement suddenly caught my eye. I leaned down, looking at a box that had several containers with a single black spider inside each of them. I looked up and found her watching me as she began smiling.

"We had a teacher request black widow spiders for a demonstration in her class. We captured what we could, but she hasn't been in to pick them up yet. I think she changed her mind once she saw how many we had," she replied with a laugh.

"Why not put them together in one container?" I asked, too captivated by them to look away.

"Black widows are known to be cannibalistic, meaning they will eat each other if given the opportunity."

"These are black widows?" My eyebrows rose in disbelief.

"Yep. We're giving it until the end of today for her to come collect them, but I don't think she will."

"Then what will happen to them?"

"We'll find somewhere safe and release them. Far away from each other," she added.

"Would you mind if I take them?" I asked before I could stop myself.

"You want a dozen black widow spiders?"

I nodded, hoping she didn't think I was crazy.

"I've been obsessed with spiders since I was little," I lied.

She studied me cautiously as she scanned the barcode on the bag of dog food.

"You know they don't make good pets, right? They'll need to be let free so they can hunt and mate."

"Not to worry. I know the perfect place for them."

I grinned as she nodded in agreement and helped to stack the containers inside a box to make sure they didn't get disturbed on my short walk home. I took my receipt and grabbed the bag of dog food, hoisting it on my hip the same way I had seen her do it, then took my box of spiders and left.

~~Officer Ozwald, Officer Contreras, and Deputy Sheriff Anderson~~

Sloane

It was nice how quiet the police station was given that it was a small town, and a lot of the officers were still out with Sheriff Dowdy collecting evidence of the crime scene where Officer Butchkins was murdered. I made sure to leave his phone out so they would find it, but *accidentally* emailed the photos he had taken to the local news station. They were sent from his personal email address, but that didn't mean it would be hard to know who they came from, given that there was only one person in Oak Creek with the last name Butchkins.

I slowly made my way inside, walking quietly down the hall as I heard male voices. I had no idea what kind of party they were having or why, especially since it seemed out of place, given one of their own was just brutally murdered. But I wasn't there to ask questions. I was there to do a job, and I was going to do it well.

I rounded the corner, and the voices got louder.

"Hang the banner higher," a deep voice said, and I immediately recognized it as Deputy Sheriff Anderson. I had thought he was so kind when I met him at the hospital when he gave me back my family's personal belongings. Little did I know that it was supposed to be kept as evidence until Everett told me.

"There. That's perfect."

"Do we really need all of these balloons?" someone grumbled, but I didn't recognize the voice.

"It's his thirtieth anniversary of working for the Oak Creek Sheriff's Department, you idiot. Of course we need them."

So that's what the party was for. Little did they know his celebration was going to start with a bang.

I pulled the gun from behind my back and held it in front of me as I quietly stepped inside the room. My eyes scanned the area quickly, making sure I knew where everyone was before they spotted me.

"What are you—" one of them—Officer Ozwald—I believe, asked, his words cutting off as a bullet pierced his forehead.

I spun quickly, firing another shot into Officer Contreras's heart as they both hit the floor. I watched as Deputy Sheriff Anderson reached for his gun, only to frown when he realized he wasn't wearing it.

"What do you want?" he asked, lifting his hands as if to appease me.

I knew it wouldn't be long until the place was swarming with cops, but I hoped that the police station was far enough away from everything else that no one would hear the gunshots.

"I came to ask you something," I replied, my voice sweet and soft.

"Okay. What would you like to ask me?"

I took a few steps toward him, my gun still drawn as I studied him.

"How do you sleep at night?"

His brows pinched together as he processed my question.

"I'm just wondering how you sleep at night, knowing that you gave me items that should have been kept as evidence. You know, back when my family was murdered at the football game. We were in the hospital, and you brought me my husband and my father's belongings and told me how sorry you were about my loss."

"I remember," he said easily, looking from my gun to me.

"You gave me their stuff knowing you shouldn't have."

"I—I—" he stuttered as I stepped forward until I was standing right in front of him and shoved my gun into his mouth before he had a chance to close it.

"You what? You didn't know you weren't supposed to give it to me? Or you didn't care because you knew there would never be a reason to need it?"

He shook his head slightly, tears forming in his eyes as I cocked my head and stared at him.

"You were in on it all along, weren't you?" I asked, knowing I wouldn't get a confession out of him.

"It doesn't matter anyway," I continued with a shrug, making sure to keep my grip on the gun steady. "What's done is done, and now all we can do is move forward."

His lower lip trembled as he stared at me, probably hoping I would pull the gun out of his mouth and regret my decision.

Instead, I pulled the trigger.

The room was painted red, as their blood splattered around it, ruining the decorations and the donuts that had been picked up from the café before I arrived.

I adjusted my dad's baseball cap on my head and hated that soon it would be red instead of white. But it didn't matter how much blood was shed when you did it in the name of justice.

Old Friends
Everett

I sat at one of the high-top tables in the back of a place called The Vine and stared at the TV in disbelief. The news was on, broadcasting a breaking story about a mass murder that happened at the Oak Creek Sheriff's Department. The images of the three officers who were shot and killed were displayed on the screen before Sheriff Dowdy appeared.

"Hey, Noah, can you turn that up?" a woman said as she wiped down the bar.

He nodded and turned the volume up as the entire place went silent while we listened.

"It is with a heavy heart that I stand here today, mourning the loss of three incredible officers in a senseless act of violence. Oak Creek has been many things over the years, but being tolerant of violent crimes has never been one of them. I have always taken pride in leading our community and protecting those who live here. Rest assured, I will find the person responsible for this, and they will pay for what they've done."

A female reporter standing off to the side raised her hand as she began speaking, but Sheriff Dowdy shook his head and walked away without saying another word.

I lifted the beer mug to my lips and took a long sip. I didn't want to automatically assume this was Sloane, but given what I knew about her these days, it had her written all over it.

"Here are your hot wings and fries," the man who people were calling Noah said as he set the plate down in front of me and nodded at my almost empty beer. "Do you want another one?"

"Yes. Please."

He smiled and tapped the table with his knuckles before heading back behind the bar to get it. It was a nice place with great vibes. Somewhere I could see myself hanging out and relaxing. It was so different than the hustle and bustle of New York City. It was small-town life, but it seemed busier than Oak Creek, almost like a happy medium.

He returned and set the glass down before nodding hello to someone who walked inside. I smiled and extended my hand as Lieutenant Buck Dickson joined me.

"How's it going?" he asked, taking the seat across from me as he glanced at the TV, a solemn expression crossed his face.

"Not too bad. How have you been?"

I had known Lieutenant Dickson since I was little. He was a friend of my parents, having grown up with my dad. When I talked to my mom about needing somewhere to lay low for a while—since I was supposed to be dead and all—she mentioned coming to Haven Brook. I didn't know she still kept in touch with Lieutenant Dickson, but I felt safe knowing he wouldn't tell anyone what was happening.

"I've been good. I would love to retire and spend my time traveling with Connie, but our grandbabies keep us plenty busy, and I love being able to spoil them. Plus, the department would fall apart if I left," he replied with a laugh as Noah returned.

"Your usual?" Noah asked.

Lieutenant Dickson smiled and confirmed with a nod of his head.

"You come here that often?" I teased, waiting to eat my food until his came.

"Every now and then." He smiled and looked back at the TV. "Sad day for Oak Creek."

My eyes lifted to where he was looking, taking in the crime scene they were still showing. I knew the minute I saw who the victims were that they were on Sloane's list of people she didn't trust. The problem was that I didn't know who else was on that list. The only thing that I could guarantee at this point was that she wasn't going to stop until she got everyone. That thought soured my stomach as I worried about her and not being there to take care of her.

"Did they say what happened?" he asked, pulling me from my thoughts.

I shook my head, trying to get my thoughts together before answering him. While he knew I was supposed to be dead and was hiding out, I didn't need him to know that my girlfriend was the one responsible for the sudden wave of crime in Oak Creek.

"They didn't get into much detail, just that someone went in and shot all of them at point-blank."

"Do they have any suspects?" His tone changed as his voice grew quieter, only loud enough for me to hear.

"Not that they've confirmed."

He nodded and looked around the room again, pausing as Noah delivered a glass of iced tea to the table and then rushed off.

"I have a friend who works at the news station in Oak Creek. He told me they received some photos and a video from the email of the officer who was killed a few days ago. They reported it to the Sheriff's department but were told it was already handled."

"That doesn't surprise me any," I mumbled, knowing how thoroughly they handle stuff there to begin with.

"What surprised me was that they didn't bother collecting his cell phone from the crime scene. It was found peeking out from beneath the dumpster they found his body next to."

"Who has it now?"

"He wouldn't say. But I wouldn't go digging around looking for it if I were you. Some things need to happen on their own time."

"But—" I started to object and then stopped when I noticed the look he gave me.

<u>Vengeance</u>
Sloane

I hadn't seen or heard much about the Lagrimas Rojas cartel since I murdered a handful of their members. But that didn't mean they were gone. They were watching me as closely as I was watching them—or at least trying to. It was hard to get close to them when they had massive security protecting the one man I needed to get to.

I called him the guy with the black widow tattoo, but apparently, his name was Juan Rodriguez, and he was the leader of the cartel. Trying to get to him was as easy as trying to meet the queen of a foreign country. It would be nearly impossible.

I sat in my bed, twirling my hair around my finger as Justice snored loudly beside me. She loved the food I bought her, though I had to convince her to leave the spiders alone. They sat on my kitchen counter, tucked away in a corner by the fridge, still separated in their individual boxes, while I googled what to feed them so I could keep them alive until I needed them. The clock was ticking, which meant I needed to get a plan together quickly.

My frustration was mounting as I struggled to figure out how to approach him without his team knowing something was amiss. It wasn't like I could just walk in with guns blazing and take everyone out. This wasn't an action movie, and I wasn't invincible. If I tried something like that, I would be dead in an instant.

I was lost in thought when I suddenly heard someone banging on the front door downstairs. Justice sat up on the bed, growling as she surveyed the room for any sign of immediate danger. I scratched the top of her head, letting her know she was a good girl before quietly getting up and walking to the window. I hated that I couldn't get a good view of who was at the door, but I could at least see if anyone was scoping out the house.

Worried that it might be Nancy and something was wrong, I grabbed a gun, tucked it into the back of my sweatpants, and headed downstairs. Justice followed, staying right beside me as we made our way to the front door.

Suddenly, I stopped and realized that if Nancy were coming to see me, she would come to the back door instead of the front. She knew that I had the front barricaded for a reason.

I watched as the doorknob turned, someone rattling it hard from the other side as they tried to get in.

I rushed to the back door, ready to block it, when it suddenly burst open.

Sheriff Dowdy stood there, panting with his face red and eyes wide with anger. I panicked for a moment, unsure of what to do. Was he there because I was in danger, and he came to protect me? Or was he the one about to put me in danger?

"You stupid bitch," he snarled, lunging forward as I took several steps back, my butt hitting the edge of the kitchen table as Justice growled and barked furiously.

I had no idea if she had any training while she lived with that dickhead, but she was rather obedient, to say the least. I tried moving out of his way, but his hands were wrapped around my throat before I could get away.

"You think you can just go around murdering my guys and get away with it?" he growled, his grip tightening around my neck.

"Not all of them. Just the ones who deserved it," I replied, trying to talk past the tightness in my throat as I lifted my hands and tried to pull his away.

A soft noise caught my attention at the door, and I looked up to find Nancy standing there with a phone pointed at us. She lifted her finger to her lips, indicating to be quiet while she desperately looked around for something to use to help me. Unfortunately, there wasn't a lot in the kitchen where she was standing, and I didn't want to risk him seeing her by having her come inside to help me.

"You have no idea what you're talking about."

"I think I do. You're not the only crooked cop in town," I bit out, trying to keep from passing out. Thankfully, my words were enough to get him to let go of my throat right before he backhanded me, sending me stumbling back.

"What's the matter? You don't like hearing the truth?" I pressed, letting Justice stand in front of me as I scurried behind the chair and table, putting distance between me and

Sheriff Dowdy. Nancy lingered in the darkness, staying out of sight as she continued recording.

I recognized the worried look on her face and knew that she was concerned about me, but I also knew how important it was for everyone in Oak Creek to be informed about what was happening. Even if I had to die to reveal the truth, at least I could leave this world knowing that everyone knew what really happened and what kind of monster Sheriff Dowdy truly was.

"Did you really think that you could get away with everything?" I asked, cocking my head to stare at him as I debated when to pull my gun out. I didn't want him to know that I was armed just yet. Plus, I needed a few minutes to catch my breath.

"Do you honestly believe the people of Oak Creek don't know the truth? You were the one who was supposed to help us get justice, and instead, you helped the cartel by getting rid of evidence. And the funny thing is that it wasn't just you. We had a whole town full of crooked people who would rather line their pockets with dirty money from the cartel than do the right thing and protect us," I continued, hoping to make him angry enough to attack me again. That way, it would feel more justified that I killed him.

"The problem is that you're going around town acting like some vigilante, but I know the real you, Sloane. I know the weak, scared little girl who never could stand up for herself. I have to admit, it's been fun watching you pretend to be something you're not, but that's over now."

"Is it?" I asked, pulling my gun out and aiming it at his head. "Because I don't feel all that weak. It's actually quite empowering and liberating to step in and do the job *you* couldn't do. I guess maybe the tables have turned, and you're the weak one now. Is that it? You weren't strong or brave enough to stand up to the cartel and tell them no?"

His nostrils flared as he looked between me and the gun still aimed at him.

"How about I make you a deal? You tell all of the people of Oak Creek the truth, and I'll make your death quick and painless. How's that?"

Okay, so much for playing this off as self-defense…

I glanced at Nancy, making sure Sheriff Dowdy didn't notice. She locked eyes with me and mouthed the word *live* as a soft smile graced her lips. I knew it wouldn't be long before whatever was left of the local law enforcement showed up to put a stop to this. I was holding the Sheriff at gunpoint, though he technically started it by showing up there to kill me.

"You're a stupid, delusional bitch if you think this is going to end with anything other than *your* body in a bag."

"Well, then, call me delusional, I guess." I shrugged my shoulders and pressed my lips into a thin line. "But at least do me one favor before you *kill* me."

"Why would I do any favors for you?"

"Because you're responsible for the deaths of everyone who was murdered that night. You failed to do your job, just like Judge Curry failed to do his. You say that you take pride in protecting and serving the community of Oak Creek, so turn around and tell them why you failed them when it mattered the most."

I pointed as Nancy stepped out of the shadows and lifted the phone higher.

"This is being broadcast live from Officer Butchkin's phone," Nancy said smugly. "The phone that *your* officers failed to collect at the crime scene. The phone where there were albums of child pornography stored, along with a list of websites frequently visited. Smile and say hi to the people of Oak Creek, Sheriff Dowdy."

I watched carefully as Sheriff Dowdy's hands clenched at his sides, balling into fists.

"There's nothing to see here. Turn that off right now," he commanded.

"I'm sorry, but I can't do that. You see, too much has been brushed under the rug, and I can't stand by and watch it happen. Because of you, both of my sons have been murdered. I have lost everything I love in this world because you failed to protect our town." Nancy stepped closer, making sure the light captured Sheriff Dowdy so no one could deny it was him.

Then everything changed in an instant as two men dressed in all black with face coverings rushed in with their guns drawn. Before I could say or do anything, one tackled Nancy to the ground as the other fired a shot. Pain exploded through my body as I fell to the floor.

Worst Nightmare

Everett

"NOOOO!" I screamed, gripping my hair as I watched the TV where a live video was being broadcast on the Oak Creek news. It had come on a few minutes ago, and I stared in horror as Sheriff Dowdy attacked Sloane at home.

My mother revealed she was the one who had the phone, and before I could process what happened, two officers rushed into the house. The phone was jostled, distorting the image right after a gunshot was fired, and Sloane's body fell to the ground. The video ended right after that, leaving me and everyone else who had been watching speechless. I had no idea whether my mother was okay or if Sloane was alive.

I had been hanging out at The Vine all day since it was where I did my best thinking and had papers spread out on the table. Noah said he didn't mind at all and to make myself at home. It was nice having real food for once, and I took advantage of the delicious meals they served for lunch and dinner while I was there. But now the place was packed with college kids pausing from throwing back shots to stare at the TV in disbelief.

The newswoman was visibly shaken as she tried to compose herself, but failed.

"I'm sorry," she said before she stood up and walked off camera, leaving her colleague to fill the silence.

"We'll be back as soon as we have more information," he said solemnly before lowering his head. "For now, we'll return to our regularly scheduled programming."

I covered my mouth and sat down as my phone immediately began ringing. I knew it had to be one of three people calling me because no one had this phone number since I couldn't use my other one anymore.

"Hey," I breathed into the phone, the shock still stunning me.

"What's wrong?" Trevor asked, his tone immediately concerned.

"They got Sloane."

My mind was spinning as I tried to figure out what to say, but failed to get more words out.

"What the fuck are you talking about? Who got Sloane? Is she okay?"

"I—I don't know. I—umm.. There was a live video. My mom took it. I don't even know why my mom was there. How did she get that phone? Did she know Sloane was in trouble? Why did she go there and put herself in danger? It's Sloane and my mom. I don't know if they're ok—"

"Everett," Trevor said softly, trying to get me to focus on the information he needed.

"Right. Umm, from what I saw, Sheriff Dowdy went to Sloane's house and attacked her. Someone barged in, and I couldn't see who it was. There was a gunshot, and then it showed Sloane's body falling to the floor before it cut out."

"Fuck. Everett, I'm—"

"Don't say it."

"What do you need?" Trevor asked.

"Nothing."

"Why don't I like the sound of that?"

"Because you know me too well?" I offered as I quickly gathered my stuff and tossed some money on the table for what I owed.

"You can't do anything stupid," he warned. "Tell me what you need, and Roman and I will be there as soon as we can. He's checking flights out as we speak."

"Find my mother and keep her safe."

"Consider it done. What else do you need?"

"Nothing. I'll handle the rest."

"What does that mean?"

"It means I'm going to do what Sloane would have done," I answered matter-of-factly as fire raged through my body. "I'm getting revenge."

I disconnected the call before he could object and shoved my phone into my pocket before rushing out into the brisk evening air.

Broken

Nowhere
Sloane

I groaned as my eyes fluttered open and I looked around, trying to figure out where I was. The last thing I remembered was being shot, but this didn't look like a hospital. A woman stood beside me, her eyes quickly scanning my face as she turned to a monitor that started beeping.

"Can you tell me your name?" she asked.

"Not until you tell me where I am," I responded, my voice scratchy as I struggled to sit up.

She gently reached out and pressed me back against the bed to keep me from moving as the blood pressure cuff wrapped around my arm started to squeeze it tightly.

"Nowhere," she answered, her eyes focused on whatever was displayed on the monitor that wouldn't stop beeping.

"Original." I sighed. "Can you please just tell me where the hell I am? I get it—the cartel finally got me. Hooray. Just tell me where this hellhole is located."

She stopped and turned to face me, her expression serious.

"You're not with the cartel. They didn't get you. You're in a very small town called Nowhere, Colorado. A friend brought you here a few hours ago. You were shot, but so far, it looks like the bullet glanced off your clavicle and exited the skin at the top of your shoulder."

"I'm sorry—who is the friend that brought me here?" I asked, more worried about who it was than what damage had been done to my body.

"Me," Keith said, stepping into what appeared to be a bedroom.

"Get him the fuck away from me," I grit out, pulling away as he approached the other side of my bed. "He's not my friend."

"I'm not the bad guy, Sloane," he replied softly as he pulled out a chair and sat beside me. "I know you don't trust me, and that's fine. But I need you to believe me. I'm not here to hurt you."

"Are you the one who shot me?" I asked coldly.

"Yes."

"Well, I hate to break it to you, but your aim fucking sucks."

The woman standing on the other side of me snorted as she pushed a few buttons to silence the monitors.

"Actually, my aim was spot on. If I had aimed even half a centimeter south, you might not be alive to talk with me."

"You. Fucking. Shot. Me. On. Purpose," I bit out, making sure each word was enunciated.

"I did it to save your life. If I hadn't shot you, someone else was about to."

"Is that so?"

He nodded, looking down at the floor.

"Are you part of them?" I asked, knowing he knew exactly who I was referring to when he refused to answer. "Are you part of the Lagrimas Rojas cartel?"

"No."

"So you're just a crooked FBI agent?" I pressed, not worried at all about the random woman who was listening to all of this. It wasn't like we were even in a legit hospital. It was apparent that wherever he took me was used to handling stuff like this with no questions asked. Hell, they probably didn't even file insurance claims or keep any record that I was here. I would just bribe them with some money, and they would forget they had ever met me.

"You'll have answers soon enough," he said dismissively as he stood up and looked at the nurse standing beside me. "She doesn't get released to anyone but me. Is that understood?"

"You got it."

"I'll be back in a few days. Rest and do as you're told."

He didn't bother to say goodbye as he walked out of the room and left us alone.

"So, you will need to stay for a few days so we can monitor you," the nurse said, giving me a sympathetic smile. "Like I was saying before, the bullet grazed your clavicle, but the entry and exit wounds appear to be just under the skin. We'll need to do an X-ray to ensure the clavicle isn't broken. Doctor Foster will be in soon to go over those results."

"If the bullet didn't do major damage, why did I lose consciousness?" I asked, hating how sore my throat was from nearly being strangled earlier.

"We can do some tests and run some labs to try to get an answer, but sometimes it's simply just the body's way of protecting itself. Given the bruises on your throat, I would venture to say that your body was already stressed and that it responded accordingly."

I nodded, stopping immediately when I felt the pain.

"Try to rest. In the meantime, can I get you anything?"

"Do you have a get-out-of-jail-free card?" I asked, wincing when I tried to move.

It wasn't the first time I had been shot, but it still hurt like a bitch.

"Go fish," she replied with a laugh. "I'll grab you some pain meds, and then Dr. Foster should be in soon."

"Is this your house?"

"No. It's a clinic that takes care of those who need help along with some *discretion*."

"I thought places like this only existed in the movies."

"Unfortunately, the bad guys tend to be worse in real life than they are in the movies," she replied softly. "I'll be back with those pain meds."

I nodded and closed my eyes as she walked out of the room and closed the door behind her. I had no idea whether anything she said was true, but she seemed nice enough. But given that Keith was the one who brought me here, I didn't trust anything. Not only had he shot me, but he was responsible for the guys who nearly killed Everett when they went looking for me the first time. Either way, I wasn't going to stick around and see what he was up to.

Retaliation

Everett

I sat outside, across the street from Sheriff Dowdy's house as I waited for the crowd of people to give up and leave. It had been an active scene for a few hours with everyone in town joining together to demand answers after they watched what happened live.

I got back to Oak Creek an hour ago, having driven like a madman, determined to find my mother and Sloane. I knew the chances of finding either were slim, but I also knew I couldn't risk being seen by anyone in town if I was supposed to stay dead. That didn't help anything because without both of them, I wanted to be dead. Life wasn't worth living without them.

Trevor had texted me a few minutes ago, letting me know that he and Roman had landed in Denver and would make their way to Oak Creek as soon as possible. Quinn stayed behind to handle some stuff she was working on, but it didn't matter at this point. The only thing I was focused on was getting my hands on the man who put his on Sloane. I didn't give a flying fuck that he was law enforcement because there was no way he would live to tell anyone what happened to him or who did it.

I took a deep breath and let it out slowly as I shifted against the tree I was leaning on. I was dressed in all black, which helped me blend in with the shadows of the night as I pulled the hoodie lower over my head. I didn't need anyone else to see and recognize me, but I wanted to make sure that Sheriff Dowdy knew it was me who took his life. I wasn't a violent person, but losing Sloane sent me over an edge I never knew existed. When Quinn tried to tell me that Sloane wasn't just grieving, that she was broken from losing everyone she loved, I didn't get it. But I sure as fuck understood it now because nothing in the world could ever heal the giant hole that ripped out my heart the second I saw her get shot.

A few hours passed before people gave up and went home. I knew it wouldn't be long before they came back, demanding answers from the man they had expected to protect them from stuff like this happening in their town. But for now, I had a small window, and I was going to make the most of it. I got up and crossed the street, making sure I stayed as hidden as possible. Honestly, at this point, I didn't care if anyone spotted me. If Sloane was dead, so was I.

I was almost across the street when I heard something and looked over my shoulder to see a dog running at me.

"Justice?" I asked, bending down to see her as she whimpered, spots of red covering her gray fur. "I know, sweet girl. I know. Don't you worry, I'm going to make him pay for what he did to her. You go home where it's safe."

I paused for a moment, not knowing whether Sloane's house was even considered safe at this point. I hadn't gone by there yet because I was blinded by rage as I drove straight from Haven Brook back to Oak Creek. Not only that, but I couldn't risk being seen there if it had turned into a crime scene.

"Come on, girl. We can't let anyone see us," I said, patting my leg for her to follow me when it was evident she wasn't going anywhere without me.

Justice was a well-trained dog, keeping in step with me and stopping whenever I stopped. I didn't know whether Sloane was responsible for this or if she had been trained by whoever had her before, but either way, it was impressive.

We walked around to the back of the house, and I crouched down as I peeked in the window, then put on the pair of gloves I had tucked in my pocket. Standing at the kitchen sink, he held a phone to his ear and shook his head. I walked around to the back door, relieved that it was unlocked. People in small towns were so trusting that they never bothered to lock their doors.

I stepped inside quietly, holding my hand down by my side to stop Justice from coming inside with me. I didn't want anything to give it away that I was there until I was ready.

"I told you that I don't fucking know where she's at," he growled into the phone. "No. They were dressed in black and had face coverings. I don't know who they were."

His head tipped forward as he sighed heavily, listening to whoever was on the other line.

"If you want to fix this, then be my guest. I went there to kill her, just like you said."

My jaw tightened as I listened, wondering who the fuck he was talking to. It was obvious that their conversation was about Sloane, which only pissed me off more.

"Thanks to that bitch doing a live video, I can't leave my house for a while. The whole town has shown up, demanding my head on a platter. If you want her dead, then you're going to have to do it yourself."

Justice whimpered softly and then laid down on the floor mat outside the door beside my feet. I needed to check her and make sure she wasn't injured, but now wasn't the time or place for it.

"I don't fucking know! If your guys can't find her, then hire someone who can because I can guarantee she isn't dead. Whoever shot her took her somewhere instead of finishing the job there. And since she murdered all of the guys that I trusted, I have no way of getting that information right now. So maybe you should have your guys figure out where she's at and finish this before it's too late."

I shook my head as I tried to calm myself before I did something stupid. I needed whatever information I could get about Sloane right now. If it was true that she wasn't dead, then I needed to find her before they did.

"Her parents' house. That's where she always goes," Sheriff Dowdy answered before looking at his phone and shaking his head. "Fucking bastard hung up on me."

His words came out mumbled, and then I noticed the open bottle of whiskey sitting on the counter beside him. He picked up the glass and threw the liquid back before rolling his shoulders and turning around.

My eyes locked with his the second he saw me standing there. Justice stood up, her posture changing as she let out a low snarl. I put my hand down at my side again and she stopped, sitting beside me.

He narrowed his eyes and squinted, making sure he was seeing me correctly.

"Everett? Is that you?"

I pushed the hoodie off my head and glared at him. My jaw clenched as I waited for him to make a move.

"I thought you were…"

"Dead?" I offered, tilting my head to the side as he studied me. "Yeah. Not so much."

"But…"

"You know, while I would love to stand here and get caught up on what really happened, I'm kind of in a hurry," I said, dismissing him as I nudged Justice inside and closed the door. "You see, you decided to put your hands on the woman I love, so now I'm here to make you pay for that."

"You need to get the fuck out of my house," he bellowed, making Justice growl beside me.

Sloane had mentioned she didn't know how the dog would react to men, so it was interesting to see how she was acting toward Sheriff Dowdy the moment he raised his voice. I arched an eyebrow and watched as Justice lowered her body into a stance ready to attack.

"Good girl," I said, ignoring my instinct to bend down and pet her head. I could tell she was in the zone, and I didn't want to be on the receiving end of what she was about to serve.

Sheriff Dowdy turned suddenly, reaching for the gun that was sitting on the counter.

"Justice, attack," I commanded, not having any clue whether she knew the command or not. Maybe it was the tone in my voice, or simply because she didn't like the man, but she listened.

Before he could reach it, she leaped up and bit his arm, shaking her head violently as her jaw clenched around him. He yelled out in pain and dropped to his knees as she held his arm between her teeth, growling as he stared at her with fear in his eyes.

I stood mesmerized by the dog for a few seconds before I noticed the power tools sitting on the kitchen table. It was as if our dear Sheriff didn't trust the people of Oak Creek not to break into his house and had begun securing the windows in the living room. There was a piece of wood that looked like it would fit the kitchen window I found him standing in front of when I came in.

"Justice, release," I said in my most authoritative voice, grinning when she did as I said.

She returned to my side and sat down, licking her lips as if to savor the taste of his blood on them.

"Good girl." I scratched the top of her head before picking up the duffle bag of tools and looking through it.

"Sit," I commanded, nodding to the chair as Sheriff Dowdy stood up and held his arm, trying to stop the blood that was pooling on the floor beneath him. Justice watched every single drop as it fell, her eyes fixated on it.

"Lie down," I directed her, pointing to a spot off to the side where I wouldn't trip over her.

She gave me one look and then did as I asked. I now understood why Sloane loved her so much. She was a damn good dog and incredibly obedient.

Sheriff Dowdy continued to stare at me as he refused to sit down, likely thinking he still stood a chance at walking away from this encounter with me. I rolled my eyes and set the bag back down on the table as I took a few steps toward him, dragging the chair with me. A flicker of worry flashed in his eyes as I grabbed him by the back of the neck and shoved him down into the seat, making sure he was situated before slamming his head into the wooden table.

"Fuck!" he growled, trying to pull away from my grip, which only made me angrier.

"Do as I fucking say," I warned, grabbing the rope that I saw lying at the bottom of the bag. It wasn't much, but it would work for what I needed it for.

He glared at me as he wobbled a teeny bit on the chair, likely disoriented from losing so much blood and getting his head banged on the hard surface. I didn't plan to keep him alive long—just long enough to get the answers I wanted out of him. I made quick work of binding both of his hands to the arms of the chair and then stepped back to admire my work. It wasn't perfect, but it would do.

"You're making a big fucking mistake," he said, spitting out a mouthful of blood as I stepped out of the way just in time.

"No, *you're* the one who made the big fucking mistake by putting your hands on Sloane. It was bad enough that you let this entire town down by working for the cartel, but where you really fucked up was when you tried to attack the woman I love."

"She doesn't love you. If she did, she wouldn't risk her life by trying to go after people who want her dead."

"That's where you're wrong."

I turned my attention from him now that he was restrained and looked through the bag to see what I wanted to use first. I pulled out a nail gun, turning it to admire it while I watched him squirm, loving that there was nothing he could do.

"The only thing I was wrong about was leaving Sloane here to take care of herself. I should have stayed and protected her and my mother," I said, more to myself than to him. "And speaking of Sloane, where is she?"

"I have no fucking idea, nor do I care. She's as good as dead, and that's fine with me." He looked me in the eye as he laughed.

My nostrils flared as anger coursed through me. I lifted the nail gun and aimed it at his stomach, grinning when he screamed out in pain as a nail pierced through his skin.

"Try. Again." I cocked my head to the side and stared at him as I held the nail gun steady in my hand. While I could technically grab the gun sitting on the kitchen counter and use it, this was more fun.

"I don't know where she is. I've already said that."

I let out a heavy sigh and lowered my head before I looked up and caught his eye as another nail went flying into his thigh.

"You mother fucker," he growled.

"Fine. Then tell me who took her."

"Again—I don't know. I wasn't expecting anyone, and they had black ski masks over their face to hide their identity," he said, this time without the disdain in his voice.

"Who were you talking to when I got here?" I asked, trying to figure out how to get the information I really needed. I could only make him talk so much, but part of that involved asking the right questions and hoping he would slip up and tell me something useful.

"None of your fucking business."

I arched an eyebrow in warning, which did nothing as he spat another mouthful of blood at me.

"Wrong answer." I moved my aim higher, this time piercing his shoulder.

His head flew back as his hands gripped the arms of the chair as he cursed under his breath.

"I can do this all day," I said, my voice light and airy as if I didn't give a fuck. "You're only making this harder on yourself."

"We both know that you're not leaving here and letting me live, so why the fuck would I tell you anything? Just kill me and be done with it."

"Why would you think that?" I asked, holding my hand over my chest in mock surprise. "Unlike you, I'm not a killer, Sheriff Dowdy."

He scoffed and looked away as my patience started to get thin. I needed whatever information I could get to help me find my mom and Sloane, and this dickhead was purposely wasting my time.

"I'm going to ask you again—who were you talking to when I came in?"

"Fuck. You."

I shook my head in frustration before lifting my hand and firing three nails into his crotch. His face turned beet red as he pulled against the rope, trying to free himself as a red stain immediately started spreading across his jeans.

"Jesus fucking chr—"

"Who. Were. You. Talking. To." I squatted down to look him in the eye as sweat dotted his brow.

"The person who is going to kill Sloane, and if you're lucky, he'll let you watch before he finishes you and your mother. Count your hours, Everett. This time, you won't be faking your death."

I knew it was pointless to keep this going since it was obvious he wasn't going to tell me anything useful. His phone began ringing on the counter, so I walked over and grabbed it.

"Answer it," I demanded, holding it in front of his face so the screen would unlock. Once it was unlocked, I slid my finger across the button to answer the call, but it didn't work with the gloves on. I lowered the phone to where his hand was bound and gripped his finger as I slid it across the screen.

"We found her," a deep voice said as I put the call on speakerphone.

I glared at him and arched my eyebrow in warning as I waited for him to respond.

"Who?" he asked, squirming in his seat as the blood continued to soak through his jeans.

"The fucking bitch who recorded you, you dumbass."

"Find out where she is," I warned quietly, so only he could hear me as my heart raced at the thought of my mother being in danger again.

He gave me a dirty look and let out a heavy sigh.

"Good. Kill her and make sure no one finds her body."

My hand gripped the phone tightly as my blood pressure rose.

"Can't do that until they discharge her from the hospital."

"Make it happen. I don't care how, just get rid of her. Make it extra painful," Sheriff Dowdy said, staring into my soul as a new darkness rose over him.

"On it," the man said before hanging up the phone.

I pulled my glove off my hand and held it between my teeth while Sheriff Dowdy watched. I knew he wouldn't be alive much longer, so I needed to deal with things right away. This meant that I needed to change the security settings on his phone so I could unlock it later. It wouldn't matter if my fingerprints got all over it since I was planning to keep it anyway.

"What's your passcode?" I asked, knowing he wasn't likely going to give it to me.

He opened his mouth to talk back as he glowered at me, so I shot another nail into his dick. My eyebrow rose as I waited for him to make a better choice.

"4485," he growled.

I smiled, pleased that he actually did what I asked this time. I worked quickly, turning off any features that would prevent me from accessing his phone later, then tucked it into my pocket.

"I'll ask you one last time, where is Sloane?" I said, leaning down to study him as I pulled the glove back on and adjusted the nail gun in my hand. I now knew my mother was in the hospital, so I trusted they would keep her safe until I could get there.

"On her way to join her husband and baby," he replied, his body starting to give up on him.

My blood boiled as fury raged through me.

"Sorry. That's the wrong fucking answer," I snarled as I slammed the butt of the nail gun into the side of his face before aiming it between his eyes and shooting. I watched as his head immediately fell forward. Just for good measure, I shot two into his heart, four into his stomach, and another one in his dick just because he deserved it.

I couldn't leave there not knowing whether he was dead or not, especially since I couldn't risk him surviving and telling anyone that I was the one who did this. So, I stood behind him, grabbed his head in both hands, then snapped his neck. As soon as I let go, his head immediately fell forward.

"Let's get out of here, Justice," I said to the sweet dog that just lay there and didn't seem the least bit bothered by what had just happened. I put the gun back in the bag and was getting ready to head out the door when my phone rang.

I pulled the glove off again and swiped to answer Trevor's call.

"Hey, we're here," he said. "Where are you?"

"I just finished taking care of something and am heading out. My mom's in a hospital, but I'm not sure which one. It might be the one here in Oak Creek, or they might have taken her to one of the ones in a nearby town."

"We'll split up and find her. Stay low, and don't do anything I wouldn't do," Trevor warned.

"Noted."

I hung up and put my phone away as Justice and I slid out the back door and walked away as if nothing had happened.

Escape
Sloane

I waited until after the doctor came to do my X-ray before I planned my escape. I didn't want to hurt the nurse, Jo, who had been so kind to me, but I also couldn't stay there and wait for Keith to show up. I didn't want to risk their lives by getting them involved in anything, so it was better to leave as quietly and quickly as possible.

Once they thought I was asleep, they left the room and closed the door behind them. I knew the pain would continue to bother me after the stuff they gave me wore off, but I couldn't focus on that right now. I needed to get moving before anyone tried to stop me.

I finished removing the IV from my arm and tucked everything away as neatly as possible, then searched the room and found a bag containing my personal belongings. I pulled off the gown I was wearing and got dressed, wincing when the motion of pulling my shirt over my head hurt like hell.

I was just about done and looking for a way out when the door opened.

Jo stood there, smiling at me with her arms folded over her chest as if she expected this.

"They're going to kill me," I said softly, hoping she understood. I had seen a gnarly scar on her neck earlier, so I imagined she knew a thing or two about running for your life, given that she had worked out of a house that was really a clinic.

"There's a black sedan outside that you can take. There's some emergency cash in the glovebox if you need it. Don't speed because you will get pulled over. But try to get out of here as quickly as you can because I can only hold Keith off for so long," she replied with a heavy sigh.

"Do you know him?" I asked as I slipped my shoes on.

She nodded but didn't say anything.

I didn't bother asking her anything else because I didn't have the time to spare. I needed to move quickly, and we both knew that.

"Thank you for everything," I said, offering her a smile as I slipped past her and stepped into a hallway I didn't recognize.

"Go out the back door. The car is already ready, and the keys are on the seat. It's unlocked."

"Thank you. I will find a way to get it back to you," I promised, knowing that I would have to deal with that later if I survived.

"I'll be fine without it. Now go. Before it's too late."
She nodded to the end of the hallway, where there was a wooden door.

I rushed toward it, unlocking it and looking back at her one last time, but she was already gone. I unlocked the metal security door and slipped outside, making sure to shut it quietly behind me. I knew that she would eventually come and lock it, so I didn't have to worry about that right now.

I looked around as I quickly made my way to the car and climbed inside. A wave of relief rushed over me as I picked up the keys and got the hell out of there.

****

By the time I made it back to Oak Creek, it was just before dawn as the light threatened to shine on a new day. It had been two days since Sheriff Dowdy had attacked me, and I had no idea what had happened to Nancy. It wasn't like I could reach out to anyone and check in on her without risking my safety or hers.

I pulled off on the side of the road a few miles away from my parents' house and turned off the car. I opened the glove box and pulled out the cash Jo had mentioned, not wanting to leave it there just in case I never came back for the car. It was a quiet part of town with thick forest and nothing around for miles. I tucked the cash into my pocket and climbed out of the car, taking the keys with me.

Birds chirped around me as leaves and sticks crunched beneath my feet. I kept an eye out for anyone who might be lurking in the shadows, waiting for me to return. I hated not knowing what had happened after I left because I had no idea what to expect when I got to the house. It was possible that the entire thing was now a crime scene, and I wouldn't be allowed to go back inside.

I worried about Justice and what had happened to her. She was such a good dog, and I hated that I wasn't there to take care of her. I prayed that she got out and found somewhere safe to go so she didn't end up in a shelter or killed. I would never forgive myself if anything bad were to happen to her. I hadn't had her long, but she had wrapped herself so tightly around my heart that I couldn't imagine a world without her.

The house finally came into view as I walked through the woods behind it, taking a moment to pause at the garage as I scanned the area. Nothing looked amiss, and I was surprised nothing was taped off, given that I had been attacked just a few days ago. Maybe they only did that when someone was murdered. But for all everyone knew, I might have been.

Since I was treated at a clinic outside of town that made no note of seeing me, there was no record that I had been treated at another hospital either. For all anyone knew, I had been murdered, and my body was left somewhere to rot. I could head into town and make sure everyone knew I was okay, but not knowing where Sheriff Dowdy was or how deep his connection to the cartel went made me strongly reconsider.

I walked slowly to the back door and pushed it open, waiting to see if there was anyone inside. I stepped in and quietly closed the door behind me. I took in the chairs that were tipped over and a new blood stain that hadn't been on the floor before. It was close to where Nancy had been standing once she made herself seen, and my stomach soured.

If Nancy were dead because of me, I would never forgive myself.

I took a few more steps, not hearing anyone in the house, and let out a heavy sigh of relief. It didn't look like things had been messed with, and thankfully, there didn't appear to be an ongoing crime scene for me to worry about. I figured most of the residents of Oak Creek were more concerned with getting answers from their beloved Sheriff, which was fine by me. I needed time to reset and figure out a new plan of action. I knew it wouldn't be long until they found me, so I needed to make sure I was ready this time.

I walked out of the kitchen and stepped into the hallway, right as a hand wrapped tightly around my throat. I gasped as my eyes widened with fear as I stared into the coldest, most evil eyes I had ever seen. His lips curled up into a devious smile as the black widow tattoo on his face crinkled.

"Hello, Sloane," he said as his grip around my throat tightened. "I've been waiting for you."

~~Juan Rodriguez (AKA Black Widow Tattoo)~~

Sloane

"You've been causing me a lot of trouble," he continued, holding me in the air as if I were a rag doll.

He sighed heavily and then dropped me, allowing me to fall to the floor as I scrambled away and sucked in as much air as I could. What was the fucking deal with everyone trying to choke me? He stood there with his hands held in front of him as he watched me intently.

"While I was waiting, I decided to take a look around. Imagine my surprise when I found a note in your bedroom with a list of names on it—including mine. Now, I can't tell you how delighted I was when I saw the ones you had already marked off. I gotta admit, it was a turn-on to see someone as frail as yourself handle some of the men you took down on that list," he said, squatting in front of me.

He watched me with a curiosity that spread goosebumps along my skin, knowing that I was staring in the face of pure evil.

"Every single person on that list deserved what they got," I said, my words sharp and laced with venom.

"Perhaps you're right. But I'm intrigued to see what you have planned for me. I couldn't help but notice that I was one of the last ones you hadn't gotten to yet. Maybe you were saving the best for last?" he teased, though I knew there was nothing playful in his tone.

"Or perhaps I wanted you to be afraid of what was coming for you, given what I had done to the others."

As if sensing a warning in my statement, he stood up and gave me an ice-cold glare before turning and kicking me in the stomach. Instinctively, I bent over, holding myself as he kicked again, this time hitting my back.

I knew I had to get up and fight him off, or I would be the first to die. A memory of Gabe holding Nicky flashed through my mind, giving me the strength to get up and finish what I started. I stumbled back a bit as I tried to get my balance as I held onto the banister.

He hadn't bothered to pat me down when he first attacked me, which meant he assumed I wasn't armed. But little did he know, I had found my gun in the bag of belongings at the clinic and it was tucked into the back of my jeans.

I pretended I was still trying to stand upright when he lunged for me. I darted out of the way, spinning around the staircase as he fell into the banister. I pulled the gun out and shot him in the knee, knowing it would slow him down but not stop him.

"You stupid, fucking bitch," he cursed, falling to the ground as he held his kneecap, trying to apply pressure as blood poured out of it.

"You should really stop underestimating me," I said, though my body was on the verge of quitting on me again. I was exhausted and in pain, which wasn't a good combination right now.

"You're dead," he warned, trying to turn to the side as his hand reached behind him.

"I don't fucking think so." I fired another shot, this time shooting him in the arm as he fell back, landing face up as he glared at me.

I knew he could still hurt me if he wanted to, but with two gunshot wounds actively bleeding right now, I knew he was going to be fading fast. I rolled him over, pulling the gun from his jeans before pushing him back down. I turned and set it on the kitchen table, knowing he wouldn't be able to get to it.

"You know, I had all of this planned differently in my head," I growled as I tried to move him, but he was too heavy. "I really hate when people fuck up my plans."

He didn't say anything, which was disappointing because I kinda liked hearing how pissed off he was at me.

"I guess now is better than never," I mumbled, kicking him in the ribs before walking into the kitchen to get what I needed.

I grabbed the boxes of the black widow spiders and put them into the larger box I had used to bring them home. Thankfully, he was still alive and lying in the same position

I had left him in a few minutes ago. While he should be weak, given his injuries, I didn't trust anything right now, and the last thing I needed was to chase him through the house and risk slipping on his blood.

I sat down on the floor beside him, making sure to keep my gun accessible if I needed it, but out of his reach.

"Do you know what these are?" I asked as I picked up two of the clear boxes and held them above him.

The spiders moved quickly, likely agitated from not having food for a few days. They could see each other and began trying to climb the sides of the container to reach the other.

"These are black widow spiders," I explained, holding one right over his face for him to see. "Just like the one tattooed on your face. Only these ones are a lot meaner than that one."

I set one of the boxes down while I opened the other one, praying the spider didn't run at me and bite me first. Insects didn't usually freak me out, but spiders were a totally different story. Once the top was open, I tilted the box and waited for the spider to slide out.

His eyes widened as it landed on his face, immediately going toward his mouth. He pinched it shut as his hands came flying up to try to swat it away.

"We can't have that," I said with a heavy sigh as I got up and went to the kitchen, bringing two steak knives back with me.

Pure terror flashed in his eyes as I held his hand flat against the floor and stabbed the knife into it, pinning it there. Then I walked around to the other side and did the same.

"There. Now you can't move even if you wanted to." I sat down and smiled as the spider walked across his neck and down toward the blood that was puddling on the floor from the gunshot to his shoulder.

"You're a crazy bitch," he spit out, fear taking over his features again as I opened another box and dropped that spider onto his chest.

"I didn't use to be. Then one day, some asshole decided to murder my family right in front of me, and things just changed." I shrugged nonchalantly as I opened another spider box and dropped that one right on top of his shoulder.

They didn't rush into biting like I had hoped they would, which left me feeling frustrated. They were hungry, and the girl at the pet shop said they were cannibalistic, so I was surprised they weren't trying to eat each other yet.

"Your husband knew what he did," he snarled. "He got what he deserved."

Anger ripped through me as I stared at him, opening the next box and holding it above his head.

"Say that again," I demanded.

As soon as he opened his mouth, I dropped the spider inside. Since he was lying down, there was no way for him to force it back out as he gagged, and tears filled his eyes. I grabbed another box and dumped a second spider into his mouth before he could shut it.

I looked down, noticing that the spiders weren't really doing anything other than walking around and likely looking for a safe space to call home. I went to the kitchen, grabbed a clear container, and then opened the rest of the boxes, releasing the spiders onto his stomach.

While his body froze in front of me, I put the clear container over the spiders and moved it until I had captured all of them, minus the ones in his mouth. Then I shook the container, aggravating them until I heard him hiss. I knew they must have started biting by the way he squirmed beneath the container.

"The itsy bitsy spiders crawled all over your body," I sang, my voice filled with happiness. "One bit your stomach and they all fought for more."

I waited a few minutes, watching as the spiders continued to move, trying to get away. I pushed the container again, making sure I got them all lined up before I got up and walked away. There was no way he could get the container off his body, nor could the spiders. Now, I just had to sit and wait for the venom to take effect.

I went into the kitchen and pulled out a bottle of water, chugging it as I tried to compose myself. The goal was to come home and rest—not come home and murder him in a sloppy manner. I wanted this one to be memorable, so I would always know that he paid for what he did to my family.

Fifteen minutes went by before I started to hear him scream in pain. I ignored it as I sat down at the table and tried to ignore the way my body ached. Just then, the back door opened, and I looked up to find Keith standing there, eyebrows pinched together.

His gaze quickly went from me to the man in the hallway, moaning and groaning. He walked past me, eyeing me suspiciously until he found who was making the sound.

"I'm too tired to kill you right now, but I will," I warned, looking at the gun sitting on the table as Keith stared at the man on the floor. His groans were getting softer, which I imagined meant he would soon be dead. There couldn't be that much left in him, given the loss of blood from the gunshot wounds.

"Well, that would be a shame, wouldn't it?" a man said as he stepped inside and clasped his hands in front of him.

I let out a gasp and covered my mouth as I stared at Gabe.

Answers

Sloane

"Did I die?" I mumbled, rubbing my eyes to make sure I wasn't hallucinating. When I opened them again, Gabe was sitting across from me while Keith spoke to someone on the phone.

Gabe shook his head, his eyes quickly scanning my face as if he were looking for something.

"How is this pos—" I stopped speaking as I quickly realized what was happening.

Gabe wasn't there because he was dead. But sitting in front of me was his twin brother, who had been responsible for Gabe's death when they mistook Gabe for him.

"You stupid, mother fucking, son of a bitch," I shouted as I jumped up from the chair and lunged across the table with my fist flying toward his face.

"Easy," Keith said as he wrapped his arm around my waist and spun me away from Hugo before I could punch him.

"The only thing that is going to be easy is putting a bullet through both of your heads," I growled, narrowing my eyes at Hugo as he sat calmly watching Keith try to wrangle me like a rabid raccoon. "My husband is dead because of YOU!"

Hugo nodded and pressed his lips together, keeping silent while I felt like I was going to crawl out of my skin.

"We have some things we need to talk about," Keith said firmly, still not releasing his hold on me. "Do you think you can calm down so we can discuss them in a civilized manner?"

I turned my head the best I could and glared at him.

"Like what? How you tried to murder your best friend? How you've been working with the cartel this whole time? What exactly do we need to talk about, other than you being as big of a piece of shit as this guy?" I nodded to Hugo, who now had a smirk playing on his lips.

"Do you think this is funny?" I asked, directing my anger back to him. "My family is dead because of you. My baby died because of you. Don't you dare sit there and smile like you think any of this is funny because it's not."

"I never said it was funny," Hugo said, straightening his back and pinning Keith with a look. "I just find it amusing how much shit you're giving Keith. It's not often I get to see someone go after him, and I have to admit, I kinda like it."

"So you guys are in on everything together? Are you part of the cartel or something?"

I pulled away from Keith, surprised when he let me go. I shot him a dirty look before I sat down at the table, rolling my eyes when he grabbed the gun and tucked it behind his back.

"No. We're not part of the Lagrimas Rojas cartel. We're DEA agents."

"Bullshit," I replied with disdain. "I'm sick and tired of the fucking lies."

Hugo reached into his pocket and pulled out a badge, laying it on the table in front of me. A few seconds later, Keith set his beside it.

"I swear to God if these are fake and you're lying to me…" I warned.

"I have nothing to lie to you about, Sloane. My brother is dead because of me, and that is a weight I carry every single day."

"Don't sit there and act like you know anything about the pain of losing him."

"I've spent my entire life knowing pain, Sloane. I grew up with a father who was heavily involved with a cartel. I watched him murder my mother after she stole drugs from him. I didn't have a normal childhood where I had friends and played with other kids. I was sent to a private school and shown little love. I didn't even know I had a twin until my grandmother told me when I was seven. She said that my mother got high at a park one day and came home with one baby instead of two. By the time my father found out, the baby was gone. He couldn't risk anyone looking into things at home, so he didn't bother trying to find him. From that day forward, Gabe was dead to my father while I spent my life making sure he never found him."

"I knew Gabe was adopted as a baby and had been found in a park, but I didn't know the rest of the story," I admitted quietly.

"I doubt that Gabe knew it either. I don't think he ever knew he was a twin. I made sure no one in our family looked for him so I could try to keep him safe. I didn't want him involved in our lifestyle. I wanted better for him. God gave him a second chance at life, and I wanted him to have it."

"Yet he was murdered because someone thought he was you," I said with a sniffle, my eyes burning as tears prickled them.

Hugo nodded and looked away for a moment.

"I didn't want to be part of the cartel. I couldn't stand what they did and hated my dad for murdering my mother in front of me. I wanted to stop him, but didn't know how. We got into a fight one day, and it escalated into a physical altercation. I knew he had been having some health issues, but I didn't know that I would deliver the blow that would kill him. He died within minutes."

Keith shuffled beside me as his fingers flew over the screen of his phone.

"They'll be here in thirty minutes," Keith said to Hugo.

I glanced at him nervously, already feeling on edge with someone else showing up.

"We have a crew who will come clean this up," Hugo explained. "I can't get into much detail, but Keith and I connected, and he offered me a new beginning. He would get me in with the DEA if I agreed to help take down the cartel that my father was working with. Word had already spread that I had killed my father, so we had a short window to work with. I accepted the offer and have been helping the DEA take down The Dark Rebels while posing as their leader."

"Let me guess, the Dark Rebels are rivals to the Lagrimas Rojas cartel?" I asked, looking between Keith and Hugo.

Hugo nodded.

"That's why they killed Gabe. They thought they were killing you," I replied softly, shaking my head as the tears ran down my cheeks.

"I spent my whole life trying to protect him, Sloane," Hugo said with emotion thick in his voice. "We had guys watching Gabe and your family in Colorado, but they killed them right before they killed Gabe that night. We didn't find out about it until it was too late."

"So what happens now?" I asked right as the door flew open, and Everett stormed inside with Justice right beside him.

His eyes wildly scanned the room, first making sure I was okay. He gave Hugo a confused look, then his features quickly changed to anger as he charged Keith and knocked him to the ground. Justice growled, holding her stance as if ready for a command.

"You fucking asshole," he gritted as he swung his arm back and punched Keith in the jaw.

"Everett! Stop!" I screamed, getting up to try to pull him off Keith.

Hugo got up and stepped between them, pulling Everett back and making sure he was steady on his feet before he extended a hand to help Keith.

"What the fuck is happening?" Everett said, his brow furrowed as he panted and looked around the room before his eyes went to the legs sticking out of the hallway.

"Everything is okay," I replied calmly, turning him so he didn't try to go look at the dead guy. I needed to check on the spiders to make sure they didn't get loose, but that could wait.

"Define *okay*," he snapped, running a hand down the side of my face as if checking to make sure I was really there.

"I'm okay. Keith isn't a crooked FBI agent. He actually works for—" I stopped for a moment, unsure whether I was allowed to tell Everett about him working for the DEA.

"DEA," Keith answered for me, nodding to their badges, which were still sitting on the table.

Everett continued to frown as he reached over and picked them up, studying them for a second while I pulled Justice close to me and scratched her head. I missed her so much and was thankful that she had been with Everett and not hurt or lost, roaming the streets.

"Are you fucking kidding me?" he growled, tossing Keith's at him.

I'd never seen Everett so furious. But heaven help me, he'd never been hotter!

"I couldn't tell you," Keith said with a shrug. "It would jeopardize everything we were doing."

"You almost had me killed," Everett snarled. "Did you forget about that? The quite literal knife in my back?"

"I had no choice. I was undercover, and we had to make it look legitimate. The one who stabbed you is a trained medic. He knew the likelihood of it being a fatal wound was slim."

"You're a fucking asshole," Everett bit back as Hugo and I watched them go back and forth.

"Keith and Hugo were working to take down the cartel his father was a part of," I explained to Everett. "Gabe wasn't supposed to be involved in any of it. The other cartel thought Gabe was Hugo, and that's why they killed him."

"And the guy in the hallway?" Everett asked, turning to face me as he tilted his head to the side.

"He's the guy with the black widow tattoo," I murmured, lowering my head as I said it. From the corner of my eye, I saw Justice inch toward him. Her body lowered, almost as if she were stalking her prey. Shit, I forgot about how much blood was on the floor, and now that she'd had a taste of it, I didn't know how she would react. The last thing I needed was for her to sit down and feast on him with a judgmental audience.

"Sloane, what did I say? I specifically asked you not to go around killing anyone else whi—"

"Shit!" I yelled, getting up and running the few feet to the hallway right as Justice tried to nudge the container of spiders off his chest. "No, girl. We can't eat this one."

"I'm sorry, what?" Keith said, stepping forward and pinning me with a look.

"It's just an expression," I lied, glaring at Everett for ratting me out about killing more than the guy I was trying to keep my dog from eating.

"The way I see it, it doesn't matter at this point," Hugo said, standing across from us with his arms folded over his chest.

"What do you mean?" Keith asked.

"Word around town is that Sloane died when Sheriff Dowdy shot her. We have a body that needs to be removed from this house. I say that we get this cleaned up and let people believe that it's Sloane."

"You want me to fake my death?" I asked in disbelief.

"Why not? Everett is dead as far as everyone is concerned," Keith said, giving his friend a look. "You can both be officially dead."

"Why? Are *you* going to kill us?" I deadpanned.

"No. However, I will assist with relocating both of you. Everyone deserves a second chance, and you've both proved that you have earned it. While I don't approve of your methods, Sloane, I can say that the death of Juan Rodriguez will be monumental in what we're doing with the cartels. You single-handedly took down one of the most dangerous men in the Lagrimas Rojas."

"While I would love to take credit for doing all of the hard work, he was already here waiting for me when I got home. I just fought back."

"That's because Sheriff Dowdy told him where you would be," Everett said, pulling a cell phone out of his pocket and handing it to Keith. "Here's his phone. There's plenty to link him to involvement with the cartel, but unfortunately, he won't be able to answer any questions."

"I'm not even going to ask," Keith replied with a shake of his head as he pocketed the phone. "Collect any personal belongings you want to take with you. We'll need to move quickly."

"What about the cartel? Won't they question where he is and what happened if you guys pretend his body is me?"

"We just need people around town to see us removing a body in a body bag from your house. That will confirm your death. Given how everything ended with Sheriff Dowdy attacking you and most of the local law enforcement being dead, we can play it off that you were fine but later succumbed to your injuries. As far as the cartel, we will make arrangements to retrieve the body from the morgue and deliver his head to the Lagrimas Rojas," Keith explained.

"You're going to deliver his *head*?" I asked in disbelief.

"As a show of force, yes," Hugo confirmed. "The Dark Rebels will take credit for the kill."

I frowned for a second, disappointed that no one would know what really happened or how I had made him suffer for what he did to my family.

"You can tell me all about it later," Everett whispered in my ear as he wrapped his arm around my waist. "We'll have plenty of time to get caught up now that you'll be stuck with me for the rest of our new lives."

I turned and faced him as I wrapped my arms around his neck.

"I can't wait." I pressed my lips to his, savoring the moment.

New Beginnings

Everett

I stood there, awkward tension filling the room as Keith and I waited for Sloane to collect any belongings she wanted from upstairs before we left Oak Creek forever.

"For what it's worth, I'm sorry," Keith said, shoving his hands in his pockets and staring at the floor.

"For which part? Trying to kill me? Lying to me?"

"All of it. I needed you to believe I was involved for the wrong reasons."

"Why?"

"Because you were getting too close to uncovering what was happening. We've worked on this operation for a long time, and I couldn't risk you blowing my cover. But please know that Sloane has always been my top concern. Her safety was as important to me as it was to you."

"Do you really expect me to believe that?"

"No. But I feel better knowing that you know the truth about everything."

I sighed heavily and tilted my head as I heard the floorboards squeaking above me as Sloane moved around.

Suddenly, my phone started ringing, and Trevor's name appeared on the screen. I swiped to answer it and held it to my ear.

"Hey, I found Sloane. She's alright," I said, hoping he had better news on my mother.

"That's great. I wish we could say the same. We searched every hospital and clinic around town, but no one has seen her. We've gone by her house several times, and she's not there."

"Fuck," I said, pinching the bridge of my nose and closing my eyes.

"What's wrong?" Keith asked.

"Not that it's any of your business, but we can't find my mom. No one has seen her since the night of the live video. Someone called Sheriff Dowdy saying that they found her and that she was in a hospital, but a friend of mine hasn't been able to locate her."

"Your mother is safe," Keith replied quickly. "She's with a friend of mine."

"And you're just now telling me?"

"There's been a lot happening since you barged in here and punched me in the face." He lifted his hands and shrugged his shoulders.

"Who the fuck did you punch in the face?" Trevor asked with a laugh.

"Keith."

"Keith is there with you?" he asked, his tone immediately changing.

"Yeah. He was at Sloane's house when I got here. It's a long story, but the asshole isn't a threat."

"We're on our way," Trevor replied before hanging up.

"Guess we're having more company soon," I muttered, putting my phone back in my pocket. "Where's my mom?"

"She's in a town called Nowhere with my friend."

"So your cartel guys found her in Nowhere?"

"No. I have a friend at the local hospital. She did me a favor and put your mother's information in the system so it would show she was there. We had one of our guys stay in the hospital room instead, so they were ready if anyone came for your mother."

"If you're lying to me, I will break your fucking jaw this time."

"I have no reason to lie to you." Keith checked his watch just as Hugo came back inside and smiled.

"Everything is ready," Hugo said, holding a manila envelope in his hand. "We need to get going. How much longer before she's ready?"

"About two seconds," Sloane answered as she walked into the kitchen. "Leave him alone, Justice."

I grinned at her, thankful that she really was okay.

"So, where are we going?" I asked, ready to get things going so I could stop worrying and just be with Sloane.

"I have a few friends who owed me a favor," Hugo said as he pulled out two passports and handed them to each of us. "These are your new identities. Accommodations are currently being set up for you in Ireland. While I wish I could send you somewhere luxurious, I owed it to my brother to keep you safe. What you do on your own time after that is up to you. But I will say that you are not allowed to return to the US under any circumstances. Do I make myself clear?"

Sloane nodded, though I saw tears welling in her eyes. I knew it was hard to start over, and for her, that's what she had been doing repeatedly since her family was murdered. But I would do everything in my power to make sure this time we were safe and that she stayed that way.

"I want to say goodbye to my mother," I said, my throat thick as emotion gripped me.

"We'll have a car take you to her," Keith said, giving Hugo a nod.

It was unclear what was being communicated between them, but Hugo pulled out his cell phone and made another call.

"It's time to go," Keith said softly.

"What about Justice?" Sloane asked, petting the top of her head as Justice sat beside her.

"The benefits of being the leader of a cartel means you have money to buy things, like private jets. I just so happened to inherit my father's after he passed," Hugo said. "I've already made arrangements, and the pilot is taking care of everything you need. Justice can fly with you, however, you will need certain things that even I can't produce that quickly."

"I know a vet in Nowhere," Keith said, pulling out his phone. "I'll give them a heads up to get started on everything so it's quick and easy once you get there."

"Thank you. I appreciate that," Sloane said, letting out a heavy breath.

"Do you want your mom to go with you to Ireland?" Hugo asked, his fingers already moving quickly over the screen of his phone.

"Is that an option?" I asked, my eyebrows raised.

"I can make anything happen. I just need to get this going if you want her to go with you."

"Yeah. She's my mom. I don't want her left by herself here, especially if we can't return to the US."

"Not a problem. I'll have a friend meet you in Nowhere with her passport."

"Don't you need—" I smacked my lips together as I stopped talking, realizing that he could create a new identity for anyone with the right connections.

Saying Goodbye
Sloane

Things felt like they were happening so fast as I went from learning that Keith and Hugo were DEA agents to having to pack things up and leave again—this time forever. It was hard saying goodbye to the place that I once called home, but given everything that had happened, I was ready for a fresh start. I knew I was lucky to have a second chance at life, and I wasn't going to waste it.

I was busy stuffing the last few things into my backpack when I heard someone knock on the back door. I tensed for a second before Everett placed his hand on my lower back and pulled me against him without smushing Justice in between us.

Keith opened the door and stepped to the side as Trevor and Roman walked in, both glaring at him before turning their attention to me.

"Oh my gosh!" I squealed, pulling away from Everett to rush over and hug them. "What are you guys doing here?"

"We flew down to help Everett," Trevor said with a huge smile on his face. "I'm so glad to see you're okay."

"Thank you. I really am," I replied, frowning when I noticed Roman's head peeking past me.

I turned to look at what caught his attention and sighed when I saw Justice had snuck back into the hallway. It was taking forever for the clean-up crew to get there, and I couldn't keep her from obsessing over the dead body.

"Justice, no. Put down that finger," I scolded, separating from them as I went to retrieve my dog.

"So, what's the plan now?" Trevor asked as I brought Justice back into the kitchen with me.

"Well, unfortunately, I didn't make it, and in a few minutes, they're going to come collect my body. Since Everett is also dead, we'll be relocating," I said with a new shakiness in my voice. I didn't really care where I went as long as I was with Everett, but saying goodbye to Trevor and Roman was going to be harder than I imagined.

Roman nodded his head, confirming he understood what I couldn't get myself to say.

"It was a privilege to know you, Sloane, and while I'm truly heartbroken by your passing, I hope you find the peace you deserve," Trevor said, his eyes glistening as tears threatened to spill over.

He pulled me in for a hug, and I hid my face in his shoulder as I cried.

"Thank you for everything you did for me," I whispered.

"Anytime, Sloane. Anytime."

"I will also miss you, Sloane. You were taken from us far too soon, but you deserve to rest. You fought long and hard, and justice was served. Rest easy, my friend," Roman said, not bothering to hide the tear that slid down his cheek.

I hugged him hard, gripping his shirt as I cried even harder.

"You were an absolute godsend, Roman. I can't ever thank you enough for what you did for me. For what Quinn did for me. Please tell her how much her friendship meant to me, even if it was short-lived."

"I will. She'll be sad to hear of your passing, but I know she would wish you peace as well."

I pulled away and wiped the tears from my face as I stared at two of my best friends.

"We should get going," Trevor said, clearing his voice.

Roman nodded.

I turned away as they gave Everett a quick hug and wished him well before slipping out the door.

"Your car is here," Keith notified us a few minutes later as he bent down to pick up my backpack. "If there's anything else you need, be sure to grab it because we won't be able to come back."

"There's just one thing I need to do," I said, taking a deep breath and blowing it out.

I felt Everett's eyes on me as I walked into the hallway and stared down at the monster who murdered my family.

"I hope you rot in hell for all eternity. I hope that your death was as painful and brutal as what you put me through when you took my family from me. I hope you never find peace.

I hope that my face torments you as you walk through the fiery flames of hell, never getting a chance to rest."

I pulled my shoulders back and then reached into my pocket and pulled out my dad's knife. Then I bent down and plunged it into his chest, knocking off the container as the spiders went running. I stepped away, knowing that I would be leaving a part of my father behind by leaving his knife in him. But I didn't care. I was ready to walk away from this chapter of my life and start a new one.

<u>Flying High</u>
Everett

I felt on top of the world as I sat beside Sloane on the luxurious plane that Hugo arranged for us. My mother sat in one of the chairs further up from us, watching a movie while Justice lay at her feet. Sloane and I sat toward the back so I could have some time alone with her. I knew my mother wanted to give us as much privacy as possible, but it was a bit challenging, given that we were all stuck together on a plane for the next eight-plus hours.

"So," I said softly, squeezing her hand because I still couldn't believe that she was okay. "I'll tell you my story if you tell me yours."

"What story do you want to hear?" she asked, turning slightly in her seat to look at me.

I gave her a look and watched her cheeks flush.

"I don't think you want to know the details of what I did." She lowered her head and tried to look away from me as I lifted her chin with my finger and brought her gaze back to mine.

"Sloane, there is nothing in the world that I wouldn't want to know when it came to you."

"Aren't you supposed to call me Lily?" she asked, purposely trying to change the conversation.

I rubbed my lips together and tried again.

"Alright, *Lily*, if you tell me what you did to Black Widow guy, I'll tell you what I did to Sheriff Dowdy," I offered, loving the way her eyes lit up.

"What did you do?" she whispered, pure happiness filling her eyes as she covered her mouth and stared at me.

"I made sure he paid for what he did to you."

"How?"

"Nail gun," I replied with a shrug.

It was strange how good I felt about what I had done, but what was even stranger was how good it felt to tell Sloane about it. It was like we had transformed into a new couple who enjoyed the horror stories of what the other did to those who deserved it.

"You shot him with a nail gun?"

"Several times. Stomach. Head. Chest. And for good measure, I even shot him in the dick."

"Everett!" she shrieked, her eyes widening as she started giggling.

"I'm sorry, I think you mean *Josh*," I said, smiling.

"Wow, *Josh*. I had no idea you were such a badass."

I grinned smugly, loving the way she looked at me.

"What can I say? I'm a totally different person these days. And I might have learned a thing or two from you."

"Did you tie him up first?"

"Nope. I made it into a game of tag and just chased him around the kitchen, shooting at him."

Her eyes widened as she stared at me in disbelief.

"I'm kidding," I assured her with a laugh. "Of course I tied him up first."

She shook her head and narrowed her eyes at me.

"Okay. Your turn."

"My turn for what?" she asked, avoiding the question again.

"Your turn to tell me what you did to the guy in your hallway."

"He was there when I got home," she said quietly. "Waiting for me, which you already know. But he attacked me first, and I fought back the best I could."

"It looked like you might have had the upper hand," I replied softly.

"How so?"

"He was pinned to the floor with knives stabbed through his hand, Sloa—*Lily*. So I'm guessing you had the edge on him at some point."

"I mean, just a little bit. I *might* have shot him in the knee first."

"And?"

"Then shot him in the arm."

"That explains how he got in the position he was in when I found him, but where did the spiders come from, Sloane?"

She took a deep breath and let it out slowly as she pulled her hand away and rested it in her lap. My mother was still focused on her movie, so I had no idea if she was listening to the conversation or not. But at this point, we had nothing we needed to hide from her. We'd all lived through the worst of it.

"I went to the pet store one day to buy food for Justice," she explained, turning her head to look out the window. "There were a bunch of black widow spiders at the front by the register. The girl said they were for one of the teachers in town, but she never came to pick them up."

"So you bought them?"

"No. She didn't sell them to me. She said they were going to release them, so I offered to take care of them for her."

"How long did you have them?"

She shrugged as she chewed her lower lip.

"I don't know. A few days?"

"You purposely saved them for him," I said, knowing it was exactly what she did.

She nodded.

"He took everything from me, Everett. I wanted to see him suffer as much as I had. I wanted him to feel every ounce of pain he caused me."

"I know," I said, reaching for her again. "I get it. I don't judge you for what you did to any of them."

She turned her attention back to me and looked deeply into my eyes.

"I didn't think I would make it out alive," she admitted. "I thought for sure I would be joining Gabe and Nicky in heaven. But then I keep getting these second chances and escaping death, and I gotta admit, it scares the shit out of me."

There was so much emotion in her voice as a tear slid down her cheek.

"Why does it scare you?"

"Because what if this is too good to be true? I've done some truly horrible shit. What if we go to Ireland, and I fuck everything up? Maybe I don't deserve any more second chances and my time is finally coming."

I shook my head quickly as I got out of my seat and kneeled in front of her.

"That would never happen, Sloane. I will die protecting you and making sure nothing bad happens to you ever again. You did some terrible things to some very horrible people, but I don't think you're being punished for it. I think you're getting a second chance because you deserve it. You've survived so much already, but now it's time to *live,* Sloane."

"I feel guilty for moving on with life and *living* it. They didn't get that chance, and now I'm moving on as if they never happened."

"No, you're not. You're moving on with life because you have to. But their memories will never be forgotten. We will live the rest of our lives honoring them by doing the things they never got to."

"This is harder than I thought it would be."

"I know." I nodded, squeezing both of her hands in mine. "But I've got you, Sloane. Always."

"I love you, *Josh*."

"I love you more, *Lily*."

I leaned forward and kissed her hard and deep, knowing that nothing would ever separate us again.

New Life
Sloane

People never understand what you're going through when you lose someone you love. Even if they've been through something similar, they still don't know what you are going through. They don't know the extent of the darkness that you choose to dwell in, just like they don't know how hard it is to appreciate a sunny day.

That's because sunny days are rare.

They're hard to find when the darkness constantly washes over them.

It's difficult to explain why you choose the darkness over the bright, sunny days because it's easier to let yourself fall into that darkness and allow it to take control of you.

But when you find the right person who is nothing but those bright, sunny days, the darkness starts to fade.

It starts to lift.

Suddenly, you feel free again.

It doesn't erase the darkness completely.

But it does allow you to have a different outlook on life.

I was robbed of everything I once loved. My world came crashing down on me, and I fell into a darkness so deep I didn't think I would ever see the light again.

What I didn't know was that his love was strong enough to lift me out of that darkness. His love was enough to make me cling to those sunny days and crave more of them.

His love was what reminded me that I wasn't broken.

I just needed love to help me put the pieces back together.

<u>Epilogue</u>
Sloane—Six Months Later

I rolled over and smiled as Everett's eyes fluttered open, and a lazy smile pulled across his face.

"Good morning," I said, my voice still filled with sleep after a long night of making love to the beautiful man beside me.

"Great morning," he corrected, pulling me closer to him as his erection brushed against my stomach.

"Great morning indeed." I laughed as I reached down and stroked it.

I loved how ready this man always was for me these days. Living in Ireland had been vastly different than what we were used to in America—killing aside. Instead of being work-driven and constantly hustling through a busy city, we were both enjoying our time at home. I didn't ask questions, but a new bank account had been set up for me, Everett, and his mother with more money than any of us could ever spend. On top of that, they set us up in a very remote area that was close enough to town for us to get what we needed, but far enough away from everyone to give us the privacy we needed. Nancy's house was behind ours and much smaller, but it was the perfect fit for her. We shared custody of Justice, who preferred to spend time with Nancy these days instead of with us.

"What did you want to do today?" Everett asked as his fingers lazily trailed over my skin.

"What are the options?"

"We can head into town for some of the St. Patrick's Day celebrations."

I scrunched my face, not really wanting to be around anyone. It was nice being secluded so we didn't have to answer a ton of questions that I didn't always have the answers to because I was no longer *Sloane*. Trying to remember who Lily was and what her and Josh's story was had gotten harder the more we stayed to ourselves locked up in the house.

"We don't have to," he said after I had stayed silent for too long.

"No, it's fine. We can go if you want to."

"I want to do whatever *you* want to do."

I didn't miss the look he gave me or the way his voice dropped as his hand dipped behind me and squeezed my ass.

"I think we both want the same thing," I replied as I chewed my lower lip and watched him.

He flipped me on my back and then ducked beneath the covers as he pulled them over his head. Strong hands pulled my thighs apart as he settled himself between them, his tongue slowly running along my slit and making me hiss.

I moaned and arched my back as I let my knees fall to the side, allowing him full access. His hands gripped my thighs, holding me steady as he sucked my clit, immediately sending me near the edge. I reached down and held his head in place, keeping him right where I wanted him as I felt the first tingle along my spine.

He sucked harder as he slid two fingers inside of me. I was so turned on that they slid in without any effort as he pumped harder, putting enough pressure on my G-spot to make me see stars.

Sex with Everett was unlike anything I had ever experienced before because no matter how many times we did it, it seemed to get better every time. He continued doing exactly what he knew I needed and chuckled when my pussy spasmed against his tongue a few seconds later.

Life in Ireland was so different from life in America, and I didn't mind that things were so much slower for us here. For once, I took the time to stop and enjoy the things that brought me happiness, like the man currently between my legs, as he brought me immense pleasure.

I grinned as he pulled away and slid up my body, grinning as he wiped my arousal off his lips. He lined himself up at my entrance and thrust inside of me, knowing how much I loved when he fucked me like this.

I wrapped my arms behind his neck, holding on as he made love to me. I glanced at the diamond engagement ring on my finger and smiled, knowing that second chances were worth taking.

****

Want more on Trevor and Roman? You can find their stories in The Dark Shadows trilogy! Be sure to start with Five Steps Ahead, as this trilogy needs to be read in order to avoid spoilers.

Five Steps Ahead (Dark Shadows Book 1)

https://books2read.com/u/38Q0gO

I love to chat with my readers and am most active on Facebook in my reader group! Come join us! I would love to have you! https://www.facebook.com/groups/2945710968775398/

Other Books By Samantha Baca

The Haven Brook Series
(small-town romantic suspense):

'Til Death Do Us Part (Haven Brook Book 1)

https://books2read.com/u/m2RJNR

The Cradle Will Fall (Haven Brook Book 2)

https://books2read.com/u/b6O0QE

The Ties That Bind (Haven Brook Book 3)

https://books2read.com/u/mqgoz8

A Very Haven Christmas (Haven Brook Book 4- Novella)

https://books2read.com/u/mvqGjj

Three Strikes, You're Gone (Haven Brook Book 5)

https://books2read.com/u/mvqL2z

The Dark Shadows Trilogy
(romantic suspense)

Five Steps Ahead (Dark Shadows Book 1)

https://books2read.com/u/38Q0gO

Ten Seconds Too Late (Dark Shadows Book 2)

https://books2read.com/u/3JRgVB

Broken

Against The Clock (Dark Shadows Book 3)

https://books2read.com/u/m2YwoR

Beaumont Creek Series
(small town)

Just One Time (Beaumont Creek Book 1)

https://books2read.com/u/3G52zK

Second Chances (Beaumont Creek Book 2)

https://books2read.com/u/4Aj6Z0

Third Time's The Charm (Beaumont Creek Book 3)

https://books2read.com/u/b5lEyG

Four-ever Single (Beaumont Creek Book 4)

https://books2read.com/u/4j5jMX

Fifth Wheel (Beaumont Creek Book 5)

https://books2read.com/u/4XwKwa

Whiskey Mountain Series
(small-town novellas)

Something To Talk About

https://books2read.com/u/4X62ag

Broken

Something To Think About

https://books2read.com/u/3GWAan

Something To Believe In

https://books2read.com/u/3yVzgB

Something To Live For

https://books2read.com/u/mllEOP

<u>Sugarplum Falls Series</u>
<u>(Holiday Novellas- can be read as standalone)</u>

Blame It On The Mistletoe
https://books2read.com/u/bw1rqe

Blame It On The Eggnog
https://books2read.com/u/38PPY6

Blame It On The Candy Canes
https://books2read.com/u/31DNo7

Blame It On The Blizzard
https://books2read.com/u/b6z6XE

Blame It On The Reindeer
https://books2read.com/u/baLAG6

Blame It On The Carols
https://books2read.com/u/me8E9z

Blame It On The Lattes

Broken

https://books2read.com/u/mB1E2A

Blame It On The Secret Santa
https://books2read.com/u/mY9dGY

Blame It On The Holidays: A collection of bonus epilogues

https://books2read.com/u/bwXRPY

The Stone Creek Series
(small-town novellas)

Chocolate Covered Mistletoe (Stone Creek Book 1)

https://books2read.com/u/3LRk9N

Candy Coated Promises (Stone Creek Book 2)

https://books2read.com/u/mldP5Y

Pumpkin Spiced Possibilities (Stone Creek Book 3)

https://books2read.com/u/bojdwV

Standalone Books

One Last Wish

https://books2read.com/u/mqg7D9

Finding Love In Apartment 2C (novella)

https://books2read.com/u/bze9aZ

Breaking All The Rules (Previously published as: Cocky Counsel: A Hero Club Novel)_

https://books2read.com/u/box2MZ

All Is Fair In Food And War (novella)

https://books2read.com/u/bp8qjX

Holiday Books

(novellas)

Snow Place To Go

https://books2read.com/u/4A560N

A Very Merry Kissmas

https://books2read.com/u/bPDgy7

A Christmas Wish

https://books2read.com/u/4EKXpE

Holiday Hijinks

https://books2read.com/u/4DP6Ze

Broken

Acknowledgments

This book was harder to write than I thought it would be, and it consumed me in ways I hadn't imagined. I'm so incredibly thankful for my alpha readers who helped me when I needed support and told me to keep going when I wanted to give up. Thank you for everything you ladies did for me. From the freak-out DMs to the phone calls where we would talk things out, I appreciate all of it!

I'm incredibly lucky to have a strong team of alpha and beta readers who helped in different ways with this book. Tamara, Valerie, Azucena, Claire, Malissa, Karrie, Jackie, and Reina—thank you all for your help with this one!

To my readers who started preordering this book when it was just a title and a cover—you're the real MVPs. You didn't care what it was about, you just wanted it. I see you, and I appreciate you! Thank you for your unwavering support over the years and with this book!

My family has been my strength since I published my first book in 2020. Their support means the world to me, and I'm so proud to see the way my daughters look at me when they see me doing all of the "author things". I know they're going to do amazing things, and I am so lucky to get a front row seat!

As always, I want to thank my husband for being there for me every step of the way. Between his unconditional love and support, and being the man who makes the magic happen with getting the book formatted, I appreciate all of it. I know I've said it a million times, and at least five times already in the acknowledgements, but I will never stop appreciating everything given to me and the support. Thank you for taking the time to read this story.

About the Author

Samantha lives in the southwest with her husband and two children, where she enjoys writing, drinking iced coffee, and watching the greatest show of all time—Friends. With over 30 books published, Samantha enjoys writing across several different genres, from steamy romantic suspense to laugh-out-loud spicy romantic comedies. She also has a sweet spot for holiday stories, so grab a blanket and get ready to binge some of the sweetest—yet spicy—holiday romance your heart can handle!

Samantha loves connecting with her readers, so here's a list of where you can find her:

Facebook Reader Group:

https://www.facebook.com/groups/2945710968775398/

Facebook:

https://www.facebook.com/AuthorSamanthaBaca

Instagram:

https://instagram.com/author_samantha_baca

Webpage:

www.samanthabaca.com

Goodreads:

http://www.goodreads.com/authorsamanthabaca

Books2Read:

https://books2read.com/ap/RQAYK9/Samantha-Baca

www.ingramcontent.com/pod-product-compliance
Lightning Source LLC
Chambersburg PA
CBHW030732310726
48969CB00005B/1204